MY TRUE AND COMPLETE ADVENTURES AS A WANNABE VOYAGEUR

MY TRUE
AND
COMPLETE
ADVENTURES
AS A
WANNABE
VOYAGEUR

by
PHYLLIS RUDIN

NeWest Press

————

Library and Archives Canada Cataloguing in Publication

Rudin, Phyllis, author

My true and complete adventures as a wannabe voyageur / Phyllis Rudin.

Issued in print and electronic formats.

ISBN 978-1-988732-12-1 (softcover).--ISBN 978-1-988732-13-8 (EPUB).--

ISBN 978-1-988732-14-5 (Kindle)

I. Title.

PS8635.U35M9 2017   C813'.6   C2017-901289-4
                                            C2017-901290-8

————

Editor for the Board: Merrill Distad

Cover and interior design: Vikki Wiercinski

Cover images: Water © donatas1205/shutterstock.com,
Paddle © marekuliasz/shutterstock.com, Fist © cunaplus/shutterstock.com

Author photo: Marcie Richstone

 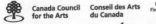

NeWest Press acknowledges the support of the Canada Council for the Arts, the Alberta Foundation for the Arts, and the Edmonton Arts Council for our publishing program. We also acknowledge the financial support of the Government of Canada through the Department of Canadian Heritage (Canada Book Fund).

 201, 8540–109 Street Edmonton, Alberta T6G 1E6

780.432.9427

NeWest Press www.newestpress.com

No bison were harmed in the making of this book.

We are committed to protecting the environment and to the responsible use of natural resources. This book was printed on FSC-certified paper.

1 2 3 4 5 19 18 17 printed and bound in Canada

To Ron

Love many, trust few,
and always paddle your own canoe.

1

There must be uniforms out there that make you walk with a spring in your step. Astronaut is one, I'm guessing. Mountie's another. But ones like mine, that look like they've been reduced to clear at a costume warehouse, well they just make you want to hide under a rock.

When I came downstairs in my new work uniform for the first time that Monday, there was some disagreement among the family. Their comments reflected the generational spread around the breakfast table. Grandpa thought the outfit made me look like a streetcar conductor; Nana, a delivery boy from Western Union. The piping around the lapels put Mum in mind of Captain Kangaroo, while my older brother Zach took in the brimmed cap topping off my skinny frame and pegged me as a Pez dispenser. Only my sister Rena was generous in her assessment. "I think you look like Prince Harry at the wedding, Ben. All you need is a few miles of gold braid and voilà." Rena seldom had anything negative to say about anyone so her comparison didn't carry much weight.

I don't know why the store didn't let me wear my own clothes. I would have dressed presentably, even worn a tie if they'd asked me to. But I sensed at the interview that dissing the uniform would be a deal-breaker. My theory? The get-up was designed to glop some class over the place by aping Ogilvy's, the glitzy department store down the street. See Ogilvy's had itself a uniformed piper. The guy wore a kilt, a furry codpiece, and a bearskin hat. The works. Every day at noon he marched through the store, starting on the main floor and working his way up to four, pumping his windbag under his armpit the whole time as if it were a misplaced whoopee cushion. The tourists were blown away by the spectacle. They'd never seen a piper do his thing on a moving escalator before. In Scotland they probably kept their musicians tethered. But even Ogilvy's, for all its snooty airs, didn't have itself a museum. The Bay did.

And thanks to my mother, who worked in Ladies' Purses, and had accumulated a shitload of brownie points with the higher-ups over the years, I was hired as its uniformed attendant. Now how it came to pass that a museum tracing the history of the Hudson's Bay Company from its seventeenth-century fur trade roots all the way up to the present day wound up crammed into a corner of the Bay's downtown Montreal department store, I didn't know and I didn't care. It was a job. Not much of a job mind you, but then it wasn't much of a museum. Don't get me wrong. Ranking it on the Pathetic Scale, it wasn't as high up there as those so-called museums you see hand-painted signs for when you're out for a drive in the country. You know the kind I mean. The ones where rube collectors set up an exhibit of their potatoes shaped like Hollywood stars and charge the tourists a dollar a pop. Uh-uh. The Bay's museum was respectable even if it was pint-sized. It had bona fide artifacts; beaver hats, powder horns, even a full-sized birchbark canoe. But for all that it was still sleepy. Sleepy? Who am I kidding? It was downright comatose. Visitors only stumbled in when they took a wrong turn on the way to the Luggage Department or Table Linens.

I did have a couple of regulars, though. Rossi was one of them. He worked in the cafeteria just beside the museum and would stop by on his breaks to escape the steam tables and BS with me for a while. "How can you stand working here?" he'd ask me. "A funeral home is livelier. There's only one explanation I can come up with. You must be going at it hot and heavy with her over there, right?" He tipped his head towards the mannequin modelling a travelling dress from the 1820s. Her wig was slightly crooked so I went over and straightened it on her papier-mâché skull, and since I was over there anyway I fluffed out her skirt too.

"Looks like maybe I interrupted something when I came in," Rossi said, elbowing me in the ribs hombre to hombre. "Tell me straight, Ben, what's it like screwing a bald girl?" Rossi wasn't exactly a Renaissance man when it came to conversation, but at least he was company. And he could never stay longer than fifteen minutes before his supervisor in the kitchen sent out a posse.

Next down after Rossi it was my mother who gave an artificial bump to my statistics by checking in on me once or twice a week.

"Mum, I see you at home every day. Why do you have to come in here like I'm a third-grader and make sure I'm eating my lunch? It's embarrassing."

"Embarrassing in front of who?" She made a great show of peering into every corner of the museum to size up the crowds of people that weren't. "Benjie, all I want is to see that you're settling in okay."

"I'm settling in fine. You don't have to worry."

Fat chance. *Worry* was her middle name. At least when it came to me. Luckily for her, my siblings were semi-well-adjusted, giving her a free pass to obsess over yours truly.

"I know this isn't a job for the future, honey, but it's a start, something to give you a little confidence. And you always look more desirable to other employers when you have a job already." She brushed some imaginary lint off my epaulets. "Something better will come along, more to your talents, to your tastes. You just have to give it some time. Don't let it get you down."

"I get it, Mum. I get it, okay? You gave me that same speech this morning before I left for work. You gave it to me yesterday before I went to work. In fact you give it to me every single day before I go to work. I don't need to hear it again. Message relayed loud and clear. Do I have to say *roger* or something to cut the communication?"

I shouldn't have been so snippy with her. She didn't deserve it. She'd always been right there when I needed her. And I'd needed her plenty once I cruised in on my teens and things started to majorly unravel in my life. I'm not talking your basic, run-of-the-mill teenage angst either. This was of a whole nuther magnitude. Suddenly, when everyone around me was marching right, I was marching left. Then Mum would have to come out with the hook and haul me back into alignment. Parent-teacher meetings ramped up to the point that school had Mum on speed dial. "Some days he's disruptive and others he's completely closed off, tight as a drum. We can't reach him," my teachers would report. "We never know which way the wind's going to blow on any given day." The school counsellor nodded her agreement. "Testing hasn't gotten us anywhere. He refuses to cooperate." This was the cue for the principal to pile on. "There's also the question of his grades. Young Benjamin is flirting with being held back if they plummet any further, I'm sorry to have to say. Such a tragedy that would be, Madame Gabai. A boy with his promise."

My mother relayed all this to me afterwards, hoping it would prod me to open up. As if. I did have moments when I thought of telling her I was gay to give her something concrete to hang all my mixed-upedness on, but in the end I decided that more lying wouldn't really help anything.

You'd figure that she wouldn't have to jump in to rescue me anymore. I was twenty-three after all. But hadn't she found me this job when I couldn't land one on my own armed with my BA (no honours) in English lit? That was the major of choice for nerdy types like me, where we all washed up on shore to die. The degree qualified you for exactly zero in the real world. No doubt you've heard the joke, my brother Zach's favourite.

What did the English major say to the engineering major?
Will you take ketchup with your fries?

It cracked him up every time. Mum didn't find it so funny. To save face with her mahjong buddies, mothers of overachievers every last one, she'd taken to calling this my gap year. I didn't quibble with her over it even though we both knew she was, shall we say, embellishing. A gap year implied some definite plan for the year after; an acceptance already in-pocket for medical school, a deferred parliamentary internship offer maybe, or something else equally parent-soothing. My gap year looked like it was shaping up to be more of a gap decade, but why parse?

The museum didn't really need a full-time attendant. Any idiot could see that. But they paid me to be there every day from ten to six all the same. The idea was that in hiring me they'd get a twofer, a security guard and a docent, bundled. I'd protect the displays against sticky fingers, and answer any questions that came up about the collection. They were sadly mistaken if they thought I'd be able to give knowledgeable answers about the objects in the display cases, although I might have misled them a bit on that score at the interview. I did take Canadian history pre-Confederation in university like I'd written on the application form. I just neglected to mention that I'd slept through it. The cold fact is that I was a blank on the fur trade, the voyageurs, and the Hudson's Bay Company's involvement in the whole megillah. Didn't know scrimshaw from scrambled eggs.

Then one day in came this kid with his mother. Mum was just my type, by which I mean she had cleavage you could suffocate in. She was trying to engage her son in this little educational side-trip when all he wanted to do was shop for the new swimming goggles and flippers she'd promised him and head for the pool. He put up a whiny protest but she was one of those teacherly mothers, the kind who sees every encounter as a golden opportunity to pack some more factoids into junior's brain pan. My own mum had the same MO so I knew he'd have to suck it up and let the didactic ritual play itself out. There was no escape hatch.

She asked me all sorts of questions about portaging canoes and grading pelts and I threw together some bogus answers out of spit and twigs to impress her. And it worked. She swallowed my explanations lock, stock, and barrel. But then the kid's bullshit meter started bonging like we were at a level crossing. Turns out his class had just finished a unit on the fur trade and he proceeded to rip my answers to shreds. Fort William wasn't on Lake Ontario, it was on Lake Superior. It wasn't the Hurons who came out on top in the Beaver Wars, it was the Iroquois. Need I go on? Being one-upped by some brat in front of his foxy mother, well, it's a humbling experience for a guy.

So while I was busy licking my wounds, didn't it happen again. People complain endlessly about the quality of the schools in this town, but they seemed to be getting something right. Anyway, this second kid who came in, not only did he bad-mouth my theme-park version of the fur trade, he had the added nerve to mock the mannequins, arrogant twerp. Now they may have been crummy mannequins, chipped and geriatric, but they were *my* crummy mannequins. It was as if you saw your sister surrounded by schoolyard bullies. Imagine you agreed with them totally that she was butt-ugly and a slut. You'd still rise up to defend the family honour and hammer them into the ground, wouldn't you?

To make a long story short, colliding with those two smart-mouth kids at the museum was all it took for the place to trap me in its spell. I was hooked. Looking at the displays through my new rose-coloured glasses, the hokey dioramas took on an air of Louvre sophistication and the moth-eaten top hats seemed to be wondering where they'd lost track of Fred Astaire.

The new me had a helluva lot of catching up to do so I overhauled my work routine which until then had amounted to counting down the minutes till clocking-out time and picking my nose. Now, in the lengthy intervals between visitors I tore through every book on the museum's shelves and there had to be a few hundred, easy. Trouble was, each one I finished left me with tons more unanswered questions. I appealed to Zach to let me double dip on his university library card and in a rare spurt of fraternal good will he agreed. Soon I was borrowing dissertations and archaeological tracts from McGill to fill in around the edges. One night in my bedroom I Googled up *the fur trade*. In three seconds flat it shot me back twenty-four million hits. Right then and there I made it my life's mission to work my way through every last one. I was a man possessed.

Even though I still had a good way to go, it only took a few months of non-stop application before I could at least answer any question the museum patrons threw at me, even the most arcane. No one could trip me up. I was the trivia king of the Hudson's Bay Company. I re-christened myself *curator*. My official job description of *caretaker* just didn't cut it. Who'd notice anyway? Or care? Enough of the letters coincided, so that if you said it fast, with a bit of a slur, you could hardly tell the difference.

When I wasn't reading, I kept busy teaching myself the back-woodsy skills. In school I used to hate it when they made us do all that fiddly historical true-to-life crap, like dipping candle wicks in tallow, but no more. I was into it. I'd even started to weave a *flèche*, the traditional zigzag-patterned sash that voyageurs tied around their waists to flash the message they were members of the clan. Unfortunately my mother dropped by while I was practicing yarn-overs on the back of a chair.

"You'll make someone a good wife," she said.

"Yeah, if one of your friend's daughters wants a guy who can give her home-strung snowshoes for her birthday, I'm her man."

Good thing it wasn't Zach who caught me being all crafty. I never would have heard the end of it.

So there I was at work on an ordinary Wednesday morning, buffing up some brass trading tokens to a nice sheen when my revelation snuck up out of nowhere and whomped me over the head. God had made a terrible chronological mistake. I was meant to have been born in the eighteenth century. The reminder window must not have popped up on His online calendar.

It explained everything perfectly. I was a French Canadian voyageur trapped in the body of a twenty-first century suburban washout. No wonder I'd been out of sync at school. And out of school too, for that matter. "It's okay, boychik," my mother used to repeat to me in those days in her most comforting tone, "your brain just has a mind of its own." Well, at long last my brain had found its true home, out on the river, hunkered down in a canoe, paddling hell for leather.

I can guess what you're thinking. That I was psycho. But I wasn't. Trust me. Rationally, I understood that I couldn't time travel to rectify the cosmic cock-up that had left me cooling my heels in lost-luggage for nearly three hundred years until my mother found the claim check. Still, I felt I had to do what I could to set things right. So I decided to take a practical approach. I'd learn how to kayak so I could paddle along the waters of the Lachine Canal and the St.

Lawrence River. It was the closest I could come under my city-boy circumstances where canoes weren't on offer, to living the life of a fur trader. And as a substitute for the real thing it wasn't half bad. I even rounded up a group of old friends and we'd go out together in our rental boats on the weekends. I played the role to the hilt, dressing the part and packing only voyageur-certified goodies in my lunch bag. The others weren't as much into the whole re-enacting business as I was, though I could generally coax them into playing along to some degree. For them these excursions were more excuses for sun and exercise and a bit of male chest thumping.

Rossi didn't come out on the water with us even though I invited him. He said that he preferred to keep his feet on dry land. But he was more impressed than any of my other friends by my newfound mastery of all things fur trade. Since I never had very many museum visitors to lavish my erudition on, Rossi became my most dedicated audience. He lapped up my lectures, never once snoozed off. Rossi hadn't been to university. His only brush with higher education came courtesy of the Cowansville Correctional Facility where he'd done some time on a car theft rap. He wasn't accustomed to being treated as a legitimate student and he liked the way it felt.

"Man," he said one afternoon, after I'd treated him to a lengthy run-down on the dating and mating habits of the beaver, that pesky wood chipper whose fuzzy outerwear had started the whole ball of wax rolling, "you've turned yourself into one major expert on the fur trade."

It was meant to be a compliment but its limp wording didn't acknowledge just how far I'd come.

"Expert nothing," I corrected him. "I AM the fucking fur trade."

2

So much for solidarity. A few weeks into our boating regime my Sunday kayaking group started hemorrhaging personnel to the dragon boats. Those guys had more glamorous rigs and Szechuan snacks biked in from the restaurant next door to their Chinatown HQ. But the biggest magnet of course was that they were coed. Plus the girls on those crews were built. Paddling down the middle of the river to the beat of their on-board drummer their barbell shoulders could scrape both shores at once. And strong? One of those she-dragons could pick up any member of my group and spin him around over her head like the blades on a chopper. Which is great. If you're into that kind of thing, I'm saying.

My kayakers were strictly male, in keeping with the fur trade tradition of propelling canoes by paddles and testosterone. This was my decision as leader of our group. In retrospect maybe it had been a mistake. We were down to only four what with all the defections, and a sorrier group of mock-voyageurs you could hardly imagine. In fairness to ourselves, we were operating under tight restrictions. It takes major bucks to play-act that you're a working shlub from the eighteenth century. For starters there's the kayak rental, thirty bucks an hour for a boat that's made out of Tupperware. Then there are the costumes. You might think that would be the easy part, but if you want to be a real stickler about it, meaning the invisibles matter too, underwear and such, then the costumes can run up a tab faster than a lush on a barstool since there's no such thing as off-the-rack.

Now much as I craved to be accurate down to the bone, with button flies instead of zippers and hand-stitched moccasins instead of Dollarama, my laughable weekly take-home from the museum didn't allow me to be so particular. But I did all that was in my power to look the part. For every outing I had my tuque on my head, my arrow-sash at my waist, and my weekend-whiskers on my face. The overall impression I was aiming for did take a major hit on account of my glasses, but I tried to imagine them out of existence when I looked at my reflection in the water. The canal did me a favour by being so murky that it made a lousy mirror.

The other guys? Well, they weren't against a little dressing up, but authenticity wasn't their top priority. Or their bottom one even. For some reason they figured that since they were out on the water pretending to be from old-timey days, that they should dress like pirates. I don't know how they made that leap but they all came to the same conclusion separately. For our first time out, Sam showed up wearing a black bicorn with a skull and crossbones that he'd scavenged from his little brother's Halloween rejects. Nick made a bit more of an effort with a red paisley bandana tied onto his shaved head at a jaunty angle, and a hoop earring to replace his usual stud. Renaud just dug a Pittsburgh Pirates cap out of his collection and considered himself appropriately attired. Without really being able to explain how it happened, I'd ended up out paddling every Sunday with Long John Silver, Jean Lafitte, and Roberto Clemente.

"I brought baklava, home-made." Nick offered it around. We'd stopped for a lunch break at a sheltered little inlet that gave the illusion we weren't within spitting distance of downtown Montreal. The leaf canopy thankfully blocked out most of the skyline. I was lying on my back, arms under my head, in the shade of what I now recognized to be a jack pine. Before I started boning up on the natural world, I couldn't tell a birch from a baobab. While I was tuned out beneath the greenery I conjured myself up a little daydream. It had us out in the bush way back when, resting our weary bones after a knock-down-drag-out with some rapids on the Ottawa River. But Nick's comment bombed my white-water fantasy out of the water.

"What'd you bring that for? Voyageurs didn't eat baklava. We're trying to be realistic here, as true to life as we can be. Won't that ever penetrate your thick skulls?"

"Don't be so pissy. They were all out of pemmican at the Super C."

See what kind of lip I had to put up with? Although I have to confess to you, in the spirit of full disclosure, that the baklava was very good.

"We could vote Nick off the island for his crime," Renaud said. "Or else leave him here stranded. Or beached. Whatever it is."

"Jettisoned, I think," Sam said.

"For your information," I said, "the proper term is *marooned*. Not that it has anything remotely to do with the fur traders. I'm just trying to educate you clowns. For the good of humanity."

"Leave it to you to know," Sam said. "Still the brainiac. Just like back in school when you aced every test. Left the rest of us in the gutter." I caught the other guys shooting him undercover shut-up looks but he rolled on, oblivious. He was wrapped up in the past just like I was, but parked at a more recent spot on the timeline. "Remember how our mothers all used to harp on us, 'why can't you be more like Benjie, why can't you be more like Benjie?'"

In the echoey silence that followed I should have kept my trap shut. A few more dead seconds and we'd have left the prickly subject of my egghead past behind, but true to form I felt obliged to open a mouth as my mother would say.

"Yeah, well, that was then. Take a good hard look at me now. A major success story, wouldn't you say?"

They made a great show of studying their shoes because we all knew exactly when their mothers ditched their Benjie refrain. It was plunk in the middle of grade six that I lost my ranking as the local poster boy and turned into a cautionary tale. The rest of them galloped on ahead on their report cards while I was busy going off the academic rails. And now that they were racking up credits towards an MBA or a CA, what did I have to show for myself? Me, the prodigy who'd popped like an overinflated bicycle tire? I'd barely scraped by with a degree in the Humanities. The Humanities, Christ! I was not unaware that for a guy in my circle the Humanities were only one step up the evolutionary ladder from Early Childhood Ed., but that's where I'd ended up once the dust settled. Mostly when we got together my old pals had sense enough to skirt around any references to my scholarly fall from grace. Today was an exception.

To lift the cloud and get us back into it, I pulled out my favourite book of voyageur lore and lingo and flipped through the pages. "Okay, you shirkers. Time to get with the program. Five points for anyone who can tell me what a tump line is."

Renaud launched his hand into the air teacher's-pet style. A trace of the suck had stuck with him over the years. "I know that one. It's that leather strap thingy that you put around your forehead to help you carry a heavy load on your back." The guys looked blank. His description wasn't clicking. "Remember Antoinette

Paoli back in grade ten?" he went on. "It's what she could have used to hold up that humungous ass of hers. Like a sling kind of." After this useful add-on the penny dropped.

"Correctamundo, my good man. Sam, you got the score card from last week?"

"Yeah, chief." He pulled his golf pencil from behind his ear to check the tallies. "Including the five he just earned, Renaud holds the lead with eighty-five points, I'm next with sixty, and Nick trails with a whopping ten. Yes, you heard me right folks, that's one-zero."

Nick's basement score ticked him off. "Hey, don't I get any points for bringing refreshments? That's gotta be worth something. None of these other jokers brought anything to share." Sam looked to me to adjudicate.

"Okay. For some reason that feeble argument moves me. Mr. Scorekeeper, give Little Nicky five points for the food, but remember Nico, that if you bring us some period dish next time, something really authentic, it'll be worth twenty to you, maybe more."

"Yeah, I'm sure you guys will fall all over yourselves with gratitude if I show up with pea soup or pig-snout ragout or whatever the hell those guys ate. Maybe I'll bring us some bark to chew."

"The bark isn't to eat, dumb-ass," Sam informed him. "It's to get high on."

"It is?" Renaud chimed in. "I thought it was to clean your teeth with." These technical debates could go on forever with them, based as they were on thin air. Next they'd have voyageurs using boiled-down bark pulp to remove unsightly body hair.

Usually I was the one to hustle them off these tangents. Who else but me cared if we strayed? But today, out of the blue, Renaud did the deed by giving us a little impromptu performance. He climbed up on one of the concrete slabs that made up the breakwater and struck a bodybuilder pose. Then he flexed his right bicep to show off the walnut that had replaced the previous month's chickpea. "This rowing is really paying off, I swear to God. I was able to open a jar of Bick's for my mother last week. In the old days she'd have gone straight to my dad. Do not pass go."

We all mocked Renaud's Schwarzenegger pretensions into the ground. But that was only because the rest of us hadn't made half as much progress in the beefing-up department. Our arms still had the muscular definition of cooked spaghettini. And not even al dente. Renaud did go a bit overboard, though, when he timed his flexes against his watch. I could have blasted him for the digital anachronism gracing his left wrist, but I didn't want to make a federal case out of it. I'd only end up having to defend my glasses. So I just let him wear himself out. Such was my life as a voyageur kingpin. You had to pick your fights.

The Sunday after the baklava debacle I woke up to a downpour, one of those climate change super-soakers that puts a monkey wrench into any outdoor plans. Now, you don't have to remind me that voyageurs were meant to share the same work ethic as mailmen, neither snow nor rain nor yada yada yada, but I tended to coddle my crew weather-wise. I would never push them to go out in sopping conditions like this. Hell, they were all I had. I didn't want them to abandon me like the others had, leaving me to operate solo. Fur trading was by definition a team exercise. You couldn't be a singleton voyageur any more than you could be a singleton volleyball player. There was no such animal. So I proposed an alternate activity. A field trip. To my museum. Dry and warm. None of them had ever been there before, a fact that put them in line with 99.9 percent of the Montreal population. The place was normally closed on weekends but the department store was open for business and I had the keys to my domain. We agreed to meet up on Ste. Catherine Street first and then I'd treat them to a private tour. It was my secret hope that this visit would accomplish what the kayaking hadn't managed to do: set them on fire, boost them up the food chain from being pissant voyageurs to full-blown members of the tribe. Believers. Committed. Gung ho.

Hah!

Mistake number one. I unlocked most of the display cases so they could see the artifacts up close and personal without even any glass interfering. Mistake number two. Stopping off for beers on the way in. Actually that should probably have counted as mistake number one, but I didn't realize the beers were a mistake till after I'd opened up the cases and by then the top spot was already taken.

So the way the visit went down was this. I circulated around the place, my tambourine-sized key-ring jingling with importance, feeling like I was the guardian at Versailles. I was planning on removing a selection of my most interesting artifacts wearing the white cotton curator's gloves I'd sprung for on the Internet. They made me look like Minnie Mouse, but I swallowed my pride and put up with them. *Nécessité oblige* and all that. I figured that I'd hold up a relic and using my best Morgan Freeman voice explain exactly how it served as a cog in the well-oiled machine that was the fur trade. In my imagination the guys would stand respectfully back so that the vapours spewing out of their awe-struck gaping mouths wouldn't threaten my artifact with oxidation.

But nope.

While I was busy across the room fiddling with a stubborn lock, Sam reached in to one of the opened cabinets and pulled out three pipes which he then proceeded to juggle. Yeah, you heard me right. Juggle!

"Hey, put those back! Those things are worth a fortune. And they're fragile."

"You can trust me. You know I always keep the balls in the air. Remember my all-time record when I went for three minutes straight in my mother's kitchen? You were there."

"These aren't onions you moron. Put 'em back." Even to me my voice suddenly sounded squeaky. Was I turning into Minnie Mouse? I didn't dare try to pluck the pipes out of the air. Sam would lose his rhythm for sure and I'd wind up with a dustpan full of clay shards to explain away to the bosses. All I could think of was to find something soft to spread on the floor under his arms just in case. There was a full-length beaver coat in one of the cases. Plushissimo. That sucker would do the trick. I turned around to grab it to cushion the floor, but the case was empty. Nick had swiped the coat off its hanger to try it on and was strutting around like a runway model. He looked remarkably like Kate Moss if only she'd been born a rodent.

Before I could run over to yank it off his back I was distracted by a shout of *ye hah* coming from behind me. Renaud was mounted astride the taxidermied grizzly that reared up on his hind legs near the back wall. He was riding the thing wild and one-armed like he was on a bucking bronco at the Stampede. His heels were digging in so tight he'd already scraped a couple of bare spots into the bear's coat. Now a specimen like that, venti-sized, was irreplaceable these days. Okay, so the bear was a bit mangy, granted, and he did have a funky smell to him if you got up close, like he needed a good run through the car wash, but it's not like I could go out and set an ankle trap for a new one if Renaud bashed this one up beyond repair. Still, I let him have at it and focused on the other guys whose pricier toys, if damaged, could have me in hock to the Bay for years to come. I could see my pathetic future rising up before me. The store would attach my wages till my hair and my teeth fell out to make up for the losses. I'd have to live out my days in a scuzzy basement apartment, eating cat food and shaving with the lids from the tins that would give me little cuts all over my face that would later get infected so I'd end up looking like The Fly. But I was getting ahead of myself.

"Are you all crazy? I'll catch so much hell if anything's wrecked. Do you want me to get fired?"

My freaked-out tone somehow penetrated their soused reflexes and the horseplay stopped dead. Or bearplay in Renaud's case. Nick hung the coat back up and brushed off all the pretzel crumbs. He draped it in such a way that you could hardly make out the new rip in the side seam. Renaud clambered off the bear and returned the *do not touch* sign to its head, and Sam caught all three pipes in his hands without a hitch. For all that my blood was pumping I couldn't stay angry at them. Clearly they were sorry. This wasn't normal behaviour for them. They weren't dudes. It was all the fault of the storm. If only it hadn't been raining buckets, if only the water hadn't been overflowing the holes in the manhole covers, if only the rainfall hadn't filled the streets so it sloshed up in waves over the curbs, then we wouldn't have hung out at the pub for so long and we wouldn't have packed away way too many beers and none of this would have happened.

My mind often swerved into the *if-only* rut. In fact it tended to get bogged down there, spinning its wheels till another line of reasoning came along and nosed it out. If only I hadn't cut Hebrew school that day to go downtown. If only I'd taken the bus instead of the metro. If only I'd gotten off at McGill instead of Guy. A good bout of if-onlying could keep me occupied for hours on end. The world could go up in flames around me in the meantime but I'd be blind to it. I was a mess.

The first of the three bells rang that announced closing time was approaching. Yes! I'd had it with playing the host. Even though we still had a good half hour before the final bell went off, I hustled the guys out of the museum, escorting them all the way down to the store's main door on Ste. Catherine Street to have the assurance of seeing it slam shut behind their rowdy asses. Me? I went back up and waited inside. Waited till the guard jiggled the museum door to make sure it was locked tight. Waited till the floor buffers stopped their whirring in the aisles. Waited till the last bits of banter between the cleaners faded away. Waited till the banks of fluorescents clicked off sector by sector. Waited till it was stone cold quiet and I was alone in the building. Except for the guard, of course. All but alone till morning.

This wasn't the first time I'd be pulling an all-nighter at the museum. I'd been doing it once a month or so when the spirit moved me. It gave me a chance to give my head an airing out and to catch up on my reading uninterrupted. And as a bonus I discovered it had an unexpected side benefit on the home front. It gave my mother some hope. She made the natural assumption, that I'd finally met a girl and had spent the night at her apartment à la Zach and Nathalie. She never said it in so many words, but I wasn't her son for nothing. I didn't tell her the truth of the matter. Let her keep her illusions.

I slept on the side of the museum that was set up to look like the Hudson's Bay Company's retail operation back when it was in diapers. It had a general store-ish look to it. Along the one wall, shelves going all the way up to the ceiling were stocked with dry goods; your bolts of cloth, your blankets and such. A long wooden counter, waist high, ran parallel to the wall. It was topped with hat stands, wheels of lace trim, and an array of the petite stuff; buttons, thimbles, ribbons, corset stays. *Notions*, my Nana would have called them. Behind the counter, manning the fort, stood a plaster-of-Paris shopkeeper, frozen for all eternity in a may-I-help-you posture. In mannequin years he was about 150, dragged up from some sub-basement catacomb of passé store dummies of the kind that were primly manufactured without boobs or dicks so they could swing both ways. All that distinguished a Will mannequin from a Kate back then, uncontoured as they were, was the wig or the facial hair.

Our shopkeeper mannequin, Alexandre I called him in private, had himself a healthy beard, dense and rabbinic, but it hooked over his ears with twists of wire that were way too obvious. Even the littlest kids who came in picked up that it was a fake. His clothing, though, was more convincing. Alexandre outfitted himself for practicality, not style. His trousers were hitched up with old-fogey suspenders, and his cuffs were kept up and out of the way with sleeve garters. His waistcoat, where he might have shown a little pizzazz if he had any imagination at all, was a dull gabardine. I had to give him full credit, though. His get-up was period-perfect. And I had lots of time to study it since I set up my nighttime base camp in the nook formed by the inner side of the counter. Alexandre was planted just beside me. If my mother only knew I was actually spending my away-nights shacked up with a eunuch, not a girl, she'd be having conniptions.

The arrangement might sound cramped and uncomfortable to you, but you'd be wrong. It was very cozy. Private too. Even if the guard did decide to run his flashlight round the museum from the front door, which he'd never once shown the least initiative to do, he wouldn't catch sight of me. I was completely hidden by the counter and the place was convincingly dark. The only light I allowed myself came from a tiny read-in-bed lamp that clipped onto the spine of whatever book I had propped open. No one would suspect the premises were occupied.

I'd overnighted enough times at the museum that I'd developed a routine. It involved a bit of borrowing from the collection but I gave myself permission. There were perks at times to being boss and employee in one skin. So first off, I'd remove one of the ladies' handkerchiefs from the shelf they shared with the shoe buckles and drape it on the floor as my picnic tablecloth. They weren't dainty like you might imagine. What with women always getting the vapours back then those things were cut plenty big. Perfect for my purposes. Next, I'd unlock the display cabinet that housed the blue and white patterned bone china that used to fit out the tables of the Hudson's Bay Company's directors. The dishes were imported from England like everything fussy in those days. And finally, I'd help myself to my favourite dinner plate. It was decorated with an oriental scene, pagodas and willows and birds, some fishermen on a bridge waiting patiently for a nibble. It relaxed me just to look at it.

I'd read up some on the china pattern as was my new habit – let no topic under the museum's roof go unresearched. The scene was symbolic, turns out. I didn't have a clue. Back at university I sucked at finding the underlying symbolism in a novel. Some English major I was. In the essays I turned in, I always went with *death* and hoped for the best. In this case I wouldn't have been that far off the mark. The birds stood in for star-crossed lovers kept apart due to their differences in station by the girl's rich prick father. The couple manages to escape to a remote island where they enjoy a few years of conjugal bliss, but they're eventually tracked down and murdered by the stiffed fiancé. End of story.

It made my secret dinner so much more special knowing that underneath my humble meal of Bonbels and crackers an entire opera was unfolding, a British rendition of a Chinese *West Side Story*. That plate, for all that it was chipped at the edges, was still elegant and eloquent. And it felt so much better in the hand than the cheapo Corelle my mother served us on. I ask you, how could you develop any affection for a plate whose sole virtue was that you could drop it off the top of the CN Tower and it wouldn't shatter? Corelle had no voice.

So there I was. All settled in. Ready to eat and read. I'd been looking forward all week to getting into *Making the Voyageur World*. It promised to be a real page turner. But round about the middle of chapter one, something started niggling at me. I couldn't put my finger on what it was exactly, but something about my picnic just wasn't right. I tried to shake the feeling off but it wouldn't stay shook. If I didn't figure out soon what was casting a shadow over my nosh the night would be shot. Great. Just great. Could the day I'd had really go any further south?

I decided to check out my set-up one element at a time, picking off the non-offenders. It wasn't the cheese. It was supposed to taste like rubber. And it wasn't the book. It delivered as advertised. The handkerchief slash tablecloth, fluffed out, was wholly unsuspicious as were the crackers. Saltines were saltines. Which brought me down to the plate, the same plate I'd eaten off of so many times before. Somehow it felt lighter than I remembered when I picked it up. It had the chintzy lack of density of one of those crap plates from home. In the cave lighting of the museum the pattern looked reassuringly familiar, all busy and blue, but when I ran my index finger around the rim, it was eerily smooth. All the chips were gone. Maybe those beers were monkeying around with my senses. It's a well-known fact that Belgian brewskis have a seriously long afterburn. I flipped the plate over so that the Staffordshire stamp on the bottom could settle the issue once and for all, but the letters were too dim to make out. To get a clearer view I disconnected my mini reading light from my book and held it up over the writing.

Walmart, it read.

3

Rossi. That scumbag. I'd gut him like a fish. It had to be him. Who else knew my habits well enough to work around them? Who else knew about the tobacco tin where I stashed my keys when they weren't hitched onto my belt? Who else knew when I left to take a whiz? Some caretaker I turned out to be. I might just as well have left the door to the museum propped wide open with a welcome-basket of fruit.

Here he'd been casing the joint all along. I couldn't get past it. I thought we were tight. Sure I knew about Rossi's juvie history; he'd never kept it a secret. But boosting cars when you're out on a bender with your pals is one thing, burgling antiquities and re-placing them with look-alikes is another. By a long shot. It required forethought, and he'd always been more of an on-impulse thief, at least to hear him tell it, a seizer of opportunities. A heist like this struck me as way too highbrow for the likes of Rossi, but maybe I'd been underestimating him all along. Could it be that he wasn't re-ally the space cadet I took him for, though God knows if he wasn't, his imitation was dead-on. This was the guy who'd asked me in all apparent sincerity which museum in Toronto had the Canadian Shield in its collection so he could go and check it out.

Sleep? Forget about it. I was too wired. I had to get started on a complete inventory of the place, to see what else that Judas in a bib apron had lifted out from under me and swapped for shlock. Now if you're ever considering doing an inventory in complete darkness, let me recommend against it. I had to bump my way around the place Helen Keller style. Christ, how'd she ever get anything done? By morning I'd only managed to check out about a quarter of the collection. It took me all the next day to finish the job and discover that out of the hundreds of items in the museum, by some fluke I'd landed on the only phony one in the place. This was good. I'd caught him early in his game. But I'd have to confront him before he made his next strike. This was not good.

Over dinner that night, my mother checked me out with her x-ray eyeballs, "You look like you just lost your best friend," she said. Were all mothers that spooky, or was mine just gifted?

"Not my best," was the most I was willing to volunteer. Rossi may have been on the dumbish side, but I'd always looked forward to his visits breaking up my day. Whenever I needed to come up for air from my fur trade shpiels, I'd get Rossi to feed me stories of his time behind bars in exchange, to plump up my education in the world of shivs and shakedowns. "You've watched *Shawshank* too many times," he'd say to me. "There weren't any bars where I was. I wasn't in for murder. It was more like a dormitory. With doors. Hey, do you think that's why they call it a dormitory?" I'd miss Rossi's company. We'd had some laughs the two of us. My mother could tell that she'd hit a nerve so she chose not to push the envelope. Instead she reverted to more generic parental carping.

"Could you please take off that tuque when you're at the table?"

"Voyageurs never took off their hats to eat."

"Voyageurs probably didn't bathe either. Does that mean that next you're going to stop washing?"

"What you don't understand is that they had good reason not to wash up. See, clean skin is a lot tastier to mosquitoes and black flies than dirty. So it paid for them not to wash. On top of that, they used to schmear their skin all over with bear fat to help keep the bugs away. And if they had any on hand they'd mix some skunk urine into it. It was the voyageurs' organic version of Off. They always kept their hair long too. For extra face cover."

Glances heavy with meaning were darting back and forth across the table. Did they think I couldn't see? I was laying another fur trade lesson on them, and one with a piss sidebar yet. I couldn't help myself. It was my kneejerk reaction to bring the uneducated masses into the historical fold.

"Honey, there are other topics of conversation for the dinner table," my mother said. She was right but what was I supposed to discuss instead? "Oh by the way, my friend's stealing from the museum and I'll probably get fired, maybe land in jail?"

Oddly it was Zach who kept the conversation from veering off to more neutral territory. He asked me an actual question about work. Normally only Grandpa and Rena feigned any interest in my fur trade fetish. "Hey, Mr. Canoehead, how much you figure all that stuff in your museum is worth?" The very question I'd been struggling with myself. Was he turning psychic on me too?

"I have no idea."

"Ballpark it then. Is it in the thousands? The millions maybe?"

"I don't know, I told you."

"Some curator you are. There must be an itemized list somewhere. Didn't they have the collection evaluated? For the insurance?"

They probably had but I wouldn't be let in on those details.

That kind of head-office paperwork never trickled its way down to the grunt working on the floor. The only time I'd ever see it would be when the cops shoved it in front of my face in the interrogation room down at the station to shape my doom.

"You're always yapping how the collection is so valuable."

"It is. It has some of the finest examples of fur trade relics anywhere."

"How do you know? It's not like you've ever been to any of those other museums to compare. Only so much is on the web. Face it. It's an afterthought operation, your place. Some kind of tax dodge I'm betting. The whole thing is probably a whim of one of the directors. Or one of the Mrs. Directors more likely."

"Zach, you are such a pig," Rena said.

Grandpa added to the firepower. "Leave your brother alone. Why must you always be ridiculing his interests? You should only be so committed."

"I just want to know about the museum's financials. Is that so strange? I am studying business, remember?"

Here Nana treated us to one of her patented snorts. Normally a great respecter of education, somehow she looked down on the study of business as a trumped-up subject of scholarly endeavour. To her it was nothing more than Money Making 101 tarted out in falsies and mascara.

"Zach, you know you're just using it as an excuse to pick a fight." Rena, my defender.

"I'm not."

"Yes you are."

"I'm not."

"Yes you are." Polished debaters they weren't.

"I'm just trying to learn more about the little jobbie he goes to every day."

"Why do you insist on running it down?" Rena said. "It's full-time, which is more than you can say about your Tuesday-Thursday slots at Future Shop."

"May I remind you that I'm still in school, unlike Sir Benjie here. I only can work part-time. Besides, I'm learning retail. It's professional training."

"Some hot-shot professional. I've seen what you do. You load TVs and computers into people's trunks."

"Get off my back. I don't see you dirtying your cute little hands with any gainful employment. Maybe you can try spreading them with bear schmaltz like your brother."

"Just when I think you can't sink any lower you always surprise me," Rena said.

"Yeah, well I'm full of surprises. Maybe you should be more prepared. Didn't they teach you that in Princess School?"

"Shut up, Zach," I said.

"Oh, he wakes up! Had enough of your widdle sister acting as your defender? You're taking over the job yourself finally? I didn't think you were man enough."

"Don't push me."

"Why? When it gives me such pleasure to push."

Mum's voice when she intervened had that on-the-edge quality that gave us all the shivers. "Okay. That's it. I give up." She stood up at her place so abruptly the chair teetered behind her. "I give up. Can't you stop tearing down? Can't you stop picking and fighting? Is it so hard? Could we manage to have a civil dinner? Please. Do I have to beg? Let me have the momentary comfort of seeing that we all get along. Or at least acting as if we do. Is that asking too much?" The only sound around the table was the metallic clunk of our stomachs clenching up. "Well is it?" I felt responsible for this flare-up, of course. My bad karma from the museum had clearly hitched a ride home in my back pocket hoping to get a crack at a wider audience.

Mum was usually such a cheerleader that when she laid down her pompoms it meant something. We'd crossed the line. Occasionally our family circle minus Dad was more than she could handle. But you could never predict. Usually a table tiff like the one we'd just had would fly right past her, but once in a while it would catch her in the gut like a cannon ball and knock her flat. There were times when we were younger when it would take her days to come back to herself, days till she'd crank herself out of bed and root around in the kitchen junk drawer to find her game face. Another shut-down like those none of us wanted to see.

Boom! The conversation shifted to upbeat. Rena came in handy here. Nana served as her second. They practically dance a hora around the dinner table. We should have taken a picture to freeze that moment for posterity. Shot from the proper angle you wouldn't even notice that the family was held together with duct tape.

Hard night, harder morning. My Rossi showdown was fixed in my mind for his eleven a.m. break. No procrastinating this time, even though I'd always thought that the mañana approach had a lot going for it. But the longer I delayed on this thing, the more treasures under my care could bolt. The museum may have been my life, but I couldn't spend every single day and night there, planted in front of the door with a shotgun across my knees. Even for a full-out fanatic like me that was too much. I had to go ahead and tell Rossi I was onto him, force him into quitting his job. I wouldn't report him to the higher-ups, wouldn't lay charges. I just wanted never to set eyes on his ugly mug again. Let him go earn his cat burglar badge stealing diamond cuff-links from Birks. It didn't matter to me who else got dinged. I just wanted him to keep his thieving paws out of my back yard.

Rossi shambled in right on schedule and plunked himself down on the rum barrel he favoured for resting his weary bones. Usually I kept right on working when he came in, chatting with him over my shoulder, but this time I swung a chair around opposite him and straddled it. I needed the spindles up against my chest to brace me. When it came to confrontation I was a wuss, board certified.

"You're actually joining me for a break?" he said. "What's the occasion? Is it your birthday or something? Should I have brought a present?"

I grabbed the flimsy assembly-line plate from the counter beside me and stuck it out in front of him, hoping he'd just come clean at the sight of it, sparing me the whole grand inquisitor bit. I kept my gaze clamped onto him. I wanted the satisfaction of catching his jolt of recognition that the jig was up. But he didn't deliver. His face expressed the same puppyish innocence it always did. I couldn't help myself. Instead of grilling him all I wanted to do was scratch him behind the ears.

"What, you're going to serve refreshments too? Could I just mention to you," and here he pointed boldly at the plate, "that you forgot to load the dish up with any brownies? Some host." He was a smooth operator, Rossi. I had to give him that. He was prepared to tough it out.

"This plate doesn't say anything to you?"

"It says 'empty.' What else should it say?"

"I know." I jacked my voice down a register, pronouncing the two words in my deepest and most meaningful baritone.

"The plate should say 'I know?'"

"No, not the plate. Me. Me. *I'm* saying *I know*." He looked genuinely foggy now. All this talking plate business seemed to have fuzzied up his reasoning powers. Or was it just show? I decided to keep things literal.

"I know what you've been up to."

"Huh?"

"Here. At the museum. Don't play all innocent. We're way beyond that you and me. I know you lifted the original of this plate out from under my nose and replaced it with this made-in-China imitation from Walmart." I knocked it against the counter so he could hear its plasticky thunk.

"What are you, crazy?"

"Where'd you offload it? That's what I'm dying to know. eBay?"

"I don't even own a computer. You know that. What are you on, man? It's some bad stuff."

"So what did you do then, sucker some antique dealer down on Notre Dame into taking it off your hands by saying you dug it up in your granny's attic? Cash on the line. You probably only got a fraction of its value that way. I hope you're satisfied that you ripped yourself off."

He shook his head slowly. "I'm on probation. One more month I've got to go. You think I want to take that kind of chance?"

"Okay, so maybe not for the measly amount an antique store would hand over out of the cash drawer. But for bigger bucks it might be worth the risk. Maybe you got ballsy and tried to flip it to another museum. The McCord maybe. A plate like that, they'd be lucky to get their hands on it. And they'd have the money. Am I getting warm?"

"What are you talking about? I don't know squat about fencing to museums. How could I just show up at the McCord's back door and try to sell them something out of nowhere. You know what I was in for. I stole cars for what they call recreational use and drove them into the ground. None of them survived long enough for me to even think about fencing them. I wouldn't know where to start from. You really think the McCord would give me a second look?"

He had a point. Provenance mattered to a place like the Mc-Cord. They wouldn't whip out their triple-tiered chequebook for a stumblebum like Rossi. They liked legit. Receipts and authentications and all that. You couldn't just stroll in and pull a bootlegged *objet d'art* out from under your raincoat and ask for their best offer. I could see him being buzzed into their administrative offices. They'd size up this guy with his pants slung at half mast to reveal his rear cleavage and before he could even show them the goods they'd have redirected him to the third floor ladies room to deal with the clogged toilet.

"Look," he said. "I know you're in deep shit over this but you're barking up the wrong tree."

I chose to ignore his various declarations of innocence, however much they rang true, and bowled right on.

"How'd you ever get the idea of substituting the plate with a phony? That was very slick, I must say. A master stroke. You must be very proud of yourself." And then it hit me. How had I been so slow to catch on? "You weren't alone in all this, were you? Someone had to act as the brains of the operation. God knows you couldn't do it with those two marbles you've got rolling around up there. How could I have thought you were doing a solo job? You. What a laugh! You had an accomplice, right? You know what that is, don't you? No? Too many syllables? Let's sound it out together, why don't we? Ac-com-plice. It means a helper, someone to do the planning when you're too big of an ignoramus to do it yourself. Oh sorry, I mean too stupid to do it yourself. Can you follow what I'm saying if I speak slow? Your silent partner, whoever the hell he was, I'm betting the guy was shitting bricks beforehand knowing the kind of material he had to work with. Why would he ever recruit a screwup like you, a loser who could barely get it together to steal a car that had the keys in it? You've got to wonder. Well, he must have spotted some shred of something in you that the rest of the world overlooked 'cause you did it."

Rossi had jumped up to give his side but I talked right over him till he gave up. I wasn't about to let him get a word in until I was damn well finished.

"I've got to hand it to you. You missed your calling. You should have gone on stage. You actually got me to believe that you were some retard wop ex-con with a heart of gold who barely knew how to rub two potatoes together. Yeah, you snowed me start to finish. You wheedled your way into my place. Got me to trust you, confide in you. Got me to believe that we were friends. And then you stick a knife in my back. As easy to you as breathing. You shat in the well of the single solitary place on this earth I could ever hold up my head. Well let me tell you something you worthless piece of slime. You think you're the first person I ever trusted to betray me? It might interest to know that you're not. I've been fucked over by someone nearer and dearer to me than you. I survived it then and I'll survive it now."

I stuck my chin right up in his face while I spewed to give him a better target. I wouldn't fight back when he took his first punch. It would be my penance for having trusted the asshole. But he didn't budge. Just stood there soaking me in. It was as if he was looking right through me. When I finally wound down he whispered "Benjie, are you okay?" He laid his hand gently on my shoulder the way you do to an old man you run into on the street who can't seem to find his way home.

Why the hell hadn't God rigged humans up with a rewind button instead of stuffing them with pointless body parts like tonsils and an appendix? "I'm sorry. I'm so sorry," I said. "No offence meant," I heard myself mutter next, as if a phrase so feeble could go any way towards mopping up all the insults I'd puked in his direction.

"None taken, man," Rossi said. He then pulled me into one of those full-body handshakes, all squeezing and slapping and pumping. It was a manshake to end all manshakes, a peace treaty of a handshake that left me feeling remarkably cleansed.

Rossi's break was over. Even at this distance his specially trained cook's ears could hear the fat sputtering in the deep fryer, calling him back to duty. For once I was in no rush for him to put his hairnet back on and take off to man the fish and chips station. And he seemed hesitant to leave. So we agreed to meet for a late lunch over pizza across the street and in a back booth meant to shelter lovers we picked up our conversation away from any possible prying ears.

"The thing that I can't figure out," I confessed, "is why whoever it is replaced the plate with a substitute. I mean why bother? Why not just steal it and be done?"

Rossi clucked his tongue at my cluelessness. "It's obvious, Benjo. You're lucky to have me and my criminal mind on the case. He was testing things out, see. The plate switch was just an experiment. To get the lay of the land. To find out what security was like. Our thief is a step-by-step kind of guy." Our. I liked his use of that pronoun. It reassured me that I wasn't all alone in this mess anymore. "He's a professional, I'd say. If he sees that pinching one little plate doesn't make any waves then he'll feel comfy coming back for the big payoff. The furs I'm guessing."

"Makes sense the way you say it."

"Of course it makes sense. I know whereof I'm talking here. So the next stop is the security cameras," my consultant on the underworld continued. "You go through the footage and maybe you hit the jackpot and identify someone." He was right. I'd watched enough police procedurals to know that's step numero uno after a break-in, but the cameras in the museum were on a par with the collection. They were so old they probably snapped daguerreo-types. Besides, I didn't want to involve security from the store and have the whole thing snowball. I was hoping to solve this on my own, behind the scenes, with no one from the Bay being any the wiser. It was my mum who'd backed me for this job. I didn't want her taking any flak on my account.

"So fingerprints are out too, then?" he said.

"Yup."

"And no DNA sampling from hairs found at the scene?"

"What do you think, I'm the RCMP?"

"Jesus. I'm just kidding. Chill."

"Sorry. I guess I'm still hyped up from before." I sprinkled extra chillies on my pizza to help blast the leftover muck out of my brain.

"You can change the locks at least," Rossi said. "That'll set the guy back."

"No can do, not without a work requisition."

"That sucks."

"Thoroughly and completely."

We ordered a couple of espressos to think our way around that roadblock. Supercautious Rossi waited till the waiter left our table before he asked me, "Any ideas who it might be? Any other ideas that is. Aside from me, your law-abiding co-worker."

I'd been so focussed on Rossi that I'd never bothered to run anyone else through my metal detector. "No, not a one. You?"

Rossi seemed to be sizing up if I'd gotten my sea legs back before he spoke, but I could sense he had a hunch.

"Come on, Rossi, you can't go that far and not say what you're thinking."

He shifted uncomfortably in his seat. "I hate to say this, but have you ever considered that it might have been one of your kayak buddies? Maybe they planned the whole thing as a sort of joke. Among friends. They're probably going to give you the original plate back this Sunday when they see you. Everybody will have a good laugh." He added a feeble *ha ha*!

"I wish. But that was the one cabinet I didn't unlock that day."

"Too bad."

"It was a good theory though, Sherlock."

"Thanks. I put all my brains into it."

Lunch hour was over and we hadn't made any progress in closing in on the perp. It was time to set up the stakeout.

4

I was determined to go it alone.

Rossi'd been pushing me to let him play Tonto, I think so he could be on hand to douse me with ice water if I ended up going apeshit again, but no way would I cast him as my sidekick. It was too risky. I didn't want to be at fault for involving him in any shady activities that could land him back in an orange jumpsuit. I'd already failed the museum. A bigger guilt trip I didn't need.

Not that he didn't make himself useful in his way. He was my chief strategist when it came to setting the trap, but even better he was my unofficial caterer, plying me with food the whole time I was holed up in the museum. Always face your enemy on a full stomach, he advised me. It was one of those jailhouse clichés he dropped whenever they served his larger agenda. And he had one I was sure of it. The tipoff was the way I'd catch him staring at me sometimes, as if he were a mechanic under the lift trying to pinpoint the loose screw responsible for the rough ride. A handy guy, Rossi, he'd give it a few quick tightening turns with the pocket screwdriver he still carried around as a souvenir of his old avocation, and I'd be good as new. Dr. Sigmund Rossi was out to cure me, but since he didn't have a couch handy, he went with the only tool at his disposal. Food. On the other hand maybe a cigar was just a cigar and his constant stream of food was simply to build me up with some fleshy armour so that in a one-on-one with my intruder I could lead with my belly. Who knew?

"Okay, let's go over it one more time," he said to me a couple days later while we were sitting at the back of the museum sharing the baked ziti he'd brought over for lunch.

"We don't have to go over it again. I have it memorized."

"We do so. You have to have it nailed down perfect. Come on. What are you supposed to do if he has a gun?"

"He's not going to have a gun. And by the way, don't you professionals call it a piece?"

"Don't change the subject. What do you do if he's got a gun?"

"I know what to do."

"Humour me. I want to hear you say it."

"Okay, if it'll get you off my case. I offer him the contents of the museum and my firstborn child. All wrapped up with a red bow. I hand everything over like a little girl."

"You bet your sweet ass you do. No heroics."

"Right coach, I've got it. I've got it."

The idea of a weapon had never crossed my mind till Rossi was obliging enough to bring it up and turn me into more of a nervous wreck than I already was. He was forever reminding me that I didn't naturally think crooked and that could put me in danger. He laid it out it to me this way. "Let's imagine it was you who was caught mid-stickup, what would you do? First instinct."

"Run?" Apparently that was the correct answer. So I could think somewhat crooked. How much harder could the questions get?

"But what would you do if you were cornered?"

Clearly this was the million-dollar question so I chewed it over for a while, putting myself in my thief's shoes. There I was, caught *in flagrante* stealing from the museum by Alexandre whose plaster-golem bulk was blocking my escape route. Would I grab at his beard which in any case would fall off in my hands?

"Try to talk my way out of it?"

Rossi squeezeboxed his palms together to fart at my stinko reply. "See," he explained to me in a talking-to-a-three-year-old tone of voice, "most crooks, growing up, their mothers never said to them 'use your words.' These guys, when they're cornered, if they didn't have enough of an IQ to pack a piece – there, you happy? – they reach for anything they can use. You have to be prepared is all I'm saying."

When the idea of a stakeout first popped into my head, it carried with it the assumption that I'd be dealing with a gentleman thief, a thief in pinstripes, a thief whose charm and good looks had always been sufficient to lubricate his criminal path so packing a piece was overkill, so to speak. I reasoned that a burglar who chose to rob a museum rather than a dépanneur was clearly an upper crust type of thief, not a shoot-up-the-joint kind of guy; a guy with discernment, a pocket square, and an above-average vocabulary. We'd talk things out all civilized and at the end of the day I'd get my plate back and he'd get his freedom, a nice you-wash-my-hands-I-wash-yours settlement. Of course that was all before Rossi convinced me that such a thief only existed on the cartoon channel.

"But what about you? You didn't carry a gun."

"I'm the exception that proves the rule. Don't count on running into a thief as sloppy as me. We're a dying breed."

The plan we cooked up was as high tech as a hula hoop. I'd

spend my stakeout nights tucked into my regular sleeping burrow behind the counter, out of sight range of anyone entering the museum. There I'd wait until I picked up the sound of the culprit approaching, and when I did, I'd reach out and grab the sonofabitch who'd defiled my kingdom. Rossi suggested I aim low, for an ankle, then yank. He thought with the surprise factor I could pull it off. It required a certain amount of muscle and self-confidence, neither of which I had in large supply, but he was convinced that by throwing the sucker off his centre of gravity I could bring him to the ground, however much he might outsize me. Then I'd sit on him and immobilize him with the cuffs Rossi'd kindly supplied. We practiced the moves together on the mats at the Y but as a crash-test dummy Rossi was overcooperative and always fell right on cue. And he didn't flail around much so getting the cuffs around his wrists was sex-play easy. But at least I had the basics down.

The weak link in our plan was that I'd have to stay awake all night every night for however long it took. To make up for it, all I could do was withdraw a few winks from the sleep bank to spend during the day on the job. Some people had a talent for power napping. I wasn't one of them. Kennedy, my grandfather once told me, was a master. Give him a five minute catnap after pulling an all-nighter with Khrushchev and he could still be trusted to punch in the right nuclear codes. Me, I couldn't be trusted to put down the lid.

By the tenth night on surveillance detail I was so sleep-deprived that if some loon in camouflage fatigues broke into the museum threatening to blow it up, I'd offer to pull the pin. But exhaustion was only the half of it. My neck had developed a permanent kink from my junior-sized hide-a-bed, my skin was bleached out from lack of daylight, my digestive system was suffering from anxiety attacks, and my personal hygiene was taking a hit. To that list Rossi added that I had a tendency towards incoherence. But not so much that I should be worried over it.

"Yo ,Benjo." Rossi warned me the next morning as I was opening up the museum. "Mama sighting at three o'clock."

"Good morning, Mrs. Gabai," he greeted her.

"Hello, Rossi. How's it going?"

"Can't complain. And if I did who'd listen?"

"I was wondering," she asked him, "was it you responsible for the daily special yesterday at lunch?"

"You recognized my style? I'm flattered, Mrs. G. I put some cumin in. Did you get that Middle Easty vibe?"

"A whiff of the Maghreb in Montreal. I loved it."

Mum hadn't come by to discuss recipes, but this was their routine and Rossi couldn't politely duck out till they went through the motions. But as soon as he left, she took one look at my sorry carcass and felt my forehead with the back of her hand. Mum was still under the impression I'd left her with that I was seeing a girl, and clearly the relationship had stepped up since I was now out every night. That I'd shifted my home base didn't bother her, but the clear evidence that the new landlord was shirking her duties, letting me go out in public looking like a vagrant who'd eaten at an iffy food bank, this was too much to tolerate.

"Honey, you're selling yourself too cheap," she started in. This was probably a line she'd been storing up for Rena but never needed to deliver. Waste not want not.

"Wha?" seemed an appropriate response although I knew exactly what she was getting at.

"Wherever you're spending your nights lately, it's not doing you any good. Look at yourself. You're falling apart." She hadn't spent all these years propping me up to let some tootsie waltz in and kick the crutches out from under me.

"I might look a bit of a mess, Mum, but I'm fine. Honest. It's my own fault if I haven't neatened myself up lately the way I should have. But you don't have to worry. Really. I'm okay." Here I was defending my fictitious girlfriend on false charges of negligence. Funny, for some reason I didn't want Mum to think I'd made a dud choice in the girl department, even if we were just talking about a figment.

"It's honourable of you to take the blame, Benjie, but you can't let yourself go on like this. You're ready to drop. You have to ask yourself if she's really worth it. You've got nothing if you haven't got your health. I know young people have a hard time realizing that, but it's true. Look at your father. There, I've probably said way too much." Not that this stopped her. "Sleep home tonight why don't you? I could use the company. Zach and Rena both have plans. And between them your Nana and Grandpa only add up to one functioning ear. It'd be nice to have you for supper."

"No, Mum. I'm tied up tonight," an expression I hoped wasn't an actual foreshadowing of the night's events.

"Honey, there's no law that says you can't make a pit stop at your own home to run a load of underwear and get a good night's sleep. If she cares for you, she'll still be there tomorrow."

"I'll take it under advisement, Mum, okay?"

"Please honey. I only say it for your own good."

"I know, Mum, I know." I gave her a peck on the cheek, put my arm around her and steered her towards the escalator. "Haven't you left the purses on their own for too long, Mum? They'll be sending out a search party."

"All right, smart guy, I'm going. But think about it, Benjie. Your bed's made up and waiting."

On night eleven I wished Alexandre good night sleep tight as usual. At least he could sleep, lucky bastard, but his un-jointed limbs meant that he had to do it standing up, like an elephant. Even though he was horizontally challenged, I couldn't help but be jealous that he was able to grab some shut-eye while I had to toothpick my lids open and grind my keys into my palm to keep awake.

I must have drifted off despite myself. I remember having a dream. My father had the starring role as usual. No other members of the family ever penetrated my subconscious. That club was restricted. Dad and I were on the beach, although we weren't dressed for it. He had on a suit and I was wearing pyjamas. I looked to be around six. We were in Florida I think, not that I've ever been there. It just seemed Floridian to me in that weird way dreams have of echo-locating themselves. Dad took me to a *cantine* by the water and bought me an ice cream cone. Then we got into one of those pedal boats you can rent. It was rough going on the ocean, but we pumped like mad and somehow we ended up in the plastic driveway igloo back at our house. Only by now we weren't in the pedal boat anymore. It had transformed itself into a Land Rover, the rugged ex-Afghanistan kind, not the suburban mommy knock-off. It was all caked with mud and had a row of those mucho-macho deer-hunter spotlights above the windshield. I turned to ask Dad where we'd left the boat, but the door on his side was wide open and he'd amscrayed.

My eyes popped open. So I could look for Dad I guess. But once I was awake it wasn't him I found. Planted just beside me I made out a pair of shoes. Connected to a pair of legs. They weren't Florsheim loafers so I could count Dad out, and they weren't Alexandre's boots. That left only one living soul those shoes could belong to. The thief was standing exactly where I wanted him to be, as if he'd read our script and knew his mark. I didn't have the time or the sense to panic. I just reached out, latched on to his ankle, and jerked with all my might as if I was trying to start a testy power mower. True to Rossi's prediction, the guy dropped like a stone, his skull knocking against the floor with an ugly epileptic klop. For all our detailed planning, we'd never anticipated that particular sound. To tell you the truth it scared the bejesus out of me. I was afraid to look down and see a head smashed on the floor Halloween-pumpkin style, brain pulp splattered like pie filling across the linoleum. All I'd wanted to do was reason with the guy. Killing him was never on my agenda. But then I heard a reassuring *oooph* waft up from the floor. I'd only knocked the wind out of him. I didn't bother with the cuffs seeing as how he couldn't help but stay earthbound until his lungs regained consciousness. I flicked on the lamp on my bicycle helmet, my new and only piece of specialized equipment, to see what type of fish I'd hooked.

A cocky one apparently. No ski mask to hide his face. No gloves even. In fact, he was dressed like my grandpa. He wore a powder blue polo shirt that clung to man-boobs that were in an advanced state of development. A white belt matched with white bucks. The few left-over strands of his grey hair were precision draped across his scalp in loving memory of its former coverage. What was this geezer doing robbing a museum in downtown Montreal? He should have been sitting around a card table in Fort Lauderdale playing rummy.

I was supposed to interrogate him in a brass-knuckles voice, but I was raised to treat older people with respect. The fact that he was an older felon didn't change anything. So again I went off plan.

"Are you all right?" I asked him. "Anything broken?"

All he could manage were gasps. When Rossi and I planned all this we figured I'd be flipping a guy in his prime, a guy who could suffer the odd lump and bounce back to steal another day, but we were way off.

I propped my intruder up against the counter into a sitting position. He was one heavy guy. Tall and built solid, with a pair of Crown Royal shoulders on him. I had trouble concentrating on what I was going to say because the knot on his skull was growing before my eyes like he was sprouting a spare head.

"Want some water?"

"No thank you." So at least he could talk now. I hadn't ruined his brain by giving him an aneurysm or something. And he was surprisingly polite, considering. I sat down opposite him and waited.

"So I guess this means you found the stuff I replaced," he finally came out with, probing the swelling on the back of his head, checking his fingers for blood.

"Stuff! You mean there was more than the plate?"

"You didn't notice the pelt?"

"What do you mean, the pelt? I checked everything."

"Shine your light over there." I put on the high beam and aimed my headlamp where he was pointing. "See the third one over?" he said. "The one that's meant to be from a fox? It's actually from your run-of-the-mill urban squirrel, *Sciurus Carolinensis*."

"You killed a squirrel and skinned it?" Trapping Hannibal Lecter's older brother was more than I'd bargained for. I was starting to feel queasy stuck in close quarters with him.

"I found it dead on the street. Must have been hit by a car. I did skin it though. I used to be a furrier in my old life. It was no big deal. I'm used to it." This explanation, assuming it was true, put me at ease. Sort of. I got up and brought the false pelt over to where we were sitting since my prisoner showed no signs of making a run for it. I studied it inside out. It was a dead ringer. I'd never have guessed. Some expert I was.

"So why?" I asked him after we'd sat for a while.

"Why? Simple. The fur business went down the toilet. All those crazy activists up north. Brigitte Bardot crying over the poor little seals. Paul McCartney and that animal-rights wife of his. The EU ban. Women wearing furs getting beaned with rotten eggs. Cripes!

I couldn't get another job. No one wanted to hire anybody my age. I had debts. Made some lousy investments. It was the perfect storm. I didn't have a choice."

This sob story was supposed to make me feel sympathy for the old-timer I guess. Forced into a late-onset life of crime by circumstances outside his control. So far it wasn't working.

"What did you do to the guard, drug him?"

"What would I have to do that for? The deadbeat spends the whole night in the mattress department. I did my homework."

"You weren't worried about the security cameras?" I gestured up to the ceiling. "You didn't even bother to wear a mask." I took it as a slap in the face that my museum didn't even merit a thief willing to go through the motions.

"Bah," he dismissed them. "Those cameras date from the fur trade. Most nights they forget to put the beaver in to run the wheel." I had to hand it to him. He really had done his homework.

"You didn't wear gloves either."

"Why would I? My fingerprints aren't on file anywhere. I've never been arrested. Never had so much as a parking ticket. Besides, I figured if they found a lot of strange prints around the stolen objects, it would take some of the heat off you."

"A real humanitarian you are."

He shrugged. "I did what I could."

All those details; gloves, cameras, disguises, I asked because Rossi would be expecting a full report. But I didn't really care about the answers in the end. Whether he doped the guard, bound and gagged him, or slipped him a bundle of hush money, what difference did it make to my life? There was only one question that gnawed away at my insides, and I left it till last. "You could have robbed anyplace. Stores with jewellery, cash, electronics. You could have stuck up a bank or a gas station. Why, out of all the possible places on earth did you have to pick here?"

"I have a particular interest in the fur trade," he said. "It's a hobby of mine, you might say. More than that really. A passion you'd have to call it. What I don't know about the fur trade isn't worth knowing." The raw arrogance of his claim made me want to grab a paddle from the canoe display and finish off the job that the head bump had started, me who had trouble squishing a spider. Who did he think he was, this fossil, to barge in on my territory and treat it like a u-pick, and then, as if that wasn't enough, to pass off my personal passion as his own. It was practically identity theft.

"Is that so?" I said, cool as anything, though my effort to sound detached cost me, let me tell you. "What were you going to rip off next then, if not the furs?"

"The coins I had my eye on. The tools too. Fine specimens. Beautifully preserved. But if I had my druthers, what I'd really love to get out of here is the canoe. She's a honey. An original. Mint condition. Probably rides the water smooth as silk. Any museum would kill to have a canoe like that in its collection."

"This *is* a museum, may I remind you." I tended to get a bit sniffy when someone dissed my place of employment.

"Sorry, son, but even you have to admit this isn't exactly the Smithsonian."

That stung.

"So what are you planning on doing with me?" he asked finally.

Good question. He'd stolen from me, insulted me, and mouthed off that he knew more about the fur trade than me.

I made him an offer he couldn't refuse.

5

I had to admit it. Even if it did burn me. My thief's stroke was beautiful to behold. Morrie skimmed across the water in his kayak like he was goddamn Hiawatha. Us? Our strokes were choppy. Pathetic. We slapped at the river as if we'd never made the connection between paddles and forward motion, lurching along all spastic. We were self-taught. From YouTube. But the video we'd studied seemed to have left out a crucial step. Either that or the splashed water on the lens blurried up the fine points. That first day out as a group, we'd corkscrewed in the water, humiliatingly unable to put any distance between ourselves and the dock. Eventually the kid at the rental shed stopped laughing long enough to give us a few pointers. Shmuck. We'd figured things out paddle-wise since then of course. Still we weren't what you'd call stylish kayakers. But Morrie. Ooh, he was smooth. And fast too. He paused at the far bend of the river so we wouldn't lose sight of him.

Things were not progressing as planned. I'd invited Mr. Big-Talking-Fur-Trade-Hotshot out on the water with us to show him up. Not the reverse. "What I don't know about the fur trade isn't worth knowing," he'd crowed back at the museum. To me, he had the nerve to say that, to me of all people on this earth. The blowhard couldn't throw down a gauntlet like that and not expect me to pick it up and smack him down with it. Hard.

Lucky for me there was more to fur trade know-how than paddling. I picked up a whack load of points on the clothing side of the board with my voyageur outfit which I'd upgraded specially for the occasion. I'd splurged on a pair of breeches on Kijiji, castoffs from a re-enactor in Winnipeg who'd shifted his allegiance to the War of 1812. This seemed as good a time as any to put them to the test. I pre-dirtied them with lint from the dryer trap and matched them up with some lisle stockings that upped my look into the stratosphere of authenticity. Morrie, on the other hand, was dressed like old people do for a transatlantic flight, in a track suit and running shoes. All he was missing was the neck pillow. To give him his due, the guy wasn't aware that this was a competition. He thought I invited him out to enjoy what I'd finally informed him back at the museum was a common interest of ours. Sap. Did he really believe that I'd forgive him all his trespasses because he was a fellow fur trade freak?

I did some serious paddling to catch up to him. My wimpy shoulders were crying out for mercy and my blisters were growing blisters, but I couldn't let them call the shots now. I had something to prove. Once I was a few lengths short of him Morrie started up again, but slower, more deliberate, exaggerating his strokes just enough. I got the message. I'd been going at it totally wrong all this time turns out, giving my torso a pass when it should have been carrying the load. I mimicked his style, matched my strokes and my grip to his, tweaked my posture, and for the first time since I'd lowered myself into one of these glorified tub toys my kayak scooted along as if I was the boss, heading where I aimed it instead of where it damn well pleased. And it zipped instead of crawled, as if it had eaten some energy bars for breakfast.

I came up starboard to Morrie and we fell into an easy rhythm beside each other. Before long we were so far out on the river I couldn't even pick out the rest of the guys as pinpricks. I'd never made it this far from our starting point before, where the river widens and makes like it's a lake. The bistros and antique stores that line the shore were completely lost from view. Nothing out there ahead of us but an IMAX panorama of trees and sky.

The water was strangely clear. Every other Sunday when I looked over the side, empty soda cans and cast-off condoms looked back up at me. Glassy-eyed fish floated belly up in the scuzzy seafoam that had knocked them off in the first place. How was it that here, not even a kilometre off my regular route, the water was crystalline, and the fish so energetic that they leapt out of the water, practically begging to be hooked? These fish were too peppy to have been nourished on lake grunge, elite athletes compared to the street-people fish that normally plied their gimpy paths under the surface of Lac Saint-Louis.

The air smelled of doused campfire, an odour I'd never picked up before. Doused campfire and pine needles. I sniffed to be sure my nostrils weren't hallucinating but there was no trace of the exhaust that they ordinarily had to snort up from those muscle-bound Sea-Doos that churned up a chop. Their hung-over owners must have been home sleeping it off.

The racket of civilization didn't reach us out here, none of the honking cars or revving motorcycles that usually poked a finger in the eye of my voyageur daydreams. Even the church bells were on mute. All we could hear was the gentle whipping of our paddles through the water, the gulls kee-keeing overhead, and the insects sawing out their backdrop buzz. But then the soundtrack changed.

Morrie heard it too. I could tell from the tilt of his head. A scrap of a song was drifting in on the breeze. It wasn't pumping out of some speaker from shore. No way. We were too far out. Besides, it had the raggedy off-keyish sound of a group of guys belting it out live. The song had a thumping rhythm to it, a real chain-gang beat. And it was getting louder and louder. I gave it a good listen and I recognized it. From my research at the museum of all places. It was "C'est l'aviron," a regular on the voyageur top forty from the 1780s. Nobody'd sung it since the fur trade went bust.

Christ! It was happening. After all my fantasizing about just such a possibility we'd actually stumbled onto the doggie door that opened up onto another age and paddled right through. We stopped advancing and bobbed on the water, letting ourselves be swallowed up by yesterday, waiting to greet our fellow travellers who now sounded almost close enough to lock paddles with. Neither of us was breathing. Who needed oxygen at a time like this? We stared straight ahead not wanting to miss the moment when they first appeared to us, our role models, our heroes.

"God, what's up with you guys?" Our heads whiplashed at the sound of Renaud's voice shouting out to us from behind. He was paddling like mad in our direction. Shit. Shit. Shit. He blew our chance, the gate-crasher. Wrecked it all. The singing stopped dead at the sound of Renaud's voice and the scene morphed back to Sunday normal. Hydro poles and cell phone towers popped back into view among the trees, the fish swallowed their valium, and those superior wet-suited assholes in their jet boats zoomed in right on top of us to douse us with spray. I could see Morrie's whole body deflating.

"Aren't you going to pull in for lunch?" Renaud asked us. "The others are already half done eating. They suckered me into going out to catch up with you. Whew, that was one helluva workout.

Now I'm really starved. You two planning on coming back for a bite any time in this century?" His particular choice of words only served to twist the knife. But what was the point of hanging around at the spot where our head-to-head with history had imploded. In glum silence Morrie and I paddled back to shore with Renaud where we picked at our lunches.

It was an odd break. My crew could tell I was trying to impress the senior citizen I'd brought along for some reason they couldn't fathom, so they toned down the goofiness, and threw around some fur trade jargon to make it look like they weren't a bunch of ignoramuses.

"You're not going to quiz us from the book?" Nick was feeling lucky and was eager to pump up his dinky score.

"Nah, I left it in my other pants."

The truth was that I wasn't in an emcee mood. Something freaky had happened back there on the water and I needed peace and quiet to knock it around in my mind. Which translated into no Q&A with the guys for the day. Their scores would hold over till next week. Without the prospect of a quiz show to keep them occupied, Sam, Renaud, and Nick drifted off to play hacky-sack, a game that I sanctioned as group leader. In all my digging through sources I never came across any evidence that voyageurs ever really played it, but it seemed plausible to me that they might stuff a beaver's stomach with sand or pebbles and kick it around for sport like a dead haggis.

Morrie folded back up the paper lunch bag from his egg salad sandwich and put it in his pocket. He made himself comfy up against a stump, pulled a plug of wood out of his tracksuit and started to whittle. It was a bird call. Nothing fancy, but he knew which side of a pocket knife was up. He put the call up to his lips and tootled through the hole once or twice to see if it fit his specs and then shaved off some surplus here and there. We didn't talk about what had just happened to us while we were out in our kayaks. He whittled. I watched. It was as if we agreed that the situation we'd found ourselves in was too fragile to be poked or prodded. If we were to put it into words, all the magic would fall out of it. At least that's how I felt.

The longer I sat there and mulled it all over, the more I decided that Morrie had his head on straight. He wasn't fixated like I was by the petty trappings of the fur traders, their food, their clothes, and all that stuff. While I had stubbornly insisted on taking a dump in the bushes, nature-boy style, before we'd set off on the water, he'd used the nearby portalet. Somehow this guy had managed to drill down to the Zen of the voyageur. I could learn a lot from him.

A sparrow showed some interest in Morrie's flirty chirping and settled himself on a low-hanging branch above us. He checked out the vicinity for the babe who'd called him over but when he saw it was just Morrie faking it, he flew off in a huff.

"So this invitation to join you all out here," he said as we watched the conned bird disappear, "it was meant to put me in my place, right? Stomp on me but good?"

"You figured that out, did you?"

"I don't have Alzheimer's yet, son. I could see I ticked you off back at the Bay. But how was I to know you were such a fanatic about the fur trade? For you, I figured it was just a job. I had no way of knowing you were a kindred spirit."

What he said was no more than true. Why should he have assumed that a minimum wage flunky would have any serious bond with the items in his charge? Tank tops at the Gap, antiquities at the Bay. To him interchangeable. I was wrong to take offence. Mind you, if I wasn't in my right mind at the time, who could blame me?

I was as sleep deprived as a new father and totally jacked up from taking a prisoner. I was well within my rights to be unhinged.

"Sorry about that," I said. "It was low. Oh, and mea culpa about the lump."

He probed gingerly around its golf ball circumference. "No need to apologize. I had it coming."

"It's just that I never met anyone who shared my interest before. I didn't even know there was anyone else out there. I thought I had the market cornered."

"I know. You get proprietary, don't you? My wife always says *you and your fur trade,* like I own the patent."

"My family thinks I'm nuts. They'd rather I pick something more mainstream to throw myself into. Something that doesn't make them roll their eyes every time I open my mouth. But that other stuff they're always suggesting to me to take its place, it's all so trivial. It wouldn't grab you by the throat the way this does. You get what I mean?"

"Exactly," he pounced on what I'd said. "There are times a man needs to have something so intense going that it helps him blank out parts of his real life. For a while at least."

He got it dead on. *Bashert,* my Nana would have said. Fate. It was fate that I came together with this complete stranger who knew me like I knew myself. It sounds crazy, I grant you, but I was starting to consider myself lucky that he'd targeted my museum of all places. Otherwise, I might never have crossed paths with my soul mate.

Now, what exactly it was in his life that Morrie wanted to blot out he didn't go into. That he'd lost his job and was seriously strapped for cash I already knew, but somehow I didn't think that was all there was to it. Still, I respected the guy's reticence. It's not like I was about to spill my guts after so many years dedicated to keeping them in lockdown.

"Your wife, what does she think of your *hobby*?" I was careful to pronounce it with quotes around it. We both knew that the h-word didn't do justice to our mutual obsession.

"She tolerates it. Says she's glad I spend my time at home burrowed in my fur trade room rather than out gallivanting with other women. Not that I would," he hurried to clarify when he caught me sizing up his potential as a golden-age womanizer. "A thief I may be, but that's the limit to my extracurricular activity. I've always been faithful to my Lena. I swear to God."

"What kind of stuff do you keep in this room of yours?"

He closed his eyes as if to bring up a picture. "You name it, I got it," he said with a re-blip of the hubris he'd shown back at the museum. "Books, maps, sketches, artifacts that I picked up here and there. A to Z. See, I've been collecting since before you were born." He was winding up a little like my Grandpa did before a lengthy dip into the pool of his youth. "Back in the dark ages, before there was any Internet, it was a real challenge to track things down. But that was the fun of it. When you did make a score it gave you such a charge. I can't describe the feeling.

"I even did a little archaeological digging when I was younger, by York Factory. God that place was the back of beyond. You could only get there by canoe, up the Hayes River. Even today that's the only route. As accessible as the moon. That's when I first picked up the paddling bug. Anyway, there was a Hudson's Bay trading post on that spot for almost three hundred years. The ground around the site was so thick with treasures, they practically jumped up and bit you on the nose. You wouldn't believe what I picked up there, dice, bone needles, a ladle, musket balls. A harmonica even. Once I cleaned it up you could still blow a few notes out of it. I came by things any way I could, and little by little my room filled up."

I hated to rain on his jaunt down memory lane since he was so clearly blissed out, but I couldn't help myself. My late lamented plate haunted me like a phantom limb. I could still feel the contours of its cracked border scraping against my fingertips.

"So why didn't you fence your own stuff then instead of raiding mine?"

"You think I didn't? Anything worth anything bit the dust a long time ago. What I just described to you? I was fudging, okay? It's how things used to be, how it still looks in my mind. All I really have left now wouldn't sell for shit if you'll pardon my French. I had to branch out. And as we both know that's what brought me to you.

"Look," he went on. "I know it doesn't make up for anything, but I'd like to invite you over to come see the place. I still have some interesting objects up there, even if it isn't a patch on what it was in the old days. No one ever visits. It's my private sanctuary. Like the museum is yours. Besides, it would give me a chance to introduce you to my Lena. She doesn't get much company and I know she'd be thrilled to have you drop by. Come. Please. Pay us a visit. I won't take no for an answer."

"So," Rossi said on the following Monday, "Let me make sure I got this straight. First you invite the crook out for a boat ride, then he invites you to his house. So now it's your turn to invite him to the prom?"

"It wasn't like that."

"Look Benjo, you've screwed this up royally, but we can rescue it. Nothing's stopping you from turning in the prick. Just because you shared a few heritage minutes with him in your canoe, that can't hold you back."

"Kayak."

"Whatever. What's his name?"

"Morrie."

"Morrie what?"

"I don't know."

"You don't know his last name? You didn't get an ID on the guy?"

Rossi's shock at my incompetence knew no bounds. He thought he'd trained me up better than that. It was the first time I'd seen him since the foiled robbery and the outing on the river with Morrie. I explained it all to him in the greatest of detail. Well, almost all. How I'd toppled Morrie, how I thought at first I'd killed him, how Morrie and me got to talking about the fur trade, and how I'd impulsively invited him out to kayak with the guys. I only snipped off the tail end. Our almost-rendezvous with the brethren out on the water was nobody else's business yet.

"But I didn't invite him out in friendship. It was to stick it to him, to show the gasbag he was no bigger an expert than I was."

"You didn't keep your eye on the ball. Didn't I teach you anything? The point of the whole exercise was to get back what he stole if you could, and scare him into never coming near your place again. Did you get your plate back?"

"No, he'd already fenced it. But he'll never come back. Not to steal anyway."

"And you know that how?"

I forced myself to say it. "We clicked." It was embarrassing to put it that way but it was true. My sixth sense told me Morrie would never bother the museum again now that he knew I was his brother from a fur trade mother. He'd find some other mark.

"You clicked? Like you hooked up on eHarmony? Clicked, he says. Benjo, wake up and smell the coffee. The guy's manipulating you. Take it from me, the manipulators are the worst. Worse than the thugs. They never leave off. He's got you wrapped around his little finger. Of course he'll come back. Guaranteed. He probably tickled all the state secrets out of you already so he can come back and loot the joint with no trouble. You'll come in one day and the place'll be cleaned out down to the paperclips. What am I going to do with you, Benjie? You're hopeless."

"I have his address," I offered up in compensation.

"What did you major in at university again?"

"English lit."

"Right, 'cause if you'd majored in math, you'd be able to figure out the odds of that address existing. Even I know it's zero and I can hardly add."

"But he came out with me to kayak, didn't he? He could have just disappeared on me. But he came."

"I can't explain it, but my advice is, steer clear of the guy. He sounds like a dangerous character to me. Unpredictable. Wacko. Maybe he's old but that doesn't mean he's a pussycat. Watch out, Benj. You're in uncharted waters here."

I was in uncharted waters with Morrie all right. Literally. And that's exactly where I wanted to stay.

6

So in my immediate entourage, which granted wasn't all that big, I had Rossi pissed off at me for being a premium dummkopf and my mother on top of the world. Suddenly I was home more, looking rested and scrubbed up. Mum was still in the dark about the whole Morrie business. I'd purposely filed that information under *classified*. The danger in unloading on her was too great. She might slip up and blab about the museum break-in to one of her co-workers and I couldn't have that. The degree of separation between my mum down in Ladies' Purses and the bosses up in the executive suites was way less than six. In no time we'd both be out on our ear. Or ears.

Mum had such a trusting nature. I had no trouble at all leading her to the conclusion that the trumped-up girlfriend and I had split up. She was too relieved to even think about gloating. Instead, she took the high road and prepared couscous merguez, my favourite. It was a major-effort meal that relayed *sorry for your troubles* without actually having to say it out loud. In the old days she would have been all over me with her consoling slobbery kisses.

She was a major gusher, Mum was. But she'd toned down her tactics with us kids over time to adapt to our teenage prickliness, choosing instead to relay her repressed maternal feelings towards us undercover, through food. If she'd lived back in fur trade times she probably would have sent us smoke signals.

Rena, Zach, and I were sprawled out on the couch in front of the TV with our ice cream. Nana and Grandpa were deep into their after-dinner dozing at the kitchen table, and Mum was flitting through the den every ten minutes modelling various outfits for one of her rare blind dates. She almost always begged off when some well-meaning friend or relative tried to jockey her off the shelf, but this time the wad of excuses she kept handy in her pocket must have slipped through a hole in the lining and out popped a yes.

"What do you think of this?" she asked, twirling around in front of us. She was blocking the screen so we all said she looked great.

"Not too tight across the tuchis?"

"Just tight enough to keep him interested." This comment from Zach sent her scrambling back to her bedroom for a wardrobe rethink.

"I hope this guy gets her in bed," Rena said once Mum was out of earshot.

"Yoy, Rena, this is Mum you're talking about," Zach said. "Keep those thoughts to yourself, do you mind?" For once I was right with him.

"Whether you two want to listen to me or not, my diagnosis is that she needs to get laid and she needs it bad. That'll unwind her." Neither of us figured Rena to have had any personal bedside experience with the subject yet, even though she was plenty old enough, but her plain talk hinted at a certain street cred. And maybe she was on the right track. Mum's meltdowns seemed to be increasing in frequency. If she didn't find some way of relieving the pressure, we'd be sitting around the kitchen table one day, me and Zach sniping at each other, and her head would rocket off her shoulders like a champagne cork.

"Doesn't matter anyway," Zach said. "You know these dates never go anywhere. Has she ever gone out with a guy more than once? In living memory?"

"According to her, nobody ever measures up to Dad, so what's the point?"

"Yeah," I said. "That pedestal she puts him on is too high for anyone else to climb up. Besides, it's a greased pole. I don't think even Dad would make it up there if he were to come back to life today."

It was ten years since Dad kicked the bucket. Plunk in the middle of my Bar Mitzvah. There I was, limping my way through my *haftorah* portion, massacring the ancient chants that were atonal to begin with, when he keeled over dead. Bang. Plotzed right in front of the *bima*. The one doctor in attendance, my mum's Uncle Jack from Windsor, a dermatologist, tore open Dad's made-to-measure dress shirt and pumped on his chest as if he knew what was what, but the zit specialist couldn't manage to make Dad's heart reboot. Dad was gone from one second to the next, and the Bar Mitzvah guests reassembled two days later at the cemetery.

Which left us with a problem. On top of his death I mean. Since Dad's untimely demise cut off the Bar Mitzvah ceremony before it was over, before all the i's were dotted and the t's crossed, technically speaking it meant that I never really became a man. None of us in the family felt like returning to the synagogue in the months that followed to finish it off. Naturally enough. Not even in the rabbi's back study, though he'd encouraged us, where we could do it privately and by the way hand over the way past due envelope. So I was left in a state of arrested development. And now here I was, out of university, working for my keep, but still not a man. All the outward signs were there of course. It's not like I didn't have hair on my *schmekel*. But I couldn't help thinking that this was why I'd never made anything of myself. I was stunted, unfinished. And who did I have to thank for my condition?

I know it's harsh to hold it against Dad, but did he have to check out at that very instant? I mean really, couldn't he have hung on for a stinkin' half hour? Typical. His timing was always off where I was concerned. Or maybe it was my timing. If only I'd been able to walk to shul faster in my toe-pinching new shoes, if only I hadn't spent so long in the crapper before my insides felt ready to face the congregation, if only I'd studied harder so my delivery wasn't so halting and sputtering, then we would have been finished by the time he croaked, and I'd be a full-fledged man today instead of a child stretched to extra tall. If I sound heartless, well, it's not like we never had our issues Dad and me.

Mum reappeared in pants, a blazer, and an Oxford shirt that made her look like Monsieur Goudreau, our high school vice-principal. "Mum, you're not even trying," Rena said. "Come on, I'll go back with you to your closet and we'll pick out something less butch, okay?"

Zach polished off Rena's unfinished Häagen-Dazs and then turned to me during a commercial. "Want to go to the car show with Eli and me tomorrow? Michael bombed out so I have an extra ticket." I had a rough time saying no to his invitation which had a certain brotherly pull to it. It was the first time since forever that he'd asked me to go someplace with him, even if I was only being invited as a pinch hitter. When I was a kid, I tagged along everywhere at his heels and he tolerated my presence with just some token grumbling. We'd throw the ball around, torture Rena together. Brother stuff. But back at that point in my life when things started to fall apart big time, my relationship with Zach was the first casualty. See, Dad started to focus so much attention on me, the son in free-fall, that Zach became all but invisible to him. And they'd always been tight those two. Among the guys in the family, Zach wasn't accustomed to being third-wheeled. That was my traditional position. If I had to sum up Zach's feelings, not that he ever expressed them in so many words, it would have gone something along the lines of *What the hell! Suddenly it's you Dad loves best and me he treats like dirt?* Now the thing is, I had it on good authority that Zach was dead wrong, and would have happily let him know so if only I'd been at liberty to say. But since I was hamstrung we drifted apart. Our relations after that were what I would generously call strained. Sometimes better, most times worse.

At first, I figured his car show invitation as a baby step towards a reconciliation. Maybe Zach was finally ready to let me back in after all these years. Nothing would have made me happier. The timing made no particular sense, but who was I to look a gift horse in the mouth? Could be the daffy Nathalie had worked him over. Civilizing the guy she'd latched onto when she fell for his ringtone on a crowded bus was a major preoccupation of hers. But then it flitted through my mind that this invitation, so out-of-the-blue, had Mum's fingerprints all over it. Like maybe she'd floated my brother the cash for a spare ticket. She wasn't above arm-twisting us into closeness. If it worked, then she'd be able to rest easy in her grave, knowing that we boys would always have each other to lean on. Mum was a major advance planner.

Whatever under-the-table negotiations prompted the invitation, no way could I accept. It would have meant bailing on my visit to Morrie's, and that I was not about to do, even if Rossi had succeeded in rattling my confidence. He almost had me convinced that Morrie'd slipped me a dummy address, and that I'd approach the Westmount number he'd given me only to find an empty lot.

Well, it wasn't the lot that was empty.

The following afternoon as I walked up the street towards the house-number Morrie'd jotted down for me, I was relieved to see the addresses increasing by neat multiples of four, mathematically predicting the existence of a house bearing the number on my slip of paper. Rossi was all wet, turned out. There was a house with that number all right, and not just your garden variety semi-detached. This was a house on steroids. Back when I was too young to protest, Mum used to drag me and Rena to Sunday open-houses. She wasn't in the market, and sure as hell not for the kind of über real estate she traipsed us through, but she loved to snoop around through the designer interiors of the upper crust. After a few years of keeping her company on those outings, I knew my carriage-trade real estate inside out. 556 Roslyn wouldn't quite qualify as a mansion. It was one of those wannabe houses that real estate agents labelled a deluxe home in the handout, or maybe a lavish stone manor. I could rattle off its amenities without even going in. It probably had a library, a butler's pantry, a wine cellar, maid's quarters, and panoramic city views. Ensuite this, walk-in that, and built-in the other. The taxes alone could pay my annual salary at the museum with a few cents change. So even if this joint didn't have all the frills of a card-carrying mansion, it was still a house and a half.

So with worry number one out of the way, worry number two, which had been waiting patiently in the wings, took centre stage. You can probably guess what it was after all you've read so far. That I'd knock on the door and whoever opened it would never have heard of this Morrie character I was inquiring after. That my thief had set me up and at this very minute, with me safely out of the way, he was having his way with my museum and it couldn't yell to me for help.

It was this image of him brutalizing my birthright that finally pushed me to reach for the knocker instead of standing frozen on the stoop like a spare gargoyle. Morrie must have been hovering behind the leaded panes of the front window because he pulled open the door after only one rap. The way he nearly shook my hand off my arm to welcome me in made me suspect that he had similar doubts to mine about us ever connecting that day.

My host led me out of the front hall into what must have been the living room, but it was hard to be sure seeing as how it was buck naked. Couches, no; coffee tables, no; loveseats, no; piano, no. Just plenty of nuthin'. It wasn't a cheerful newlywed emptiness either, a freshly-painted emptiness open to a future of Ikea possibilities. It was an emptiness of removal. Puncture marks in the walls signalled where paintings used to hang, with little anthills of plaster dust on the floor underneath each one. A darkened oblong on the floorboards marked out an area rug's former turf. The only sign of life was a framed wedding photo sitting on the mantle, but I couldn't get near it since this maybe-living room wasn't our immediate destination. We kept right on going and passed into what was theoretically the dining room, but again, no tables or buffets or breakfronts to hint at its former vocation. I mean nada. I checked it out as best I could as Morrie hustled me through. A room like that, in its golden olden days had probably hosted sitdown dinners for thirty guests, maybe forty. Silver and crystal. Baccarat or some such. Nowadays the only way to serve a meal in there would be picnic style, butts against bare floor.

But not our butts apparently. We weren't pausing there either. Morrie opened a pair of sliding doors at the far end and motioned me to go into the next room. At least it was clearly identifiable as a kitchen. Whoever'd cannibalized the other rooms hadn't sunk his incisors into this part of the house yet. Now this was a room that gave a hint at the house's former glory, even if the lonely table in the gigundo eat-in area was a fifties bridge table with two mismatched chairs. Size-wise it more rightly belonged in Jerry Seinfeld's apartment. It was at that rickety bridge table, shimmed with a matchbook, where Morrie eventually sat me down.

"Can I offer you something? A beer? Coffee?"

"No thanks. I'm good." He helped himself to a Schweppes from the fridge and settled in opposite me.

"This is a little awkward, Ben," he began.

I helped him along. I was a super soft touch now that I'd tramped through the empty barracks he had to call home. My family's bungalow may have been modest, Morrie's garden shed was probably roomier, but it was cozy, no denying. "Well, we're used to things being awkward between us, you and me, wouldn't you say? With our history? So just start in. Go for it."

"Right. You're right. It's not like we got to know each other in any conventional way." He fingered the purplish bumplet on his scalp that was the memento of our first meeting.

"Well, it's like this. Before I introduce you to Lena, I just want to mention a couple of things. Ground rules sort of. Maybe that's not very hospitable. Lena would treat me to a matching bump on the head if she ever caught wind that I was stage-managing your visit, but here goes anyway.

"You remember back at your museum that day, I told you that my business washed out?" I nodded my recollection. "Well, when I couldn't find another job after, I didn't know what to do. Lena's condition was deteriorating. The house was mortgaged up to the hilt. I needed cash. There was no one I could get to float me a loan.

So what I did, I started to sell things from the house. Little things at first, some candlesticks here, an Inuit carving there. A print, a watch. Bits of my fur trade collection. And that kept me afloat for a good long while. But eventually, in the way of things, the money I picked up doing that ran dry so I had to move on to the big stuff, the furnishings, the chandeliers, the rugs, all that. The stars out of my collection. I sold everything that wasn't nailed down. I'm telling you if I could have peeled the paint off the walls and stuck it back into the cans for a refund, I would have. That's how close to the edge I was running by then.

"Lena, she never knew. She hasn't been able to leave her room for anything other than a doctor's appointment, it's been years now. I only keep up what she sees or feels; her room naturally, the A/C, the heat, the garden. The adapted van. And living in this neighbourhood I can't let the exterior of the place go to pot. The neighbours wouldn't put up with it. So the landscaper and the stonemason do tag team to bleed me dry."

"So you're saying she doesn't suspect anything?"

"Nope. Not a thing."

"She never asks to go into the rest of the house for auld lang syne?"

"Never. You'll understand when you see her. She's very weak. And the pain is tough to control. Just getting her out of bed is a struggle. She trusts me that everything beyond her room is the way it always was. She has no reason to think otherwise."

Okay. So I'd never met her. But it seemed impossible to me that this Lena, if she had even a gram of intuition, wouldn't clue in that hubby was selling the house out from under her in dribs and drabs. How could he keep an operation like that secret from her? But then if I was any kind of expert on the inner workings of families, I would have been better at repairing the broken widget in my own. God knows the fix I'd tried to apply was a flopola of grand proportions. Yet didn't I persist with it till this day?

"Doesn't she have nurses, aides, I don't know, therapists coming in, someone who might spill the beans?"

"There's a suite built onto the back of the house, next to the garage. That's where she stays now 24/7. I had it done up years ago when things were different. It was going to be her studio. To paint in. There's an entrance from the garden. Anyone who comes to look after her comes and goes that way, off the driveway. They don't have access to the rest of the house. That door's locked. You're the only one in years who I've let in through the front door." I could already feel the weight of the baggage my front-door status bestowed on me.

"So here's the thing. Those ground rules I was mentioning? You have to swear to me not to let slip anything about the house to Lena. Nothing that might make her suspicious. And for sure nothing about the thefts! If she had any idea.... She's very, what can I say, rigid in her standards. That's how she was raised. If she ever suspected I'd been involved in anything even a fraction not on the up and up, she'd never forgive me. Of that I'm positive. To her there are no shades of illegal. Don't talk to her about mitigating circumstances. No exceptions. No loopholes.

"Lena's father was a furrier. That's how we met. He had a business card, and above his name it was printed *honest, conscientious, and reliable*. That card said it all. And it didn't apply just to him alone. It was their family motto sort of. They lived by it. So she can't know. Do you understand? She can't." He ran his hand nervously over his forehead as if to second guess why he'd ever been foolish enough to invite over this chink in his armour.

I'd come this far. And it wasn't like I was making a pact with the devil. "Your secrets are safe with me."

By rights it should have looked clinical in there. The hospital bed at the centre of the room was studded with a cockpit's worth of levers and controls. You could probably raise it, lower it, or set it on the spin cycle. The owner's manual for that baby must have been a good half-inch thick. A wheelchair was pushed up against the wall, and I caught the corner of a porta-potty type contraption hidden behind an oriental screen. But somehow, for all that, you didn't feel like you were in a sickroom. Lena took care of that.

Morrie led me over to the bed and introduced me to his wife. She was a tiny little thing, pixyish I guess you'd say, with her dyed carroty hair cropped short and shooting out from her head at funky angles. Her lips were perked up at the corners as if to mock all the medical gizmos that had clearly stumbled into the wrong room. Her eyes had a cheeky glimmer to them. If only she were wearing the little green hat and matching tights, you'd have sworn at first glance she was Peter Pan's great-grandmother. But that illusion got a kick in the teeth when you stopped to take in the dramatic curve to her spine. It was as if she were trying to perfect some advanced yoga pose that demanded she stretch her chin down to touch her knees.

I screwed up right off the bat by sticking out my hand for her to shake. It was too late to retract it when I noticed her hands were balled up into permanent fists, the knuckles all knobbly and swollen. They looked like hunks of ginger from the market. Lena was unfazed by my gaffe. She just shrugged her shoulders as if she were the one at fault, raised her right arm as best she could and gave me a friendly dap. With that one move, which I had the sense cost her her full energy quota for the day, she made me feel welcome when I really deserved to be booted out the door as a grade-A shmuck, an insensitive young punk that her husband had been sucker enough to drag in from the street. But she was too fine, choosing instead to flick my blunder away and put me at ease in her home. She must have been an incredible hostess back in the days before her dining room went the full monty and her body started to feed on itself.

"Hello, Mrs. Shukert. I'm happy to meet you."

"Likewise. I've heard so much about you, Benjamin. And please, call me Lena."

"Thank you for inviting me over. Your house is very beautiful."

"I hope that my Morrie gave you the grand tour?" There was a trace of Eastern Europe in her diction, a little hand-me-down shtetl underneath her *t-h*'s.

"Just the downstairs so far."

"He didn't take you up to show you the view? That's what I've always loved most about this house, the way you can look out the windows at the back and see forever, like you're God in heaven if you'll pardon my presumption."

"Don't you worry," Morrie assured her, "he'll get the full upstairs tour when we go up to my room. I guarantee it."

"That room," she dismissed it with sham irritation. "His mancave. Isn't that what they call such a place? It's not a term I ever heard until recently. I learned it from the television. I watch it far more than I should now that my gymnastics team has dumped me for some reason." I'd always been a great admirer of a slow-pitch wiseass delivery, and this Lena was a pro. "Although," she continued, "maybe I have the term wrong. A cave must mean that it has to be in the basement, no? And Morrie's is not."

I was able to offer some clarity on the subject. "I think it can be on an upper floor. But then you have to call it a mantuary."

Even if her illness was wasting her away, her body had forgotten to mention it to her laugh. It packed a healthy wallop, a great brassy whoop that shed years off her and let me catch a glimpse of the fireball Morrie had married.

"A smart boy my husband brought me home. You can teach me all sorts of useful things. I hope you won't make yourself a stranger. I don't get much company. What my loving husband does to put people off, I don't know, but they don't come around like they used to. But you, I have a feeling you'll come again.

"Now, when he takes you upstairs, dear boy, I hope you'll find that it's been cleaned up to my standards. I haven't been able to supervise the upkeep in a while. If there are any dust bunnies in that room to shame me, I'll have this one's head." She eyeballed Morrie who smiled down on her withered frame like the sun shone out of her *pupik*.

"Nothing like a few dust bunnies to make a place feel like home." I reassured her.

"It's kind of you to say so. You're well brought up I can tell. I know my husband tries to clean up in there in his way. He refuses to let the cleaning woman go in. She might disturb his system. Destroy the perfect order. But he's not cut out for mopping and scrubbing, my Morrie. His talents lie elsewhere. The other day he bumped his head on one of his display cabinets and it left him a good lump. Next time I'll send him up there with a helmet." So that's how he'd explained away the knot on his head, this guy I'd sized up as shrewd? A feather-dusting accident? Not too inspired if you ask me but she seemed to have fallen for it.

"So I hear you're in charge of your own museum," she said. "Not many men your age can boast of such an achievement. You must be very accomplished."

"It's not actually my museum, Mrs. Shukert." Morrie's earlier speech about his wife's honesty fixation had a truth-serum effect on my replies.

"Lena, please."

"Okay, Lena. See I'm just the hired help. Morrie must have exaggerated my importance."

"Don't demean yourself. My husband tells me you're extremely knowledgeable about his pet subject. He's been waiting all his life to come across such a person, and now he's found you."

"I'm flattered he thinks so."

"So, Benjamin, remind me how you and my husband met exactly?"

Such a simple question. And it had a simple answer. I just didn't know how much of the simple answer Morrie would expect me to lay on the table because my coach wasn't there to semaphore me any clues. He'd stepped into the bathroom to get some water for his wife's pills. I tried to stall. After all, how long does it take to pour a stinkin' glass of water? But he stayed away for what felt to me like a good, long stretch. The door to the bathroom was closed. He must have stopped, as long as he was in there on pill duty, to take a quick piss. At least I hoped it would be quick. I knew from hanging around outside the bathroom waiting for my grandpa to vacate the premises that a quick piss wasn't something to take for granted at that age.

The seconds were ticking themselves off. I had to offer up something. I made the strategic decision to start off with fact, inch out from there, and see where it took me till the flush came that would save my hide. What else could I do? "Well, we met at my museum one day this summer." I took a little dogleg to drag things out a bit. "We don't get all that many visitors in the summer normally. Attendance goes way down starting in June. November's our biggest month for some reason. Maybe people are in the store doing early Christmas shopping and run across us while they're there. I don't know. We've never done a questionnaire for visitors but it's something I'm considering. I've written up a prototype. I can't distribute it though without submitting it to my supervisors upstairs first. But if they give it their stamp of approval then I can have it ready to go out as early as next month. It has the usual kinds of questions. I've been doing some research. First there's your demographic stuff, age bracket, sex. That kind of thing. Then I try to pin them down on how they spend their discretionary income on culture, how many museums they visit per year, how many movies, plays. How did they come to hear about the museum, what kind of displays they prefer. And I leave room for comments in case they're in the mood to give a suggestion."

By the time Morrie came back in I was gibbering about parking. How I got there I couldn't tell you. I was operating on autopilot. He put the meds on his wife's tongue and followed them up with a straw since her frozen posture prevented her from tilting her head back to swig. I paused during the pill popping to catch my breath and Morrie caught my eye. I read the request to cut the blathering and bring him up to speed.

"I was just saying how you and I met at the museum."

"Right." He took over. "Remember I told you darling that I was at the Bay one day to pick up a new bed jacket for you and I passed Ben's museum and went in to look around?"

"Oh yes, you did say. My head is like a sieve these days with all the medicines I take. I do remember now. You said it was right in the middle of the store. How unusual. How many stores do you think would sacrifice retail space to allow for an actual museum inside?" she said to me.

"I don't know for sure, Mrs..., sorry, Lena, but I don't think it's very common. Not anymore anyhow. My mum says there used to be a museum in the old Pascal's Hardware Store down on St. Antoine. But the condo developers scooped that place up a long time ago."

"Well, there can't be many stores that go as far back as the Bay does, at least not in North America, and with such an extraordinary history. A store that had a role to play in creating this country of ours. I wish I were able to see your museum. Such a story it must have to tell. Morrie says it's a very impressive place." Of course I thought it was impressive, but it wasn't that often that I met up with someone else who shared my view.

Lena drew me out on all the details, showing more interest in my place of employment after a ten-minute acquaintance than my own flesh and blood had ever managed to dredge up since day one. She asked me about preservation techniques and hands-on displays versus hands-off, real museological-type questions. Did I think we should set up small outpost museums in other Bay stores or go out to local schools to demonstrate how the voyageurs lived? Her curiosity seemed to help put her discomfort on the back burner. She acted as if there were no subject more fascinating than my museum, that if a fairy godmother bopped in and tapped her with her wand so Lena could uncurl and walk away from the straitjacket that was her body, the first place she'd head to would be the Bay to check it out.

How did she do it? If I were in her condition, twisted into a permanent U like my titanium bike lock, I'm pretty sure I wouldn't have the grit to engage in conversation with a stranger the way she was doing. I'd take those bed controls in my teeth if that was the only way I could manage it, set them to the eject setting, and let that bed fling me against the wall with enough g-force to whack the life right out of me. I wasn't brave like she was.

"If you'd like, next time I come I can bring pictures of some of the really special pieces. Give you a sense of what's there." Her enthusiasm over my fur trade fixation seemed so genuine, no sign of the glazed-over eyes I was accustomed to facing when I started to unreel. It turned me into putty in her hands. If she'd asked me to hoist her over my shoulder like a sack of potatoes and cart her down to the museum for a personal tour, I'd probably have scoped out the room for a burlap bag. Morrie's actions all made sense to me now. This little sprig of a woman who hardly made a dent in the mattress was not a person you'd want to let down.

Morrie cut things short. "And now I'm going to take him up to see some of the special pieces in *my* collection like I promised when I invited him here, and we'll let you nap."

"Oh, don't go yet. Benjamin and I haven't had chance enough to talk. A new gentleman-caller for me is always an occasion."

"What," Morrie said in what I took to be a running shtick of theirs, "you're looking for a replacement?"

"Right, I'm thinking of turning you in for two thirty-five year olds."

"Well, I'll leave you to dream about the possibilities, dollface. In the meantime we're heading upstairs." They kissed each other goodbye. And I'm not talking the pro forma peck that my staid grandparents delivered when a photographer at a wedding or Bat Mitzvah bludgeoned them into rustling up a display of affection for the album. This was a serious smackeroo of the type that soldiers endowed on their sweethearts before heading off to the front to crush the Nazis. And the leave-taking still hadn't spun itself out. "Bon voyage," she called after him. It seemed like an over-the-top farewell for a trip that would take him up a single stairwell. It's not like we were off to Kazakhstan. I looked to him with the question in my eyes once we'd left the studio.

"She always wishes me bon voyage when I'm going off to my fur trade room. She knows that once I close the door on myself in there I might as well be in another world."

I guess I'd seen too many old movies. I expected Morrie's refuge to be on a par with the wood-panelled studies of ex-safari hunters. You know, zebra-skin carpets and elephant-foot umbrella stands.

But of the North. He'd have Hudson's Bay blankets thrown artfully over a couch, a fur press retrofitted into a magazine rack, crossed snowshoes mounted on the wall instead of tusks, and a deep, cracked leather club chair to sink into so he could pore over the last unsold remnants of his library.

I couldn't have been further off base. What I had in front of me was a workshop. The type you'd usually see set up in a basement or garage. The tools were neatly hung up along the walls on pegboards according to their size, the profile of each one outlined in black marker to guide it back to its proper home after use. A bit OCD it struck me at first, but what did I know? Probably Norm Abram would approve. They seemed to be woodworking tools mostly, sanders, chisels, saws, clamps. And all of the elbow-grease variety, no power gizmos that I could spot, no pneumatic anything. The only visible electrical cord ran off the Mr. Coffee. This was a purist's workshop, a workshop that made a statement.

The smell was delicious after Lena's studio. I'm a dick, I know. Her room was filled with bouquets working flat out to send up their perfumes, but as maskers they didn't quite get the job done. The underlying sick-scents still managed to wiggle their way into the air. Morrie's room, though, smelled pure and fine, woodsy through and through, sawdust, wax, and cedar planks.

It looked like he was deep into some project. And not just another dinky bird call. This was major. He had a tarp thrown over some beached-whale bulk in the middle of the room. It took over almost all the available floor space. Luckily Morrie was trim across the gut. If his belt line were any thicker, he'd hardly be able to work his way around the thing, whatever the hell it was. I was dying for a peek and he knew it so he whipped off the covering like he was a game-show host pulling back the curtain on my grand prize Audi. Then he stood back like a proud papa and let me take it in.

It was a birchbark canoe. Old style. Maybe half-way done. I ran my hand lightly across it. It was calling out to be touched. "This is one handsome boat. Made the traditional way?" To my know-nothing eyes, it looked like a scratch canoe, constructed of roughhewn materials Mother Nature had served up fresh.

"Nah. It's from a kit. The voyageur model. Much as I'd love to make one from the ground up, how am I in a position to go out and dig up spruce roots or climb to the top of a birch tree and shave off the rind? No, this is imitation, but good quality. Epoxy instead of pine pitch, rope instead of roots."

"You'd never know."

"Nice of you to say so, but it's obvious if you look close. Everything's too perfectly milled. It all lines up exactly right. But according to the manufacturer's run-down it should be able to walk the walk." He jerked his thumb towards a set of plans he had tacked up on the wall. "They say that fully loaded it can carry as much as four tons of goods. Just like its ancestors."

"That should do you all right."

"I know. It's overkill. But at the time I wanted top of the line. Big as life."

"You're lucky you have enough room to put it together up here. If it were my house we'd have to knock down some walls to fit it in."

"Space I've got plenty of."

"It's amazing. Really. I had no idea you were an artist."

"Let's not exaggerate. I just follow the instructions. That is except when it comes to the look. That's where I grant myself some leeway. What I do, see, is I rough things up as I go along, to try to make it look original." He gave me a little demo with a length of chain that he whipped against the outside of the canoe like he was a plantation overseer, pocking up the finish with authentic-style nicks and scratches. "I have some other little tricks I've developed. Not that it's necessary, but I like it to look well-used, not straight out of the box.

"The kit cost me a fortune, but I was part-way through building it when times got tough, so what could I do? I plug away at it little by little. It relaxes me. And it's not like I have other choices of how to pass my spare time. I can hardly put my feet up in the living room and watch TV, can I?" It was the first tinge of sourness I'd heard come out of him. I didn't know the guy all that well, but Morrie seemed to keep his issues, and granted they were many and varied, pretty well bottled up. Join the club.

"I could use a second set of hands," he added quickly to get us off the negative. "If you're willing that is."

"Suits me." I was more than happy to sign on as his apprentice. "But just so you know what you're getting yourself into, my father used to send me down to the basement for a crescent wrench, and I'd come back up with a plunger. He'd only risk using me as a helper when my brother wasn't around to do things right."

"I'll take my chances," he said. "Stick with me. Maybe you'll pick up something."

7

At long distances I sucked. But ask me to sprint and I was Usain Bolt. I didn't have the oxygen-tank lungs of a marathoner like Morrie did. He always came out on top when he pointed at a distant buoy and we'd shoot out across the water for it. That guy never ran out of wind. I took the early lead every time, but once he'd inch out there ahead of me Sunday driver style, looking for all the world like he was advancing in slo-mo, somehow I'd never manage to catch up.

We'd gotten into the habit of going out for a crack-of-dawn kayak workout on Sundays. We invited the other guys to join us, but they weren't too crazy about the idea of cranking themselves into gear at sunrise just for the pleasure of paddling themselves into exhaustion. Thanks but no thanks. They'd show up at the usual time. So I took advantage of the freebie master classes Morrie was offering one-on-one. After a couple of intro sessions, it got so I couldn't get enough water time to suit me. Those endorphins snuck up on me out of nowhere and goosed my metabolism till someone who didn't know any better could watch me paddle and almost take me for a jock.

We were way out from shore, bobbing on the water, resting up after our practice when out of nowhere Morrie started to chant. "*Acabris, Acabras, Acabram.*"

"Pardon?"

"*Acabris, Acabras, Acabram*," he repeated.

"Well, fee fi fo fum to you."

He sat quietly in his kayak, looking up at the clouds, unimpressed by my comeback.

"Do you mind telling me what we're talking about?" I asked him.

"It's from the *Chasse-Galerie.*"

"The what?"

"The folk tale. Do you mean to tell me that in all your reading and research about the voyageurs you never came across the story of the *Chasse-Galerie*? Say it ain't so."

My brain must have been fried from all the exercise. Otherwise it would have come back to me sooner. "You mean the story about the canoe?" I couldn't dredge up all the details. "It's haunted or something?"

"So these guys are making camp on the Gatineau River," Morrie began. "It's winter. New Year's Eve in fact and they've all knocked back a few. Late at night this one guy, Baptiste, shakes awake his friend Joe and puts a proposition to him. 'Want to go home to Lavaltrie tonight? We'll celebrate réveillon, get a little New Year's smooch from our girls, and be back in time for breakfast.'

"'Are you nuts?' Joe says to him. 'Lavaltrie's three hundred miles away. It would take us months to get there through the bush. And can I remind you it's winter?'

"'I'm not talking about slogging there on foot,' Baptiste tells him. 'We'll travel by canoe, there and back in six hours tops.' So by now the cobwebs have cleared a bit from Joe's brain and he's clued in to what his pal is suggesting, that they fly home in their birchbark canoe, navigating through the sky under the devil's protection.

"'No way José,' Joe answers, 'I'm not risking my immortal soul for a quickie trip back home, a slice of tourtière, and a kiss. Count me out. I'll celebrate here with everybody else.'

"But Baptiste badgers him. See he needs an even number in the canoe, and so far he's only been able to brainwash six others into signing on. With himself that makes seven. 'Don't be so yellow-bellied,' he says. 'I've done it five times before and the devil hasn't bagged me yet. All you have to do is obey a couple of simple rules. That's it. First, whatever you do, you don't pronounce the name of *le bon dieu* during the trip. How hard is that? And second, you don't touch any crosses on the steeples that we pass. If you can just manage those two things, then the devil will whiz us home through the air and bring us safely back here in plenty of time. So what do you say man, are you in?' At the sight of the others waiting to take off, Joe knuckles under and joins the crowd. They all get in the canoe and Baptiste recites the incantation that will get the show on the road. '*Acabris, Acabras, Acabram! Fais-nous voyager par-dessus les montagnes!*'

"Bam, next thing they know they're up in the air paddling like hell through the sky, singing at the top of their lungs, making for Lavaltrie, the full moon lighting their way. They slalom around the steeples and don't nick a single one the whole way. In just under two hours they spot the spires of their destination from the sky and bring the canoe in for a landing in a snowbank, soft as you please. They find out where the New Year's celebration is being held in the village and head that direction, but before Baptiste lets his crew loose on the house party he issues them a stern warning. 'No liquor must pass your lips while you're in there,' he says. 'You need to keep your wits about you. Understood?' The guys all swear to stick to the fruit punch and they go in and have a high old time.

"When four a.m. chimes, the pre-arranged time to start heading back, all the crew members quietly slip out of the house, all that is except for Baptiste, who, as it happens, is drunk as a skunk. They have to drag him out kicking and screaming. Now this is a problem, as you might imagine, since he's the one who's meant to steer the canoe. And beside that, how can they count on him, in his condition, not to blurt out the name of the lord and damn them all to hell? Well, the clock is ticking and it's not like they have much choice in the matter, so they plunk him down in his spot at the stern and hope for the best.

"'*Acabris, Acabras, Acabram! Fais-nous voyager par-dessus les montagnes! Take us over the mountains.*' The canoe shoots up into the air and they paddle for their very souls. The moon isn't nearly as bright as it was when they set out, and the pickled Baptiste is seeing double. He steers like a wildman, avoiding steeples by a hair, giving his crew a collective coronary. His luck runs out over Montreal when he drives them smack into the side of the mountain. They pick themselves up out of the snow and assess the damage. No one's hurt and the canoe's still in one piece. They'll be able to finish the trip. But before they set off again the fellas get into a quick huddle and decide that they can't stick with Baptiste as their pilot. He's too big of a risk. They tie him up and gag him and dump him into the bottom of the canoe.

"'*Acabris, Acabras, Acabram! Fais-nous voyager par-dessus les montagnes!*' Up again. For the last time. Joe takes over the steering. He sets their route by the Ottawa River below, and then veers off towards their camp guided by the north star. Everything's going according to Hoyle until they're a few miles short of their destination. That's when Baptiste bolts up in the middle of the canoe.

He's wriggled out of his gag and bonds. Swearing a blue streak, he holds his paddle out from his body and starts to swing it around and around. Joe ducks down like everybody else, to keep from getting his skull bashed in, and in that second of lost concentration, he lets the boat dip and they crash into the crown of the mother of all pine trees. The boat flips over and they all fall out, bumping and crashing their way to the ground against the branches that never seem to end.

"Next morning, Joe wakes up in his own bunk, bruised and scraped some, but none the worse for wear. Same for the others who shared his midnight adventure. Turns out that their stay-behind *camarades* from camp found all of them in a snow bank at the foot of a great pine tree, out cold. They dragged them back in to sleep off what they figured was an overdose of last night's rum that the camp boss let flow.

"Joe doesn't breathe a word. Keeps his close shave to himself. But years later on New Year's Eve, at a different camp, he treats everyone around the fire to the story of his true and complete adventures as they unfolded on that night. And he repeats it every year after that, the old man doing a public service for the young bucks who might be tempted. 'If someone comes up to you,' he cautions them, 'and offers you a journey like mine that's too good to be true, remember what I told you this night. Beware of the devil.'"

So ended Storytime with Morrie. He turned his kayak around and started a slow piddle-paddle back to where we'd meet up with the guys. I caught up with him after a few strokes and then stuck my bow out ahead of him to block his way. "So you're telling me this why exactly?"

"You know why."

I knew why all right. I just found the whole subject, now that we'd finally looped back to it after all this time, downright scary.

I'd stashed it in the long-term parking area of my memory, but now he was nudging me to pull it out into traffic.

"You're thinking," I said, coming out with it slowly, "that it wasn't some freaky kind of shared delusion that first day we went out kayaking together, when we heard that voyageur song floating on the wind. That our ears weren't just playing tricks on us. You're thinking that they were really there." That's actually what I thought too, but I couldn't admit it out loud just yet. I needed Morrie to take the first steps and then drag me by the hair towards the conclusion I was fighting against. "That's crazy."

"We know what we heard," he said.

"So you believe in this kind of woo-woo stuff, Roswell and all that?"

"Nope, never did. A lifelong cynic."

"Same here."

We mulled it all over for a while in our separate heads.

"You know," I said finally, "technically, those guys in your story, they travelled through space not time."

"What, you're niggling with me about the details? The point is, those voyageurs we heard came to us. Somehow. I'm not saying the *Chasse-Galerie* is the literal truth. I'm saying more that it suggests a truth. That things in the world are kind of, I don't know, porous. Never in a million years would I have thought I'd hear myself saying something like this, but I believe that on that day, if Renaud hadn't blundered in and messed things up for us, we would have met up with them."

"With a fur-trading crew."

"Yep."

"From way back when."

"Uh huh. That's what I think. A hundred percent."

If Morrie believed we'd had a close encounter of the third kind, then maybe I could finally let myself believe it too. My own version of what happened that day varied from his in some of the particulars. The way I remembered it, we were the ones who'd travelled through time to meet with the voyageurs on their own turf. But like he said, why quibble about the details?

"So is that why you keep coming out here with me? Hoping it will happen again?"

"Halfway, yes, although I don't suppose you can force these things. It's not like you can make an appointment. Probably if you miss your chance, poof, it's gone forever."

If only there were mulligans in time travel, but Morrie was most likely right. No second tries. Shit! The day of that fateful outing, when I heard that canoe making straight for us, the beat of the rowers' chorus pounding against my eardrums, I'd felt the buzz of an adoptee who's about to meet his birth family for the first time. All would be revealed. So that's where that nose came from. But now my lineage would forever remain a closed book.

"Why do you think they picked us to reveal themselves to, you and me?" I asked him. I had my own theory as to why those jet-setting voyageurs had set their GPS to zone in on us and I wondered if Morrie's jibed. In my mind it was because we were devotees *pure laine*. Zealots you might even say. Probably nowhere else on the face of the earth existed another pair of fur trade fanatics as extreme as we were and that's what earned us our just reward. To me it was open and shut.

Morrie wasn't so puffed up. "What makes you think they were coming to see us? Maybe they were just plying their old routes and dropped in to check out the old neighbourhood. Or maybe they came down to do some fishing. Hook a nice fat walleye or perch for their supper. Grilled over an open fire, nothing can beat it."

"Why would they have to eat, if they're, you know, otherworldly."

I was still looking for flaws to skewer my own argument.

"Well if they're otherworldly," he said, "then by extension so are we. And we eat." He had a point, but in this whole train of events logic had long ago escaped my grasp. We sat in our stilled kayaks, our ears cocked to what we hoped was the voyageur frequency.

"Morrie."

"Hmm?"

"Do you believe in the devil?"

"I try not to think about it."

Avoidance. Normally that was a mechanism I could get behind. Just look the other way. But it seemed to me that if we were really buying into this whole visit from the beyond business, and it looked like we were, then we couldn't sidestep questions of the devil and his upstairs rival. For sure metaphysics wasn't my thing, but lately I'd started to dip into questions of life, the universe, and everything. I was dying to thrash it all out with Morrie, but in this matter our obsessions didn't mesh. Or at least he wasn't owning up to it.

I tried to tickle him into a round of amateur philosophizing, and maybe I could have gotten him to bite, but Renaud paddled up and interrupted us. Yes again. If there were an Oscar for Best Buttinski in a Supporting Role, Renaud would win it hands down, but at least he planted us firmly back in the present day. We all had our regular workout and lunch, a little fur trade round robin to keep the guys on their toes, and then I drove Morrie back to his place in Mum's car. In exchange for the lift he invited me in for a visit and a bite with Lena. It had become a regular part of our Sundays.

It got so I looked forward to these tea parties with Morrie and Lena. It's not so much that I was craving grandparents. I had a matched set of my own at home. But mine, no disrespect meant, seemed to have been born old. Even as four year olds at the playground they probably worried about breaking a hip, whereas Morrie and Lena would still be barrelling down the slide on their stomachs today, mentally, that is.

Morrie made the tea party a festive affair, silver tray, china teapot, walnut strudel, the works. He measured out loose tea, a twiggy substance I'd never set eyes on at my house where my mum bought Red Rose tea bags in the value pack. The stuff Morrie spooned into the pot looked like it belonged in a joint, but it brewed up nice and aromatic and I felt like my hosts were giving my taste buds a European education.

As promised, each week I brought a picture on my phone to show to Lena, something from the collection that I thought she'd go for. Morrie pretended to be jealous. "You never showed so much interest in my fur trade stuff."

"Well, maybe if you were to take a picture with Benjamin's fancy phone of all the beautiful objects in your room to show me, I'd ooh and ah over them too. It's been so long since I've seen them."

That request gave us both a major jolt, the sum total of Morrie's beautiful objects having long since vaporized. It was an idea we hoped she'd lose track of in the druggy haze that sometimes played fast and loose with her concentration. For the time being luck was on our side and it did seem to fall off her radar.

"So, Benjamin," she said, staking out a fresh topic of conversation, "tell us who is it you take after? From which of your parents did you pick up your history genes? From both maybe since the affinity is so strong?"

"Neither that I know of. My mother was math right down the line. Majored in it at university. Wanted me to take calculus, can you believe it? She thought it would discipline my mind. She always planned to teach after she finished school, but she met my dad before she graduated. Then we kids came along, I have a brother and a sister, and somehow she never did get her degree in the end. Never made it back to finish up. She works at the Bay too. In the Purse Department. But anyway, getting back to your question, history was never her thing. For Mum it was always numbers, numbers, numbers."

"And your father?" Lena asked.

"Dead."

Okay, so as an answer to a polite inquiry it was kind of bald. I tried to fluff it over a bit. "I guess I picked up my interest in history from the mailman." But she got the message. For my protection, Lena rerouted all future conversation neatly away from my father, for her protection Morrie kept the chat away from their hollowed-out house, and for his protection I shut up about Morrie's second career. On Sunday afternoons, everybody had to play nursemaid. This perverse triangle of watchfulness got us to be way more invested in each other than we otherwise might have been, and it didn't take long before I let Morrie and Lena put down roots in the corner of my heart that my father had left vacant, and they welcomed me into the corresponding spot reserved for a son, if only they'd had one. Now, if this all sounds too warm and fuzzy to be coming from me, what can I say? I just let myself slip into it like you would a warm bath.

8

Something was up with Rossi. He wasn't his old self. He didn't drop by the museum half as often as he used to and when he did find his way over he barely said a word. I wondered if maybe he had a bug up his ass over all the time I was spending with Morrie. Before we two bonded, Rossi had been my main man on all fur trade matters. And it was true that Morrie had gradually outstripped him on that score. Was he jealous? But after I let that notion percolate for a while, I had to reject it. It was unworthy of Rossi who'd always been there for me, even when I didn't deserve it. How many times had he picked me up, dusted me off, and wound me up to face another day back when I had the robbery hanging over my head? Pettiness wasn't his thing. I couldn't see him playing one of those tweeny schoolyard games of but-I-thought-*I*-was-your-best-friend. There had to be something else going on.

I didn't have much to go on now that he'd swallowed his tongue. Rossi'd made it through probation, so that was off the table, and his supervisor in the kitchen had played kissy-kissy with the notoriously tight-fisted Ange-Aimée in payroll to coax her into signing off on the pay hike Rossi'd been angling for. The chef had even offered to put in a good word for him at some upscale restaurants around town, or at least up the scale from the Bay cafeteria, which effectively left the field open to just about anyplace. Girl trouble? Not likely. Rossi's life was a constant whirl of girl trouble. He thrived on it. So what was left?

Only one stubborn idea kept coming back up on me like a wonky curry. I hoped I was as flat-out wrong about it as I had been the previous time I'd confronted him with an accusation, oh so sure of myself. But I had to find out.

Next time he wandered in, same old same old. Washed out. Jittery. And he could hardly meet my eyes when we spoke. Correction. I should say when *I* spoke. On his end there were only grunting noises which for all I knew might not even have been replies, just the audio from his digestive system. He volunteered absolutely nothing to the conversation unless he couldn't avoid it.

"Haven't seen much of you around here lately. You got something better going?"

"Been busy."

"What with?"

"Recipes. Stuff."

"So they're letting you show off your own creations? Run the show a bit more over there? About time. Now you can zap them with some quinoa or kale. Some bok choy maybe. Let them know there's more to life than red jello."

"Yeah."

That was it? 'Yeah?' Things were worse than I thought. Even a reference to jello, that never-fail-to-perform chain jerker, failed to perform.

"How about school, classes going okay?"

Rossi'd finally gotten his nerve up to register for some night courses at the Institut d'hôtellerie, the city's flashy training school for professional chefs. He'd hesitated at first. The uniform they required intimidated him. Too chic, too cool. In their stainless steel teaching kitchens you had to wear the whole schmear, black-checked pants, double-breasted chef's coat. Even a white toque on your head tall enough to tickle the fluorescents. That outfit was Paris. His Bay uniform Sudbury. The baggy whites the Bay doled out to its kitchen staff hovered in style midway between grand-daddy long underwear and psych-patient jammies, all of it topped off with a bakery-lady hairnet. Talk about humiliating. And I sympathized all the way. When it came to uniforms the Bay's choices ground you down. It was a struggle to rise above the feeling that the clown outfit they had you put on every day wouldn't define you for life.

But to Rossi's credit, he shook off the department store's uniform curse and moved up in the world to the classy dress code of the Institut. And once he started chopping and puréeing in its kitchens, it slipped his mind that he'd ever suffered from stage fright. Used to be that when he'd stop by the museum on his daily visits, he'd jabber a blue streak about the place; what regular guys his fellow students were, how he'd learned to seed a pomegranate faster than a speeding bullet. No more.

"School? No problem."

"Got anything else new and exciting going?"

"Nope."

I was fed up with these question-and-answer visits. They made me feel like I was his mother, trolling for personal tidbits he wasn't eager to cough up. This new Rossi, the tight-lipped Rossi, was driving me round the bend.

"Come on. Out with it. What's eating at you?"

"Nothing," he said in a touchy tone that translated to me as its opposite.

"You're back to boosting cars aren't you?" I'd been planning to wheedle it out of him, let him come clean of his own accord, but I had no patience left for a leisurely lead-in. "You let yourself be sucked back into it, right? You went out drinking with your old crowd again, got the urge, and they didn't lift a finger to stop you. They egged you on, am I right? Just like before. You swore you'd cut off from those guys."

"Again you're thinking I'm a thief? For a guy's who's supposed to be so smart, you sure have a one-track mind."

"Don't get all bent out of shape. It's the best I could come up with. Look at you. You're a mess. Don't try to deny it. Something's gnawing away at you. You're jumpy like I've never seen you. Can't look me in the eye. If I'm wrong about the whole car thing, fine, my bad. But all I'm asking is that you tell me what's up with you. It's gotta be better than keeping it bottled up, boring a hole straight through your insides."

"I'm fine. Same as always. Right as rain."

"Yeah, you're fine and I'm the tooth fairy."

"There's nothing wrong with me. Cross my heart. Give your imagination a rest. You're working it too hard."

"You think I don't have eyes to see? You're falling apart right in front of me. A total basket case. Look, you know that anything you say won't go any further. I'll take whatever it is to my grave. You can tell me."

"Benj, I've got to get back to my station. I'm already way late."

"Your soup kettles can wait five more minutes. They won't explode. You're not going back there until I know what's up. Who knows, maybe I can help."

"You can't," he blurted out. I could tell he wished he'd kept his mouth shut, but too late. Now that he'd let that much slip, more stonewalling didn't make much sense. Rossi did a deep breathe-in before he spoke again. "So you haven't heard then."

"Heard what?"

"The rumours."

"Rumours? What rumours?"

"I didn't want to be the one to spread them, see. I've been wait-ing, hoping I'd find out that there wasn't any truth to them, and that would be it."

"What are you talking about?" If I thought Rossi looked lousy before, now he looked like he needed a sick-bag. He took his good old time starting out. Whatever gossip he'd been sitting on all this time, for sure he wasn't keen to be the one responsible for giving it wings.

"Remember a few weeks ago when Antoine was off with a stomach flu?" he said. "So Eric sent me in to replace him in the executive dining room. The big bosses from six were there with the new American owners. They were having an all-day powwow. I served them lunch and then when I came by after to clear the table they were slow to clam up and I overheard part of their con-versation."

"And?"

"Well, I thought, I mean I might have heard them talking about cutting back."

"Layoffs, you mean?"

"More like shutting down certain non-performing depart-ments."

"They're closing the cafeteria? Just like that? After all these years? I can't believe it." No wonder he was thrown off balance af-ter a sucker punch like that. Rossi griped about his job like we all did, claimed he didn't get enough love, but deep down he was de-voted to the place. When he made the job rounds after he'd served his sentence at Cowansville, a hundred other interviews told the car thief (reformed) thanks but no thanks. The Bay took him in. That first job was at the sinks, but he worked his way up to unofficial second banana. Everybody knew that Eric, the chef en chef, wouldn't switch the celery in the Waldorf salad from a slice to a dice without sounding it out on his underling. The Bay took the raw ingredients that were Rossi, spun them around in the commercial mixer, slapped them in a mould, threw them in the convection oven, and out came a man. The cafeteria was the making of him.

I felt Rossi's pain. Didn't my job help me crawl out of the hole that was my old life too? But it was my role in all this to be upbeat. "You'll land on your feet," I told him. "Once you get your fancy-ass new cooking degree you'll be able to write your own meal ticket at any restaurant in town. They'll be fighting over you and I'll be stuck here alone. I'll miss you when you're gone, you know. Who else listens to me the way you do?"

"No, Benjo," he said, back to giving my eyes a wide berth. "Not the cafeteria. They're closing the museum."

At first it didn't compute. His words were making their way through my brain all right, but coming out the other end as gibberish. Wasn't I too young to be having a stroke? Rossi wasn't taking any chances. He dragged me over to a chair, forced me into it, and pushed my head down between my knees. Maybe not a stroke remedy, but a remedy for something or other. And it helped. All that extra blood up there flushed out the blockages and Rossi's message untangled itself. I knew exactly what I had to do. I repositioned my head back on top where it belonged and tore out of there, heading straight to the Purse Department. No rumour would dare go round the store without checking in at my mother's counter. It would be a whopping breach of etiquette after all the years she'd put in at the Bay for a piece of gossip to flit right by without even stopping to say hello. It simply wasn't done. If anybody'd have the skinny, she would.

Mum was nowhere to be seen when I got down to her corner of the first floor, but I knew that if Madame Dolce & Gabbana wasn't on duty shilling handbags, there was only one other place she could be at that hour, under the canopy on Union Street, enjoying a cigarette. It was the hangout of choice for the smoking minions. The metal overhang prevented the smoke from fleeing wasted into the stratosphere. It kept it concentrated and super toxic, just the way they liked it. I'd never come looking for her before. Not once. It was always the reverse. So when I swooped in like a bat out of hell and dragged her away from her friends, her face immediately took on a who-died look.

"I've got to talk to you," I said, pulling her to an unpopulated corner of the church garden across the street. I let go of her wrist when we got there. I'd cinched it hard enough to leave a mark.

"Benjie, what is it? Are you all right? Did something happen at home?"

"Is it true?"

"Is *what* true?"

"That they're closing the museum on me?"

She blew smoke slowly out of her nostrils in two plumes so great they looked like power-plant exhaust. Her body seemed to shrivel as it left her. It struck me then that all the experts had it wrong, that cigarettes were all that were keeping her going. Without the smoke to fill in all that empty real estate around her bones and organs, giving her lift, she'd just collapse in a heap.

"Where did you hear that?"

"I sure as hell didn't hear it from you, Mommie Dearest. Is it true?"

"Benjie, it's only a rumour, not a sure thing. Don't get yourself all uptight."

"Right. They're slitting my throat and I shouldn't get myself all uptight. Maybe I should just sit down and have a cup of tea and a crumpet."

"Benjie, my darling boy, don't do this to yourself, please."

"I'm hardly doing it to myself. I'm not the one bringing down the axe."

"You know that's not what I meant."

Yeah. I knew what she meant. Don't let yourself backslide. But backsliding felt pretty damn good just now.

"So you never saw fit to tell me? To give me a clue? Didn't I deserve at least that?"

"Oh, Benjie, you think it slipped my notice that the museum is everything to you? I just didn't see any point getting you in a state when it might not even come to pass." As usual she and Rossi were on the same wavelength. I sometimes thought that he seemed more like her natural son than I did.

"In a state? In a state? A *state* is for when someone nicks your bumper. If I lose this, I'm left with a shitload of nothing."

I glanced across the street at my co-workers gathered under their nicotine umbrella. "Am I the only one who was in the dark?" I had visions of all 872 employees tsk-tsking behind my back. "The whole world knows, right? I'm the only dope who didn't have a clue. And why not? Because my own mother, who you'd think you could count on, held out on me."

There I was. At it again. Letting her have it not because she was guilty but because she was handy. And she took it. Always had. Whenever I got wound up like this growing up, her self-defined job was to let me lash out at her till I wore myself out. How could she stand me?

"Benjie. Get a hold of yourself. Nobody knows anything. It's all just hearsay. You know how it is whenever the new owners come in on a flying visit. Everybody's on tenterhooks and the rumour mill starts churning. It's only natural. But that's all they are. Rumours. Nothing's been announced. Nothing's been signed. Nothing's closing down yet. Nothing's for sure."

That repeat repeat repeat technique of hers swept me back in time to my teen-aged feral days. Mum used to pull it out when she wanted to soothe me. It was the oral version of a back rub. Maybe it used to work when I was a younger, but now it drove me up the wall.

"Don't pull that Om crap on me. I'm not twelve."

"Honey, I never meant to hurt you. You believe me, don't you? I guess I was trying to will it not to happen by keeping it to myself, under lock and key sort of." I did believe her, but it didn't help anything.

"What am I going to do?"

"There's nothing *to* do. Just go to work as usual. Keep the place running. I know it'll be rough, but just you wait. I'm betting all my many millions that it won't even turn out to be true."

"From your mouth to God's ear, as Grandpa would say."

9

Well, I guess God's ears were in need of some serious irrigating because it did turn out to be true. They were shutting me down. RIP.

Nobody from HR came over and told me about it to my face, me who was most intimately affected. None of them even put themselves out to phone my local. How did I get word in the end? A fuckin' memo. The bosses blamed that all-purpose punching bag, the economy. My little museum, whose monthly expenditures didn't amount to a hill of beans in the grand balance sheet of the retail giant, my little museum was closing because of pig futures and the world debt crisis? Give me a break. Oh, and by the way, thank you for your service.

I didn't go postal. How could I when it felt as though my whole body was shutting down?

Inside my skull I could hear all the little switchmen in my brain flicking their levers to *off*. But before the cease and desist order made it down to my feet, I got them to walk me over to the cafeteria. I looked through the window to the kitchen where Rossi was elbow deep in bread dough, communing with the gods of leaven. He was too engrossed in his kneading to notice me, but Bernard gave him a you've-got-company nudge and he glanced up. When he saw me miming my neck suspended from a noose, he shot right out of the back to join me.

"Come with me, Benjo, what you need is to lose yourself for a while."

He didn't ask any questions which was okay by me. As embarrassing as it is to admit, I wasn't sure I'd have control of my voice. Rossi just led me out of the store and into the first bar we came to. It was one of those chains with fakola country antiques mounted all over the walls, washboards, and ox yokes, and lanterns. The walls were panelled in bleached pine boards that looked like they'd been pried off a homesteader's privy. If Rossi'd been intending to get my mind off the museum, this wasn't the best choice. Everything my eyes landed on, except for the big-screens, reminded me of my about-to-be-dismantled collection. We should have walked further when we left work, towards a no-nonsense corner taverne, dim, still reeking of cigarettes smoked ten years before, and where the only effort towards décor was the queen's portrait on a twenty.

Rossi did some corrective ordering. When I asked for a beer, he nixed it over my head with the waitress and had her bring us a couple tequilas. In his expert opinion I was in need of something more muscly than beer, a drink that came out swinging. It was only after I downed my fourth that he calculated I could handle some conversation.

"Did they say when?"

"No exact date was mentioned. *Imminent* was the word they used."

"I'm guessing you've got some time. Everybody knows that the monster facelift they're planning isn't going to kick in for another five, six months. So you can probably sit tight for now."

"What difference does it make, a week, a month? My specific expertise in fur trading doesn't exactly set me up for a future career anywhere else, does it? When I leave that place, I'm done for."

"Come on, Benjie, there's lots of things you could do with your education." I noticed he didn't suggest any. He was doing his best to buck me up, but let's face it, he didn't have much substance in me to work with.

"Look on the bright side," he said. "You won't have to wear your elevator operator uniform anymore."

"Yeah, maybe I'll have a ritual burning in my back yard."

"I hope I'm invited."

"You can light the first match."

"Call it a date."

After clinking glasses to that crumb of a silver lining, we sank back into broody silence for a while, but then round six, or was it seven, seemed to wake Rossi back up.

"How are they going to dispose of the stuff I wonder?" he asked.

"Do you think they'd divulge that information to me? A mere nobody?"

"Do any of the stores in other cities have a museum to transfer it to? Winnipeg maybe?"

"Nope. We're the one and only."

"Maybe they'll sell it all off in a job lot to a joint like this," Rossi said, gesturing around the room at all the phony historical *tchotchkes* that were the franchise theme, "someplace that's always looking for a pipeline to a source of fresh antiques." He was talking out of his ass but in my admittedly sloshed state of mind, I couldn't rule it out. Those geniuses upstairs knew what to do with sweaters and jeans that didn't move, but they'd never had to dispose of one-of-a-kinds before, priceless artifacts that documented the birth of a nation. The thought of my precious collection being offloaded like last year's fashion blooper made me want to barf, although I guess it could have been all the shots. I signalled the waitress for another to help me chloroform that worry and that's when Rossi cut off the flow. In his esteemed judgment it was time to head home.

I could still walk, just not in a forwardly direction, so instead of splitting up at the metro like we'd planned, Rossi escorted me all the way to my front door. He reached in and took over with the key when matching it up with the keyhole proved to be beyond my powers of coordination. His too, turned out. We might have spent the whole night on the front gallery if my mother hadn't heard all the scritch-scratching against the door and let us in.

"Thank you for bringing him home in one piece, Rossi."

"You don't really want to thank me, Mrs. G. I'm the one who got him tanked in the first place. See, he got some bad news at work today." I could see him flailing his eyebrows with meaning. "I was just trying to dull the blow."

"You're a good-hearted guy."

"I'm a bum. But sometimes I get it right."

"I hate to hear you run yourself down, Rossi. You've got what it takes. Don't let anyone tell you otherwise. They'll have to answer to me."

While Mum was busy extolling Rossi's inner mensch, I curled up into a snail on the living room carpet. In addition to my Bar Mitzvah, getting drunk was a rite of passage I'd somehow missed out on along the way, but now that I knew how it felt I was glad I'd never before had the pleasure. I would have been more favourably inclined towards this whole getting hammered thing if only some oblivion went along with it. I'd always thought that was part of the package. But my memory of the memo was in no way blurred by the copious amounts of Jose Cuervo I'd knocked back. In fact the letters spelling out the memo's message now popped up extra clear before my eyes, magnified into a font so humongous it could have been used for skywriting.

I studied Rossi from my vantage point at his feet, talking all serious to my mum. How was it that he was still upright?

"Did you hear?" he asked her.

She nodded. Watching her bobbing head made me dizzier, if that was even possible. "It was all over the store in a flash. By the time I got up to the museum to check on Benjie he was gone. I called his cell but he wouldn't pick up. I've been worried sick. I'm so relieved to know he was with you all this time. I was afraid that.... Well. Never mind. The important thing is that he's home safe."

"Do you need any help getting him upstairs?" My mum always brought out the gentleman in Rossi.

"No thanks. We'll manage." Her focus on me dropped for a second while she let her breathalyzer gaze rest on Rossi. "You're welcome to stay over on the sofa-bed if you want. Continental breakfast included."

"I'll take a pass. I think I'll just make my way back home. It's not so far. Thanks anyway. Oh, and sorry for your loss." You could tell Mum thought Rossi's funeral-home farewell was over the top, but to me it sounded right on target for the circumstances.

Mum didn't even try to get me up to my room once Rossi left. She could have called Zach down from upstairs to do the heavy lifting, but I guess she figured I was comfy enough where I was. Besides, she knew what was what. Why give Zach added ammunition? She tugged off my shoes like they always do in the movies although I never understood why, dragged the granny square afghan off the couch to cover me with, and slipped a throw pillow under my head.

"Do you need the bucket, do you think?"

"No. I'll be okay. As long as I don't talk. Or blink. Or breathe."

"My poor Benjie. What am I going to do with you?"

I think I felt her kiss on my forehead before everything faded to black. Finally. All that alcohol was delivering. Yes!

10

The suits didn't waste any time. A delegation from the sixth floor came down for a tour of inspection the very next day. Needless to say I wasn't at my best. I wasn't even up to my worst. Not that it mattered. My input wasn't being solicited by my esteemed employers who barely acknowledged my hungover presence. Monsieur Duhamel, the *capo di tutti capi*, skipped clean over the hello-how-are-you niceties. He just nodded in the direction of the official keychain hanging from my belt, and then held out his hand for me to give it over. I doubt if Dreyfus could have felt any more of a wrench when they marched him out in front of all Paris and stripped the medals off his chest.

Once I gave up custody of the keys for their visit, they shut me out. I had the impression they'd been planning on asking me to clear out for a while so they could poke around without a peanut gallery, but it was one of those rare times when the museum was jammed with visitors, a set of laissez-faire parents and their four sugar-amped kids, so the higher-ups had to put up with my presence. It's not like they were about to play babysitter. The bosses went about their business kicking the tires of the collection, their pin-striped backs turned to block me out, murmuring to one another with the volume tuned to low. I had my eardrums fully cranked up to wiretap mode but the kiddies kept badgering me with questions, little brats, so I could barely pick up any of their discussion. When the execs handed me back the keys on their way out, (no thanks or goodbye to the hired help, of course), I was none the wiser.

Which was why when I next showed up at Morrie and Lena's, I couldn't fill them in on any of the particulars. It was a Sunday of wild winds hitched onto the butt end of a stubborn storm front, no day for kayaking on the river, but I dropped by all the same hoping they'd have the kettle on the boil for me as usual. And they did.

I'd spared them the rumours. Didn't they have enough to deal with? So the news of the closure, coming unpadded as it did, clobbered the pair of them. Maybe that had been the wrong strategy, crueler than keeping them in the loop. Well, it was done now.

Enough time had elapsed since the memo that at least I was able to relay the news flat-voiced. That was because before coming, I'd stashed all my misery away in my usual hiding place, somewhere due south of my ribs, and slammed the door shut on it. Which wasn't easy. After so many years it was getting pretty crowded in there. But it was wasted effort putting on a brave face. They could see right through me, those two. Lena was horrified on my behalf and offered me the solace only a fur trade widow would know how to provide. She understood how the prospect of losing my beloved museum was tearing me apart.

"I know it would kill my Morrie to have to part with even a fraction of his collection from up in his room. He simply couldn't do it, not even with a gun to his head. He'd give up an arm first. How you must be suffering my poor, poor boy."

Okay. A little aside here. The comfort is what I came for and Lena was delivering it in bulk, but it was getting all muddied up in my mind with guilt. So call me selfish but that angle I hadn't anticipated. Morrie'd had to go through the same kind of withdrawal, the same kind of pain as me. A zillion times worse probably, because he'd tracked down every single item in his collection on his own, built the whole thing up from nothing. He told me once that in the pre-Lena days, if it came down to a choice between spending on a must-have map or artifact he'd come across, a real hole-filler, or buying food for his supper, he went hungry. Like those Impressionists and their paint tubes. The nitty-gritty of every separate acquisition was burned on his brain; the hunt, the haggling, the documenting, the restoring, the displaying. He could rattle it all off. I'd heard him do it. Selling off his precious collection bit by bit, well for Morrie it was death by a thousand cuts. The megadose of sympathy Lena was shovelling my way rightfully should have been lavished on him. But the secret life he'd been leading meant that now he could only listen in on her there-there noises and absorb them second hand. A cost of business.

Lena stroked and calmed, knew exactly what magic words to choose that would grant me an afternoon's vacation from my troubles. Hard to believe she didn't have kids of her own. She seemed like a real pro, although I guess it's easier to give that kind of credit to people who aren't your own parents. Her husband didn't pitch in.

"Morrie, dearest, you're very quiet."

It was true, he'd barely said a word. Usually when we got together there was no dead air. This was a couple with what to say. They springboarded off each other's sentences so regularly you could hear the boings. "I guess the news just hit me hard," he said.

He sat in his usual chair at his wife's side, his head bowed in thought. What was running through his mind? I took a stab at it. That he should have emptied out the museum when he had the chance? He would have made a decent buck or two and now where was it all disappearing to anyway? My fur trade treasures, surrogates for his own, wouldn't even be there for him to visit. Then again, maybe I was way off base. At mind reading I was no expert.

Morrie stood up suddenly. "Ready to go upstairs?" he asked me. It was our Sunday routine to plug away on the canoe once Lena's eyelids started to droop, not that she had a clue what we were up to. With the two of us working on the project together, it was really starting to take shape.

"Darling, use your head," she whispered to him, clearly still wide awake, and with an opinion or two to put into play. "Isn't it a bit insensitive to rub Benjamin's nose in your collection when he's about to lose his own?" Morrie ignored his wife's unsubtle *zetz* to steer him in a more compassionate direction and asked me again. "Are we going upstairs?" The upswing for the question mark was there, but still it came out sounding more like an order. Blunt. No coddling from him. Lena pursed her lips in disapproval. Maybe not a flashy show of anger but enough. That she was even capable of being p.o.'d at him came as a surprise to me but then a breach of politesse under her roof was beyond the pale.

"Yeah sure," I said to him. "Let's go."

"You needn't go up just to please him," she said in a steel-toed voice aimed at hubby, not me.

"Really, I don't mind at all."

I headed upstairs ahead of Morrie to give them a chance to make up in private. Too bad he'd long ago sold off the Iroquois peace pipe from his collection. I'd heard him describe it, all quillwork and feathers. One of his gems. This would have been the perfect time for the two of them to take a toke, see if it still performed as advertised.

Up in his room, the canoe was already uncovered and waiting for me, the tarp neatly folded away. I did my usual walk-around to admire our handiwork. Before this whole canoe business fell in my path, my experience with woodworking was minimal. I'd made a popsicle-stick truss bridge for a science fair project once, if that counts, but it collapsed in the very first round of weight trials. So I think it was fair for me to assume that if I couldn't construct something out of friggin' tongue depressors that would hold up, wood and me weren't a match made in heaven. But looking at what Morrie and I had accomplished, the boat's perfect curves, its gutsy bow, I treated my self-image to an upgrade. This was a rare event for me. Down was my more usual direction.

We'd done all the binding which seemed to take forever. That day's step was laying the tiers of planking to make ready for the ribs. It was a satisfying step, closing in on the finish line. Morrie had the planks all laid out to dry. They'd been soaking for weeks in his special sauce, his personalized swill of tea, ammonia, shoe polish, saffron, and whatever the hell else that would age the planks to the eye, but not eat away at them. It was a delicate chemical balancing act, but he'd finally hit on the perfect formula. In his next life he could run a meth lab.

When he showed up to join me a good half hour later he had zero interest in getting down to work. All he wanted to do was talk. Or grill I should say. He did a rerun of every question they'd asked me downstairs, the identical questions that Rossi had plied me with. There wasn't much opening for originality in the situation.

"So you don't know if they're going to split it all up or sell it en masse?"

"Like I told you, I couldn't make out what they were saying. Believe me, nobody wishes more than me that I could have."

"Or where it's going to go? A private buyer? To a museum someplace? You didn't pick that up either?" I thought I'd made myself pretty clear downstairs, but then I'd had a few days to absorb the whole mess. To Morrie it was still raw. He needed to hear me repeat it, to have all the facts pinned down. His second profession had turned him into a details kind of guy.

"Nope. They were too far off to listen in on, and it was noisy."

He stood up and made his way around the perimeter of the room, bumping into the planks that we'd laid out so carefully on sawhorses, knocking some of them to the floor. His shoulders were jerking up and down, like his nerves up there had short-circuited. Even after that time I'd caught him flat-footed at the museum he wasn't half this discombobulated.

"But you could see them, couldn't you?" he asked me. "Did you notice if they showed a particular interest in any one thing? If they lingered in front of something or other for longer?"

I brought up the instant replay of the visit in my mind. The video was jumpy, like from a handheld, thanks to those kids bouncing off the walls, but I could still make out the action. "Well, the furs I guess. They unlocked the cabinets and gave them a good once-over. Laid them out on the counter and ran their hands all over them. Rubbed them against their faces. That kind of thing."

"Idiots. They think they'll get something for them? I can tell you my friend, they're in for a rude awakening. You can hardly give them away."

It was his usual furrier rant. But once he got it out of his system he seemed to calm down. He quit pacing and his shoulders clicked back into their sockets. He stooped down to rescue the tipped-over planks and set them back where they belonged. With the room restored to order, he sat down beside me.

"So that's it then, the furs."

"Yeah, that's it," I said, relieved to see the old unruffled Morrie back. "Except for the canoe."

"The canoe? What about it?" He shot back up to his feet, all his senses on high alert.

"You talked about lingering. Well, they lingered in front of the canoe. For a good while now that I think of it. I remember them squatting down in front of it as if they were eyeballing a putt. Got right up close. Lots of laughing too. Who knows, maybe they were planning a fishing trip. That would solve all my problems, wouldn't it? They'd take out that canoe and sink straight to the bottom in under five seconds."

"You wish. It just needs some upkeep."

"Get serious. You know how old that thing is."

"I am aware thank you. But those canoes were built to last. It's not like they could trade one in at the lot if something went haywire while they were out in the bush between Nowhere and Been-there. And as well-preserved as yours is, a little TLC would have it floating like a dream. Not like the crap you buy today." He took a spiteful kick at our project that tipped it onto its side. I felt sorry for our canoe as I used all my muscle to right it on its work stand. It couldn't help it if it was a prefab, not the genuine article. But I knew what Morrie was getting at. The museum canoe had the sweat of actual voyageurs soaked into its ribs, the blood of New World beavers staining its gunwales. For all the deluxe staining treatments and artificial roughing up he'd done on the kit canoe, it would never be anything more than a B-actor pimped out for a role.

That was it for the day's conversation. Morrie made getting-down-to-work motions and I followed along. We put in a good few hours and then I helped him tidy things up and got ready to go. He walked me down to see me out as usual. Just before he closed the front door behind me he left me with this. "Ben, it would be very useful if you could find out exactly when it's all going to happen."

Useful? What the hell was he getting at?

11

Morrie's cryptic prodding to get me on the *when* case did me a good turn. It gave me a kick in the butt, pushing me to start thinking outside my self-pity box. The guy got me cranked up. I damn well deserved to know when. Christ, wasn't it my life the bigwigs were screwing around with?

So now the only question was how to wring the information out of them. A full frontal attack on head office? Bold, but too risky. A move like that might just drive them to slap a padlock on the museum's front door even sooner than they'd planned, fumigating their resident shit-disturber right out of the joint. No. Cagey was the way to play this, go at it more out of left field, get someone else to do the Mata-Hari-ing on my behalf. And I had the perfect candidate.

Life among purses had become a bit of a yawnfest for Mum, ever since she'd had a brush with glam at her counter, thanks to none other than Céline Dion. Now Céline, Quebec's homegrown little cabbage, didn't just walk in off the street. Uh-uh. That's not how superstars operate, Mum explained to us after the fact, now that she was our household expert on the shopping habits of the rich and famous. What Céline had done, or one of her flunkies to be precise, was to book the entire store to stay open after hours for the exclusive use of her extended family. Considering Céline is the youngest of fourteen children, and that she was backed up by the full chorus line of nephews, nieces, cousins, husbands, wives, aunts, uncles, and hangers-on (that would be your nannies, your protection, your drivers, and your bag-toters), well you can do the calculations if you can count that high. Let's just guesstimate that the full Dion clan out-populated PEI. It paid for the Bay to stay open overnight when these folks had cash enough in their pockets to unswamp medicare.

Anyway, according to Mum, it was somebody or other's birthday in the family and they were all on the hunt for gifts. That's what kicked off the whole outing. Now deep-pocket types like that, they don't automatically think gloves or scarf like us earthlings. They might want to offer, say, a six-burner stove or a full dining room set with a sparkler stuck on top. Which is why every department in the store was staffed with its A-1 sales force ready to rake in the bucks. That included Mum, naturally. For her this was not the ideal shift. She was the very definition of a morning person, but the time-and-a-half they dangled in front of her was too tempting to pass up.

By eleven-thirty on Céline Night Mum was longing for her bed, but it was just at that low ebb that the chanteuse herself stopped by at Mum's station. Her sudden appearance lit a fire under her and flicked her back to morning mode. The singer had her oldest son tagging along, a very well-mannered boy according to Mum who'd witnessed enough of the opposite in the store to put you off reproducing for good. Turned out Céline was a bit of a purse junkie, and after the two of them had an intense cocktail bag consultation, the diva dropped four thousand bucks in Mum's department without batting an eye. The two of them hit it off so well that Mum ended up squiring Céline all around the store for what was left of her inbred shopping blitz.

Around three a.m., a moving van pulled up at the loading dock to collect all the purchases. At the same time a line of stretch SUVs with tinted windows lined up at an anonymous service door on Aylmer to likewise siphon up the super-shoppers, but not before Céline had left Mum with an autographed CD and a bottle of her namesake eau de toilette. It could have been a reality TV show.

Mum had never kvetched much about the humdrummery of sales clerking before Céline showed up and left a trail of fairy dust on the Bay's linoleum, but now she was finding her days ultra blah. A little cloak and dagger work on my behalf would make for a nice break in her routine. Besides, she thought that the organization had royally fucked me over (my translation) by informing me I'd be pink-slipped when the museum closed, rather than offering me a placement in some other department. Now which one of these reasons motivated her to go undercover on my behalf, I couldn't really tell you. I just moved on, leaving it all in her capable hands.

"See you later alligators. I'm out of here." Morrie kissed his wife on the tip of her nose, picked up his briefcase, and headed off. Every now and again I sat and visited with Lena on those evenings when Morrie had to be out "on business." I tried not to obsess too much about whether that made me some kind of accessory, but in the end I figured probably not since he never actually revealed to me the identity of the bird he was out to pluck, kept me safely in the dark on all his illegalisms. But as an enabler I was guilty as self-charged.

So why did I do it? Well, I fell into it, you might say. The first time it happened it was totally accidental. Morrie took advantage of one of my impromptu evening visits to slip out on a job he already had lined up. With me on the spot he wouldn't have to worry about leaving Lena home alone, which is what he'd been planning on doing. It affected his concentration, he explained to me later, and of course in his particular line of work staying sharp was a primo consideration. He always dosed her with an extra pain pill before he headed off, just in case, but even so, he couldn't completely settle down to business wondering if all was well on the home front.

This I only learned after the fact. That first time I played lifeguard for Lena I didn't have a clue what he'd really gone off to do. He said he had an appointment with a client. Fine. To me that meant he was still selling off the dregs of his own stuff. You could have blown me over when he admitted that he'd been out burgling. I thought that the museum heist, which left him black, blue, and busted by yours truly had hammered home the lesson that he wasn't cut out for larceny. Apparently not.

I guess I could have said no the next time, but the guy's bank account was clearly running on fumes and what he was asking of me wasn't much. I really didn't mind passing a few hours with Lena while Morrie was away. She was terrific company, a born yakker. I know, I know, my life was warped. What normal guy in his twenties prefers to spend his time chatting up a senior citizen to doing almost anything else? Well, I guess I wasn't a normal guy in his twenties. That, I believe, if you've been paying any attention at all, I've already proved.

"Are you feeling okay, Lena? Do you need anything?" It must have been around my fifth time on night detail and she wasn't her usual peppery self once Morrie left. I hoped she wasn't coming down with something. I had no way of getting in touch with him if there ever was an emergency. He didn't have a cell. Cell phones cost, as he reminded me, and what was the point anyway? It's not like Lena was capable of punching the numbers with her frozen fish-stick fingers. No wonder he held his breath every time he left her.

Not that I could give her much hands-on help if she had a health issue while I was at her bedside. We fur trader types had only rough and ready first-aid skills, enough to deal with rheumatism aches and frostbite, a sprained ankle from portaging maybe. If Lena needed a poultice, I was her man. But at anything higher level I was toast.

"Can I tilt your bed up a bit? Give you a better view?"

"I'm fine dear, thank you. Just a little preoccupied. That's all."

"Would you like me to put on the TV or some music to take your mind off whatever it is?"

"Absolutely not. Those toys I reserve for when I have no company. I'd much rather talk to you."

"That's what I'm here for." I waited to let her call the conversational shots since none of my feeble efforts so far had managed to get her engine running. "Ladies first."

"So polite you are."

"We aim to please."

She didn't open up right away. Instead she took her time looking me up and down. It made me sit up straighter. I could feel that I was being measured somehow and I didn't want to come up short.

"Benjamin," she said eventually. "May I ask a small favour of you?"

"Sure, name it."

"I've had such a craving lately."

"Well if it's in your fridge, I'd be glad to bring it over. What're you in the mood for? Some fruit? If it's ice cream you want we can split, as long as it's not peppermint."

"No, not an itch for something to eat. It's something else."

"What then, a little spin on the dance floor?" Usually it cracked her up when I bopped her handicaps on the kisser, but today there was no lightness in her.

"What I want ..." she started but then sputtered out. She took a minute to firm herself up and then gave it a second go. "What I want," she spilled out in a rush, "is to go into my house. The rest of it I mean. It's been ages since I had the chance to see all my lovely things and I miss them. It would give me such pleasure to pass my eyes over them one more time." This was definitely not in the nature of a small favour. Small favours meant a sip of juice or a pillow plump. This was a huge favour, a massive favour, bigger even than the ultimate dreaded favour, her needing to use the bedpan on my watch. This was a can-of-worms favour to end all favours.

"I don't think that's such a good idea."

"Why ever not?"

"Well, I don't think I could move you, for one."

"I weigh nothing, dear boy. With your strong rowing arms you could easily lift me into the wheelchair."

"But I might hurt you. I don't know the right way to carry you."

"I can tell you how. You could manage. I bend at most of the usual places. I guarantee I won't break."

What a dope I was resorting to a logistical argument. It had no wiggle room in it. If I could move her then I could move her. I had to change tactics.

"But I have a feeling Morrie wouldn't like it."

"I don't know about that. But in any event Morrie wouldn't have to know. It would just be between us. Our little secret. You could have me safely tucked back in bed before he comes home from work." She was trying to paint her request as a fun little escapade, an after-dark sneak-out to La Ronde when the parents are asleep. But I wasn't buying. This extra level of anxiety I so didn't need. Even if I enjoyed them for the most part, I'd be a liar if I said these evenings with Lena didn't have a certain bass thump of tension running under them, never knowing if the next sound you'd hear would be Morrie's key in the lock or the phone ringing from a bail bondsman. Besides which, I wasn't comfortable with the idea of lying to Morrie. So I'm sexist. Sue me. The fact that I'd been lying to Lena all this time, or at least keeping secrets from her, which I suppose amounted to the same thing, didn't give me the least ethical twinge. After everything real and surreal that Morrie and I had lived through together, I guess you could say we had a bond that trumped all that equal opportunity stuff.

"To tell you the truth, I feel not right going behind his back in his own home."

"But it's my home too."

Wasn't she ever going to drift off? Had she switched meds or something? Usually her chemical cocktail started to fog up her concentration before an hour was up but we were way past that and she was still fast awake. I didn't know how much longer I could stall waiting for her pills to kick in with the mallet.

"You don't think you could just put it to Morrie tomorrow? He'd probably cave if you pressed it. I've never seen him say no to you."

"I've asked him over and over lately. He doesn't think it's a good idea. He worries that in balance it would make me feel worse rather than better to revisit everything I'm missing. And without his cooperation I'm stranded."

"Maybe he's got a point. Better to leave the past in the past."

"My past is all I have left at this point. My body's been giving me signals me that there's not much future out there for me. Please Benjamin. You wouldn't deny me this one thing I ask of you, would you?"

Reader, I gave in to her. You'd have to have a heart made out of stone to hold out on someone staring their own mortality in the face and all they want before meeting their maker is a stinkin' ride in a wheelchair around their own house.

"You promise you won't tell Morrie?" I said. "No matter what?"

"I won't if you won't."

"Then we have a deal."

I'm not as stupid as I look. I knew this wasn't a deal to bet the farm on. Once Lena took in that all her furniture was MIA, she'd forget she ever promised to keep our outing under wraps. She'd nab Morrie the second he came in the door and bash him with her discovery.

But I'd given her my word. Even if it meant that after today my precious little sanctuary would roll up the welcome mat. And I had it coming I guess. Wasn't I breaking one of the bedrock rules Morrie set out for me right at the start, never, under any circumstances, let Lena know anything about the emptied-out house. The best I'd be able to offer in my defence would be that at least I'd stayed mum about the thefts (bedrock rule number two). But that wouldn't matter. Spilling half the beans had the same effect as spilling them all. It meant that their lives and mine would never rub against each other again.

I edged the wheelchair up against the bed and locked the wheels the way Lena told me to do. Picking her up was a bit of a feat. I'd never realized always seeing her in bed just how little her limbs obeyed her. She couldn't contribute anything to the effort. When I finally managed to cup her awkwardly in my arms, she scuffed up against me like a bundle of kindling. My balance wasn't all it could have been, and I practically dropped her sideways into the wheelchair, but she was a trooper. Didn't complain, didn't cry out.

"Let's go, Benjamin. I'm ready." That made a grand total of one of us.

I tried to tuck a blanket around her. Not so easy when she skewed out at angles never intended by nature. The cover refused to stay put. It was way too long and kept catching under the wheels every time I wanted to move us forward. So instead I snitched a little fringed shawl-type thing whose usual job was covering her side table, and I draped it around Lena's back. She took a glimpse of herself in the mirror as we passed it. "I look like a gypsy fortune teller, don't I?" Good thing the outfit didn't lend her genuine crystal-ball powers to foresee what we were about to get into. That discovery I wanted to put off as long as I could. I walked us as slowly as humanly possible towards the connecting door. Easy enough if you're busy kicking yourself for being such a pushover. I mean how many things can your legs be expected to do at once? I was still half-hoping I'd hear snores rising up from the wheelchair before we crossed over into the rest of the house, but no such luck. She was too revved up to conk out now. Unless God pulled a pillar-of-salt move on me in the next few seconds, our expedition was okay'd for takeoff.

Lena didn't bat an eye when I rolled her into the suctioned out living room and parked the wheelchair smack in the middle. I stayed behind her (yeah, yeah, I'm a coward), bracing myself for the outburst. I'd been wondering before we got going if it would come in the form of tears or shrieking, trying to advance fine-tune my strategy depending. But it turned out to be neither. What I mean to say is that there wasn't one. All she did was say "the dining room now Benjamin if you please." In there, ditto. She gave her surroundings a brisk inspection and asked me to move her on to the den. And that's how we worked our way along, pausing a beat in each room for her to take in the nothingness that was the new decorating scheme till we'd covered the entire first floor.

"Is it the same, the second floor?" she asked me since we both knew I wasn't about to do moguls with her on the stairs.

"Pretty much, yes."

"Including Morrie's fur trade room?"

"Emptied out. Or nearly."

She took one last glance around, swallowing the whole sorry scene. "Let's go back please, Benjamin. We're through out here."

I rolled her back to her studio and resettled her in bed. We sat quietly for a while. I wish I could say it was our usual easy silence, but it wasn't. It had some bite to it.

"You knew," I finally said to her. "You knew all along."

"I suspected."

"How?"

"The mail. I hear it drop through the slot in the front door every day and it echoes when it plops onto the floor. It didn't used to. I just needed your help to confirm that I was right."

I should have felt played but somehow I didn't. "Maybe I'm reading this all wrong, but you seem to be okay with it."

"Okay? Well, in a way I'm relieved to know for sure. The uncertainty was worse. But you're wrong. I am definitely not okay with it. Not in the least okay."

"He just didn't want you to have to worry is all. He was trying to spare you that."

"I understand exactly what pushed him to do it Benjamin. I just wish he'd opened up to me. That's too heavy a burden for one person to carry alone." Then she added, "or almost alone."

That last little jab was aimed at me, the interloper who'd edged in to help bear what should have been a conjugal burden. But I couldn't fault Morrie on his decision to cut her out. Her wasted shoulders were hardly up to the job.

"I suppose he thought, well, that you'd be disappointed in him. In how he handled the financial end of things when his business went under. That he should have been shrewder. Avoided this whole mess somehow. Taking care of it this way, well, you wouldn't have to know." What was I doing blabbing so much? Morrie hadn't authorized me to be his mouthpiece but my tongue was going rogue.

"He could have told me. After a whole lifetime together he should have had that much faith that I'd be behind him. That's what hurts, Benjamin. Not losing the chairs and the lamps and the tables. You think I really care about some sticks of furniture? It's that he held back from me when there was no godly reason for it. None. Even with me sick. Strange, isn't it, as much as couples think they know one another, there's always some little corner of each person that's unfathomable to the other. The fact is, I wouldn't have minded living in a smaller place if he'd ever said he couldn't afford all this. Not one bit. He could have sold everything with my blessing."

"Why don't you just tell him now? Let him put the house on the market. It's only for you that he's holding onto it."

"No. Too late. I have to leave him his pride. It's all he has left."

12

Mum was smitten. Who'd have thunk?

It was Rossi who tipped me off. "Your mother's acting strange. All, I don't know, fluttery."

Fluttery. This was not Mum. "You ought to get yourself down to Optical and have Hélène do some tests on those eyeballs of yours. It can't be mama mia you're talking about."

"I'm not wrong on this one, Benj. She's out and out, well, bubbly. You mean to tell me you haven't noticed?"

"Nope. Because there's nothing to notice."

"You're way wrong there. Because you're her own kid probably. Kids are blind to that sort of thing. It takes an outsider to see it. And as your inside outsider, I'm willing to put myself out on a limb here and give you a reason why her personality has suddenly shifted like 180 degrees, or however many means just opposite."

"Theorize away my friend. I could use a laugh this morning."

"Well, I'm guessing, based on the contents of my evidence

bag, that your mother has put herself back in the game. She has the hots, your mum, for Serge."

"The hots? My mum doesn't get the hots for anyone. I don't think she even knows what the term means. She isn't one to look, let alone partake."

"Suture self said the doctor to the patient."

Okay, so he'd piqued my curiosity. "This Serge character, who is he anyway? How come I've never heard of him?"

"You've got to keep up with the times around here, my man. He's the brand new guy up in head office, the one they brought in to ease the transition. She's always hanging off him. How do you account for that?"

Actually, I had a very definite idea of how to account for that, but wasn't she going a bit overboard? When I'd asked her to serve as my secret agent, I figured she'd use her brain not her bod. I mean this was Mum after all. I expected her to pull in a few markers, put out some discreet feelers, that kind of thing. What was she thinking?

It wasn't only Rossi who'd picked up on Mum's libido defrosting. The news had even hopped a bus out to the suburbs. Rena, Zach, everybody knew. Everybody but me that is. I was the self-absorbed asshole who couldn't see what was going on right in front of his face because my eyes were always tied up playing after-images of Lena surveying the house that her beloved husband had attacked with an enema nozzle. Everything outside of that was a blur to me.

At breakfast, Rena tweaked Mum. "So do you care to tell us who's this mystery guy you've been seeing? Twice already this week I've caught you sneaking in late. If this goes on I'll have to ground you. What do you have to say for yourself?"

"He's nobody, okay?" Mum said. "Just a guy from work. He's new to Montreal. I'm showing him around town a bit. Getting him acclimated. Telling him where to buy his bagels."

"A lot of time you're investing in a nobody," Rena said.

"He's a nice enough guy. I'm happy to help him find his feet."

"Give us some particulars if you please. Where's he from for starters?"

"Blanc-Sablon originally."

"Ooh, a small town boy. That explains it. He really does need you to show him the ropes," Zach said. "He's probably more used to eating moose."

"He didn't just fall off the turnip truck, smart guy. He used to work in the Quebec City store before he came here."

"So he's smooth then?"

"Smooth enough."

"What department is he in?" Rena asked. "Furniture? That's where they usually put the guys with some grey in their hair. Am I right? Or appliances maybe? One of the big-ticket departments?"

"That's assuming he's older," Zach said, "and Mum's not cougaring around." Zach's comment was beneath Mum's notice. She stuck with Rena's line of questioning.

"Well, no department exactly."

"So how does he pull in a paycheque then, if I may ask?"

"He's in head office actually." Mum looked a bit embarrassed by this admission to Rena. She usually hung out with the plebes.

"Head office, whoa. Sleeping our way to the top, are we?"

"Get your mind out of the gutter, Zach, will you? I thought I raised you better. We've just gone out to eat a few times. To Upstairs once for jazz. A movie or two. Tapas. End of story."

"That adds up to a lot of nights," I said.

"Point being?"

I backed off. "I'm just saying."

"If he's from head office, then maybe you can get him to give

Groucho here his job back," Zach said. "It would be a public service. Stop him from moping and moaning and making our lives even more miserable than before. I didn't think anything could be worse than Lord Beavertail's endless yammering about the fur trade, but listening to him count down the days till they shove him out of that place kicking and screaming, that's a helluva lot harder to take."

Zach had a knack for knowing where to apply the electrodes. "Lay off," I said. "When I need assistance from you I'll ask for it, and you can bet that'll be never."

"Fine by me. I was just trying to make a helpful suggestion. Put this Serge dude to good use."

"Your humanity is duly noted."

"You can't accept that I might be on your side."

"You sure have a strange way of showing it."

"If you could manage to put that chip on your shoulder away for five minutes running," Zach said, "I think I can speak for all of us in saying we'd be grateful for the time off."

"On *my* shoulder. That's rich. You never stopped to wonder why you list to one side? That's no chip you're carrying, it's more like a meteorite."

"You can't see yourself for what you really are, can you? Maybe it's time I spelled it out. Gave you the reality check you so richly deserve."

"So tell us how you two met, Mum." Rena barged in and hijacked the conversation before it took an ugly slam into the boards. Even through our locked horns Zach and I could make out the wisdom of her move. Things were on the verge of boiling over brother-wise. Between that and all our nosing around into the Serge situation, we were entering the danger zone. We'd seen Mum go ballistic before with half as much provocation. But this time she didn't. Instead she blushed. Maybe Rossi knew what he was talking about.

"I'm not about to go into that with you bunch of yentas. You'll never let me hear the end of it. That's all you're going to learn about Serge for now. Case closed." She started stuffing the cereal boxes back into the cupboards. "Don't you all have somewhere to be? How is it that in most North American families they don't ever sit down together at the table, and in this family I can never get you to leave it? Where did I go wrong?"

I cornered her after breakfast in the laundry room. "Mum, you haven't forgotten your mission here have you? You're just supposed to be finding out when the museum's closing, that's all. It's not exactly industrial espionage what I'm asking. Don't feel you have to, you know, put out to get the info." Christ. Did I really just say that? To my own mother?

"Relax, boychik, I'm just doing research. All above board and outside the bedroom, not that it's any of your business. I remember precisely what it is I'm meant to do. And Serge is perfectly placed to get me the information. I'm just easing in to the whole thing so he won't suspect. Don't get yourself all hyper over it. Everything's on track."

She left me no choice. I couldn't pull her off the job now that she was so into it, not when I knew from personal experience what that felt like. So I backed off. I'd done my due diligence. Mum was on her own. I shifted my attention over to the other woman in my life.

Lena was good to her word. That dame was no stoolie. Of course I only found that out later. Meantime I was plenty worried, let me tell you.

On the night of our hush-hush field trip, Lena was dead to the world by the time Morrie came back. I'm saying zonked. Usually she stirred when he gave her a little honey-I'm-home peck on the cheek, but that night he didn't get a rise out of her. Morrie asked me how the evening had gone and I told him it was uneventful. That was a lie you're thinking. But I saw it as more of an exaggeration than an out-and-out lie. I figured that by comparison, the serious *eventful*, the blow-the-shingles-off-the-roof *eventful*, would wait for later, once Lena woke up and tongue-whipped her hubby to within an inch of his life.

The following Sunday I showed up at their place at the usual time. We'd been keeping to our tea-time schedule even though the weather had turned too frigid to kayak. This was the time of year that fur traders hung up their paddles and caught up on some face time with the missus, treating the beavers and themselves to a little R&R. Before heading off home they'd strop up the old straight razor to give their faces more kissability and chop off the season's growth of hair, forcing their pet lice to stake out new lodgings. It was family time till the thaw.

For me and the guys, winter saw us go our separate ways. We didn't replace kayaking with a cold-weather activity of any kind. None of us was into ice fishing or snowshoeing and to be honest, we didn't mind a bit of space. It was clear to everyone that with Morrie added to the mix I was less dependent on them to scratch my fur trade itch. And they were okay with it. It's not like they were ever rabid voyageurs like I was. They'd always just been humouring me. So when I made the winter swap, the three of them for the one of him, they saw it as it only logical. We'd start our kayaking Sundays up again come spring.

That meant that the way things shook out amigo-wise, for the time being Morrie was my one and only. If we were still on speaking terms that is. And that was a big *if*. After that fateful night earlier in the week when Lena'd poached me for her team, odds were that I was now top dog on Morrie's shit list, my name bolded and asterisked. I was probably wasting my time even going to his house, but I had to find out where I stood.

While I faced Morrie's front door, my finger poised to ring, the different scenarios I'd imagined up during the week for this moment came flooding back to me. First there was the one where Morrie would let me stand outside and ring and ring and ring till my index finger went numb. In doorbell talk it said *get the hell off my property you bum you*. Moving up the intensity scale was the one where Morrie did unlock the door to me, but only to have the pleasure of tearing a strip off me face to face before booting me out into the slush. Bad enough that one was, but the worst of them all, and don't ask me where it came from, was the one that had Morrie punching me out in the entrance hall. Bare-knuckled and merciless, street thug style. Farfetched I grant you, but occasionally your subconscious feels the urge to take some artistic license. Like in the extended overnight version of the punch-out storyline when Lena would leap out of her bed and drag him off me. Sometimes she had wings, or maybe they were antlers. Whichever. That last one was a killer. I could never get back to sleep again after.

I went ahead and rang. Zilch. Rang again. Zilch squared. Looked like I hit it right on the money with scenario number one. He couldn't even stomach the sight of my two-timing face. I'd been hoping that he would at least open the door a few inches. Give me a chance to wedge my foot in and make my plea. But Morrie'd wiped his hands of me. He'd set up clear boundaries for our friendship, ones that I'd signed off on, and I'd gone and taken the wire cutters to them. What did I expect after that? That he'd forgive and forget? Maybe Zach was right. Reality and me, we weren't what you'd call buddy-buddy.

Before I turned to leave, I peeped through the mail slot to grab one final glance at my now ex-refuge, to fix it in my mind. I was just lowering the flap when a flicker of movement caught my eye. I sharpened up the focus. It was Morrie ambling towards the door doing up his fly. What with my nerves going full tilt I'd been too impatient. He was wearing his at-home moccasins and his flannel work-shirt, tucked in to adhere to Lena's dress code. She was a formalist, Lena. You don't entertain in shirt-tails, I'd heard her lecture him before. She was anti-flannel too, but he'd managed to get her to back down on that point. Even through my tiny view finder in the front door I could make out that there was no tightness to his posture, no anger backlighting his eyes. Lena hadn't squealed. Everything between Morrie and me was still *chorosho*. At that instant the anchor that I'd been lugging around since the Lena tour slipped off my back and crashed onto the stoop. Lucky it didn't crack the cement in two, I knew Morrie wouldn't be able to afford the repair. When he opened the door, my host circled his arm around my shoulders father-son style like he always did and led me back to the studio. No sly co-conspirator glances passed between Lena and me. We were both happy to stow our recent adventure six feet under without a marker.

The room was toasty warm even though the electric logs glowing in the fireplace were all show. It had the feel of a campfire at dusk, with everyone joking around and trading stories. Somehow that afternoon the tea tasted mellower and the pastries sweeter. Lena drifted off more quickly than usual though she struggled against it; she hated to be the one to break up the party. In the few days since I'd last seen her, she'd already started slipping, just as she'd predicted. Her skin was drawn even tighter over her bones if that was possible, as if her skeleton was wanting to switch spots and push itself to the outside for a change.

We left Lena to her siesta and headed upstairs to the canoe

where it was business as usual. Our conversations ebbed and flowed as the banging of our tools allowed. We didn't restrict our talk to the fur trade. Uh-uh. We branched out in every direction, struggling between us to resolve all the ugliness that flared up in the headlines week after week. But that day world hunger wasn't on the agenda. The issue Morrie wanted us to discuss was more up close and personal.

"You haven't found out yet have you, when the museum is closing?" Morrie asked me. It had been a while since he last prodded me for an update on the closure. I suffered a bit of a pang that it was taking me so long to root out that one simple fact, but now that the subject was up for grabs again I wasn't about to let it go.

"I'm working on it," I told him. "Things seem kind of dormant right now on that front. They aren't making any moving noises or packing up crates or anything. But I should know for you soon."

"So no one's seen fit to enlighten you."

"Are you kidding? They'd confide in Alexandre before they'd ever speak to me. But I have my spies in the field. It shouldn't be long now till I get a report."

"What's with those bums that run your place? They don't even have the courtesy to keep you au courant, you of all people? That's the thanks you get for being a valued employee? Here you slave for them for peanuts. You care for that collection better than any trained professional. You take every visitor on a trip back in a time machine, give them a real feel for the history, and still they're prepared to toss you out like yesterday's fish." His mini-rant corresponded with my own way of thinking but it was gratifying to hear it spewing out of someone else's mouth for a change.

"Retail's the only language those guys speak," I said. "History to them is a waste of space. If it's history you want, then go to the library, if it's a parka, then go to the Bay."

"You're defending them?"

"All I'm saying is that I get where they're coming from. They're dumping us for the square footage. They probably want to squeeze in some more of that igloo drek that the tourists eat up. Those dopes upstairs probably went to the same business school as my brother."

Morrie grunted and reapplied himself to the canoe. I followed suit. It would be easier to pump him if we both had our eyes focused on our work rather than each other.

"So all this insistence of yours about finding out when the museum's closing, I'm guessing it's not because you're planning me a farewell party."

He kept right on sanding. "Just curiosity, son, that's all." His answer was clearly bogus. Did he really think I'd swallow it and move on?

"I remember you saying it would be useful to know exactly when. Not *interesting* or *satisfying*. *Useful*. That's the word you used. You as much as put me on the job to find out. Don't tell me it was all just to satisfy some idle curiosity. I don't buy it."

"Don't go probing too close, Ben. I wouldn't want you to get burned."

So he was shielding me. Forget that. When I babysat Lena, okay. I was happy to be kept in the dark. I had no connection with Morrie's patsies on those nights. But now we were talking about my museum. Keeping me in the dark wasn't an option.

"I'm already involved, aren't I?" My voice was inching up to an unmanly upper range I'd never hit before. "Even if I don't know exactly how. I'm doing some kind of prep work for you, research, snooping. So out with it. I have a right to know." I wasn't sure what right I was referring to but it gave me a leg to stand on even if it was only prosthetic.

"You can calm down, Ben. I'm just considering a little project, that's all."

"By *project* you mean *job*."

"Strictly speaking, no."

"So tell me what it is then, un-strictly."

"Really, Ben. This has nothing to do with you. Take my advice. Keep yourself safely out of it."

"What about keeping *your*self safely out of it? Seriously, I'm having a bad feeling about all this. Just what exactly are you planning? Tell me. If you can't trust me who can you trust?"

"It's not a question of trust, it's a question of exposure. The less you know the better. But anyway, what I'm planning, it's more on the order of borrowing than stealing. So you don't have to worry. Satisfied?"

"If it's simply borrowing, why can't I know about it then?"

"Well, I guess, if you want to be completely accurate, you'd have to call it unauthorized borrowing."

"Cut the semantics. We're not talking borrowing with an expired library card. We're talking stealing here right? And from my museum."

"No, not stealing really. Like I said."

"You know, I've had it up to here with this runaround you're giving me. Just spit it out. I warn you, I'm not leaving this house till I hear the full story, so you might as well start talking." I jumped out of my chair, climbed up on the work platform, and plunked myself down in the canoe. It was the first time either of us had actually sat in it. We were saving that photoshoot moment for later when it was completely done. It was kind of nervy on my part. By rights Morrie should have had first stab at it. But I felt like it put me in a position of moral authority, as if my demand for the truth was backed up by all the generations of fur traders who'd come before us.

"I'm listening."

"Okay. Okay. Calm yourself," he said. "Get down out of there and I'll tell you everything." He lent me a hand for support. I sat back down beside him and waited. He was so slow to wind up I was afraid I'd have to make another stand, but for the life of me I couldn't figure out what it would be.

"It's the canoe," he finally said. "The one at your museum. I want to take it out on the water. Just once. Know what the real thing feels like. Live in the skin of a voyageur for a couple of hours. And then I'd return it. No harm done to it. I swear. You of all people should understand that craving, no?"

It was worse than I thought. He was delusional.

"And how were you expecting to get that thing out of the store, huh? Explain me that. It's as long as an RV and must weigh as much as what, the Statue of Liberty? Were you just planning to come in, hoist it up onto your head like a giant matador hat and then walk out wearing it? With no one noticing? Or I know, maybe you were going to attach a rope to it and tow it out like a toboggan. Throw a bedsheet over it for cover. That I'd pay good money to see."

Funny. Even as the words were leaving my mouth it struck me as strange that my first impulse wasn't to attack his premise. Just the mechanics.

"I know. It's idiotic to even consider it. But it kills me to think of that canoe being dumped who knows where, someplace you can bet it won't get appreciated. That boat deserves one last shot at the water before it gets locked up behind glass again to waste away for another few hundred years."

"The boat deserves? Are we being totally honest with ourselves here?"

"Hell yes. You think that canoe doesn't have a soul? If it could speak what do you think it would vote for? To be stuck in a display case next to a pair of styrofoam beavers or to be out cutting through the water where it was born to be? And we both know, you and me, that there's a good chance it might not even make it as far as some other museum. I wouldn't put it past the Neanderthals at your place to chop it up into firewood and have a weenie roast over it. The thing is, Ben, I know it sounds nuts, but I can hear that boat calling out my name to save it."

Nobody could match the guy for chutzpah. There was no way anyone could do what he was proposing. The number of roadblocks was mind-boggling. Why not spring the Unabomber while he was at it? It was mission impossible, this crusade he'd set up for himself.

"Okay, we're on," I said.

"We?"

"Of course we. You think I'd leave you hanging out to dry?" It would be a risky as hell, but I was beyond caring. My employers had screwed me every which way but up. I didn't feel I owed them much in the way of loyalty anymore. It was rationalizing, I know, but I'd hit my limit. Besides, that canoe wasn't just calling out to Morrie. Some days back at the museum, in the late afternoon quiet, I could swear I heard my own name floating around among the dust motes. I just never realized till now where it was coming from.

13

Two heads working together should have meant that the planning would take half as long, but I'd always been dim in math. Somehow, even with both of us running off at the brain towards the same goal, our drawing board remained depressingly blank. Something weird was going on. Our imaginations seemed to be telling us that if we were too stupid to scrap this crackpot idea, then they'd step in to do it for us. So they went on strike. Soon ideas weren't just in short supply, they were in no supply.

Our negative progress was getting me down. "You do realize don't you that if they dismantle the museum while it's still winter, we're screwed. We can't take the canoe out on the frozen river and we can hardly snitch it and hide it under the bed till the thaw. That'll be the end of it all. Kaput."

"Keep faith, my friend," Morrie said. "They've dragged their feet this long haven't they? Chances are we'll make it till springtime. And remember we have global warming on our side. Whatever puny layer of ice there is capping off the St. Lawrence will melt like nothing once spring gets it in its mind to show up."

Who was this Mr. Upbeat? This side of my partner in crime had never surfaced before. No surprise there. The guy carried around so many troubles he needed a roof rack. But ever since we'd become birchbark blood brothers he let his repressed Pollyanna side peek out from time to time. And sure enough his optimism was rewarded. But not in the way we'd anticipated.

What happened was we caught a break when a city water main burst and flooded the Bay's metro level so that all of Men's Clothing and Accessories was going blub-blub. Now this wasn't just any old water main. It was a whopper. I'm saying huge. As big around as Alaska and dating from the stone age. Okay, so maybe I am fudging its age a bit, but that sucker was old. The graffiti on its outside read *Samuel de C ♥ Hélène B*. It's amazing the thing had waited that long to pop. Anyway, this particular water main led off the city's central reservoir that was perched just up the mountain from the McGill campus. When it blew, gazillions of litres of H_2O whammed into downtown landslide style. Pedestrians were swept right off their feet and concrete traffic barriers switched streets of their own free will.

How often do you think that you get an urban flash flood on a completely unrainy day? Nobody was ready to deal with it. It took the city's emergency work crews forever till they managed to pull their collective thumbs out of their asses and stick them into the dike where they belonged. By then, the lower level of every last building in the downtown core was doing a fair to middling impression of Lake Champlain.

Once the torrent slowed to a trickle, the Bay's higher-ups got out their waders and went sloshing through Men's Wear, trying to get their heads around the damage to their kingdom. For sure they were going to be run ragged for the next little while overseeing the sopping-up strategy; namely dumping the waterlogged stock, draining and dehumidifying, testing for mould and, you'll pardon the expression, fecal contamination from the sewers. Then there'd be the paperwork nightmare, the heaps of insurance forms to plow through and the lawsuits against the city and its papier-mâché infrastructure. And on the tail of all that would come the retiling, the rewiring, the replastering, the repainting, the recarpeting, the re-everythinging. Good luck snagging a contractor. The Bay would have to battle it out with all the other buildings downtown that got their tootsies soaked. Management was going to be way too preoccupied to fuss with my museum for the time being. Morrie and I figured that the flood gave us a good month in the bag, maybe two. Meanwhile we'd put our thinking caps back on.

"So how's my main squeeze?" I asked Lena.

"Ready to rock 'n' roll." Her patented answer.

Morrie was still making after-dark strikes to fill the family coffers. As much as he wanted to hunker down and hatch a plan undistracted, he couldn't afford to devote himself full time to our canoe conspiracy. They'd starve. So I kept Lena company as usual while her light-fingered husband did his bit to keep the bailiffs off their back.

"I hear you had some bad luck down at your place," Lena said to me on one of Morrie's pilfering nights.

Bad luck? Bad luck? It took me a few seconds to pin down what she was talking about. "Oh, the flood you mean." To Morrie and me the flood qualified as downright excellent luck, a gift from the gods, but a normal person like Lena whose mind was pure, not rotted out like ours, wouldn't necessarily see the upside of a tsunami.

"I saw it on the news. What drama. Who'd ever imagine downtown to get hit by a tidal wave? It was practically biblical."

"Locusts might be next. I'd keep a can of Raid handy if I were you."

"I'll file that tip away, thank you. Nothing was damaged in your museum I hope."

"No. We were lucky. We stayed dry. The water didn't rise anywhere near that high. The damage was pretty well restricted to the lower level where Men's Wear is. It was something to see, though. Cash registers and computer monitors were bobbing on the water. The cologne bottles in the display cases were floating around like fish in an aquarium. The water was up to here on me," I said, indicating my armpit. "If you'd wanted to, you could have gone from men's pyjamas all the way over to dress shirts at the far end doing the breast stroke."

She took me over-literally. "Why in the world would I want to go swimming through a department store?" This was a problem lately. Lena's beautiful brain, which used to execute flawless loop-the-loops and triple axels, now had a habit of crashing down to earth mid-manoeuvre. She flip-flopped in and out of clarity without any warning, one minute razor sharp, the next all fuzzy. But that day she snapped back into lucidity with a vengeance.

"You have to get Morrie to stop stealing, Benjamin. One of these days he's bound to slip up and get arrested. I won't be around much longer. I don't want to have to look down from up there and see him in prison stripes because of me."

"How did you find out?" By the time I snapped my mouth shut to keep that question barricaded behind my teeth the words had already sneaked out. Only in my twenties and already my reflexes were slipping. I should have laughed away her assumption, I should have flipped us to a safer subject; I should have run for the hills, but the should-have ship had already sailed and I was left behind on the pier to deal with the truth.

"Is that really important?" she said. "The point is I know. And I want you to convince him to give it up."

"Why me?" I sounded like the whiny little kid who gets nailed by the teacher on the playground when all the other hair pullers were savvy enough to scatter.

"Because I don't want to squander the short amount of time we have left together hectoring him. That's not the memory of me I want to leave him with. You'll have to do it. There is no one else."

Now I didn't much like the idea of mucking around in the guts of a couple. It seemed to me that a couple, especially a long-in-the-tooth one, is an intricate piece of machinery, finely tuned and balanced over years of trial and error. Its instruction manual is all scribbled over with complicated work-arounds, the yellowed pages dog-eared and studded with Post-its. Then along comes some third party, gives one element the slightest tickle, and next thing you know the whole thing's gone kablooey. And here Lena was telling me to stick my rusty pliers into the couple's Rolex gears? She was probably figuring I'd done it before when I chauffeured her around her empty house against Morrie's decree, so what was the big deal? She didn't know the half of it. When it came to playing shortstop with a husband and wife on base, hell, I wrote the book.

I didn't ever play hooky from elementary school, straight arrow me. But Hebrew School? That was a different story. Four days a week after school in a language that didn't even have enough sense to use the Roman alphabet? I mean I ask you. Those late afternoon classes were soul-crushingly boring and the way I recall it, our teachers wouldn't lift a pinkie to pep things up. They were operating under some weird illusion that the subject matter alone would turn us on without any carbonation on their part. Either that or they were stoned. They had to be aware that we'd just come from spending eight hours chained to a desk at the elementary school across the street where the grade-six menu of history, geography, math, science, French, and English had already bulldozed all the oomph right out of us. If we were going to stay awake on their watch, they'd damn well have to do some bumping and grinding. But I guess their hourly rate didn't leave them so inclined. It used to kill me to watch all my *goyische* friends, those lucky buggers, go home from school at three-thirty to veg out on the couch while we chosen people had to put in an extra two hours *aleph-betting*. It was enough to set you down the path to self-loathing.

So it was free-cone day at Ben & Jerry's. Now what kind of choice was that? A scoop of Cherry Garcia on a waffle cone (ten-cent supplement) on the first warmish day of the season, or reading aloud in our crippled Hebrew about the wardrobe trials of Rivka and Dovid as they try to put together a knockout costume for their Purim party? Like I said, a no-brainer. I'd worry about forging a note later. Zach was usually obliging at imitating Mum's signature. It was his main creative outlet. He'd honed his skills on Rena during the term she was stuck with gym first period. Forty minutes of running laps and doing squat-thrusts with only five minutes in the locker room afterwards to reconstruct herself left her looking like a shlump for the rest of the day. Gym, in her mind, was the underlying reason why no guy at school would give her a second look. So every now and again she appealed to Zach to crib her a note in my mother's crabby, back-slanted script. *Please excuse Rena from participating in gym class this week. She has female problems.* He'd do me the same favour, but I'd have to vet his work before he sealed the envelope just to make sure he hadn't written out of habit, *please excuse Benjamin for missing Hebrew School on Monday. He had female problems.*

The Ben & Jerry's in my neighbourhood was out. Too big a risk that my Aunt Josie who spent her whole life at Second Cup shmoozing clients over moccaccinos might spot me, and then I'd catch hell. So I hopped on the metro and headed downtown where B&J's had three scoop shops to choose from.

Even though it was a weekday afternoon, the streets downtown were jumping. It always worked that way when a freak summery day popped up out of the slush at the tail end of winter. The boots and the Kanuks and the gloves would have to come back out of the closet the next day but in the meantime the weather had everyone pumped. The café owners hustled their tables and chairs out onto their terraces chop-chop and the sidewalk musicians and jewellery hawkers crawled out from wherever it is they hibernate. For no good reason that I can remember looking back, I settled on the Ben & Jerry's near Concordia. I suppose it was the first one I passed and I just tacked myself onto the end of the line on autopilot.

The line snaked way down Crescent but it moved along pretty snappy. And even when it stalled out every once in a while, it didn't bother me. I was AWOL and soaking up rays. Life was good. I'd get there when I'd get there. No worries. There was a cluster of slightly older Traf girls just ahead of me who'd flounced down the hill for the event and they deigned to suck me into their group. They had their kilts hiked up after-school style revealing huge tracts of bare thigh and their ties were loosened come-hitherishly at their throats. They were gloriously pouty. The sun glinting off their braces blinded me, but in a good way. When they offered me a cigarette I was able to take my drags without embarrassing myself. No coughing. No gagging. I'd been snitching from my mum's stock for a year or so just to practice up for an event such as this and finally it paid off. To see me you'd have sworn I'd popped out of the womb with an Export A between my lips. I shot out a lasso of smoke that curved around them in an embrace my pipe cleaner arms would never have had nerve enough to attempt on girls like these. They looked like they'd been teleported in from some upscale new planet that the ratty old science textbooks at my school had yet to register the existence of.

When we finally reached the counter to put in our orders, way too soon to suit me, I lost track of them temporarily. See, their server knew his way around an ice cream scoop. Mine was brain dead. By the time she figured out how to get the ball of ice cream to sit on top of the cone without crushing it, my new friends had taken off. But their musky little cloud hung over me even after they'd gone, giving my nostrils a vicious hard-on. Their quick getaway did have me semi-peeved. Would it have killed them to stick around and wait for me? But I guess it was a test to see if their new little lapdog would follow.

Woof woof. It was easy enough to pick up their track. Our kindred hormones were texting each other. The group was heading east on Maisonneuve. I'd catch up with them before my ice cream had even begun to dribble down my fingers.

They turned left onto Mountain and then hung a right onto Sherbrooke. I figured they were heading for the benches on the McGill campus. There were worse places to shlurp a cone and watch the world go by. I was about a block and a half behind them. I didn't close the gap even though my legs could eat up that much sidewalk no sweat. Why rush? I was at the perfect distance to cop an excellent view of the pendulum action of their asses. It was one of the great miracles of physics.

But it wasn't long before the rear view lost its pull on me. I was too charged up to see what effect gravity and velocity were having on their forward body parts. I picked up the pace just a bit and by the time they were passing the Ritz I was nearly within shouting distance. This would have been much more useful of course if only I knew their names but we hadn't yet gotten around to introductions. Since I couldn't call out to them, that was the moment when

I finally decided to step on the gas so I could wedge myself back into their glittery circle. Instead, once I sped up, I slammed smack into the Ritz doorman, cone first. If this were a comic book instead of the serious memoir I'm writing, the balloon above our heads would say SPLAT!*!. The poor guy couldn't chew me out like he was dying to do because for all he knew I was the spoiled property of some guest at the hotel. Goodbye tip if he didn't keep it zipped. The most he could do was glower at me from under his visor. Still his glower was impressive. I guess he had a lot of practice working at a place like that. When he abandoned his outdoor post to go into the lobby and sponge himself off, I followed him in to apologize. I wasn't raised as badly as he figured.

If only I'd kept on trailing those girls, if only I'd gone against my instinct to say sorry to the doorman, if only I hadn't turned towards the elevator in the Ritz lobby when the ping announced its doors were opening, then I wouldn't have seen my dad wrapped around that slut planting an epic kiss on her lips, and I'd be on my rocker instead of off it today.

Did I want to tear out of there and crawl in a hole to retch in private? Hell yeah. Trouble was, my legs refused to obey my orders. And then my arms, my hands, my head, they all got caught up in the mutiny. I couldn't even close my eyes. They were stuck fast on the open setting feeding in an endless stream of images that I had no desire to process. But what else could I do? I was a witness despite myself, chronicler of record of the first step in my family's disintegration.

Why did it have to be me? Couldn't he have shown his true colours in front of someone halfway capable of dealing with it? So I was smart in school, so what? They didn't give classes in this. All I knew on the subject (and what exactly was the subject?) came from TV. Fidelity and in-, guilt, blame, treachery. Scriptwriters knew how to untangle all those threads in twenty-two minutes, not me. I just wanted to take those threads, wrap them around his throat, and strangle the breath out of him.

I sized up Dad's hook-up while their eyes were still closed, checked out her packaging. She seemed a different style of woman from my mum who was petite, a bit scarce on the flesh. Or maybe Mum wasn't so brittle back then, and I was just backdating the later version. Anyhow, this woman was lusher, cut full. I earmarked her to be a little younger than Dad, even though I was crap at estimating such things. Looks-wise I couldn't give her high marks. Not gross, but she wouldn't turn any heads that one. My mother, the high priestess of damning with faint praise, would have called her presentable. Dressed to sell RRSPs or cemetery plots.

Her plainness nagged at me. It forced me to re-adjust my first call. A slut? Nah. She looked, well, regular. Standard issue suburban. Neighbourish. I couldn't pin most of the blame on her. No way had she bedazzled him armed with her short stack of attractions. Not that it would have made all that much difference who initiated it, I guess, but at least Dad being lured in by a cover-girl type I could understand, even if I couldn't forgive. Whatever this was, though, totally freaked me out.

They finally came up for air. Dad untangled his hand from her hair and repositioned it on the small of her back (towards the low end) to steer her out of the elevator. That much solicitude I'd never seen him show Mum. He must have figured that his wife had a good enough sense of direction to find her own way out of an elevator without any manly leadership needed from him. Out in the lobby he gave her ear a quickie nibble. Hadn't he noshed on her enough up in their room? Now that was a scene it grossed me out to imagine so I turned off that channel for the time being. It was already hard enough for me to grasp that said unimagined room was situated in the Ritz of all places. What must that have run him? When our family travelled, it was loyal to Econo-Lodge. All five of us squished into two double beds and a fold-out. No liveried doorman ever greeted us when we piled out of the car there. The Ritz was as remote from our family consciousness as booking a stay on Mount Everest. Mum sucked the marrow out of every pay-cheque Dad brought home as she'd told us kids time and again, intending it to serve as a lesson, and here he was living deluxe. And on his dime. Even in all my mighty ignorance I knew you didn't go dutch in these circumstances.

The two of them parted company without exchanging a word, which made me think that either (a) they'd said all they had to say upstairs, or (b) this road-show of theirs was a routine, not a one-off, so no words were needed, they had their moves down pat. I didn't give a flying fuck which letter it was. I was just grateful to see her clear out and put some space between us. Dad gave her a one minute lead towards the front door so they could make their exits separately. A true gentleman he was, my dad. He wouldn't want to tarnish milady's reputation. Never one to waste time, Dad profited from his enforced stay in the lobby to check himself out in one of the mirrored columns. He tugged on his shirt cuffs to make them peep out the precise quarter-inch fashion required and then fiddled with his moustache. That was the move that did it.

The Ritz lobby was all-over mirrors. It was going for the Versailles look. Reflections on top of reflections on top of reflections. The hotel's spray-tanned, tooth-bleached, Bowflexed clientele clearly liked to see itself coming and going. Dad fit right in. When he reached up to his moustache to redirect a stray hair that was pointing up his nose, kissed out of formation no doubt, he caught sight of something he didn't expect reflected in that mirror. Me.

He wheeled around to confirm the apparition. I would have

been happy to oblige him and disappear in a puff of smoke but I was still bolted to the spot. Tough luck Dad. He didn't say a thing, not even my name. He was too busy making calculations to talk. I could read his brainfeed right through his forehead. I'd seen him with Madame, it told him. No point spinning any tales. Of course he was reading inside of my head too. And since I hadn't yet reached the age of majority, he had rights as my father not only to read but to muck around in there too. Lay some subliminal groundwork. So he did. Only then did he open his mouth.

"I guess you'll be needing a note," he finally said.

And with the promise of that signature I let myself be bought. The whole sorry Ritz episode would be wiped from the record. Shredded. Fini.

If only. That much secrecy turned out to be way too heavy an albatross to dump on the back of a twelve-year-old, and it didn't take long before I started sinking under the weight of it. I'd never realized before how much energy it took to keep your mouth shut. I had to work at it every single minute of the day. No let-up. School? I couldn't be bothered anymore. Had to stay focussed on job one. It's a slog holding a family together all on your own.

Mum was mystified. Where had her old Benjie disappeared to from one day to the next? Poor Mum. We kept her on the run back then. With one hand she'd be practicing life-support on me, and with the other she'd be soft-boiling Dad's eggs for two minutes and twenty-three seconds every morning as if nothing had changed between them. Maybe I'd screwed up totally agreeing to keep her in the dark. Didn't she deserve to know Dad was sleeping around (although he swore to me it was over)? Should I tell her? Shouldn't I? All night every night the PowerPoint slides with the bulleted pros and cons would flick past on my bedroom ceiling, but all I ever got for the exercise was no rest.

Oh, you poor, innocent kid, you're thinking. He really did a number on you, your dad. The decision was never in your hands. You were like one of those child soldiers. The rebel leader comes up to you holding a Kalashnikov and says *my way or the highway*, so you salute and say yes sir. That was me and Dad. More or less.

You'd figure things would have taken a turn for the better for me once Dad croaked. I'd be free. But by then the knots he'd tied me up in were too complicated to be unpicked and my future as a write-off was set in stone.

So if Lena thought I would ever again allow myself to be positioned between a husband and wife, she had another think coming. If Morrie was bent on stealing, even if it meant he'd have to live out his days on bread and water, I wasn't about to advise him otherwise. But in the end, my stance on this issue turned out not to matter.

14

Pall-bearing is a bit like portaging a canoe. You need to round up a set of guys of a similar size. You can't have one way tall, say, and the others shrimpy so that it puts the coffin off balance and you can hear the corpse shifting and rolling around in there since your ear's right up against the wood. Same goes for portaging. Everyone of equalish stature so you can hoist the canoe up on your shoulders and have it sit there even-steven while you march it past the rapids. There were height requirements for voyageurs back then. 5'4" tops. It wasn't as hard to find guys that size as you might imagine. They grew 'em short in those days.

This comparison came to me, I'm ashamed to say, during Lena's funeral service. Not that I had to worry personally about heaving the coffin up onto my own shoulder. She was cremated, according to her wishes. But my mind wandered off in that direction. I had no control.

It pained me to picture how they'd managed to fit her into that pine box that sat before us in the chapel. I'd have thought she'd need some specialty shape, a trapezoid or something, the way her poor body was twisted and kinked. But it must be that undertakers are on the order of physios or chiropractors. They're trained to noodge rigid spines and limbs posthumously into submission until they conform to the space restraints of a standard casket. In any event, it was a closed-lid affair as tradition dictated, so we'd never know how they'd jammed her in.

My mum always took the attendance at my dad's funeral as a testament to what a great guy he was. Overflow seating no less. Paperman's had to pull a last minute switcheroo to the heavy-duty chapel so everyone could be comfortably accommodated. Lena's funeral attendance was tiny. So I guess Mum, the renowned math scholar, had that correlation back-asswards. I was the youngest person there by a mile. A few rickety couples clustered in the front. Afterwards, they kissed Morrie, whispered their consoling words, rubbed him on the back, and then they were gone.

No shiva. Not officially anyway. I offered up my house. Morrie declined. He was right, I suppose. No one at home had ever even heard of him. Too much explaining. And he could hardly welcome callers into his own house, setting up the platters of lox and bagels and *mun* cookies on plywood panels set across sawhorses in the empty dining room. It would be too shaming to Lena's memory to let their friends witness what they'd come to. None of them had a clue. Morrie'd made sure of that. He was an master planner, Morrie was.

As soon as he started selling off their possessions, Morrie got to work on a parallel divestment campaign. A human one. Their friends would call up and invite themselves over for a little visit with their dear Lena. Morrie said no. She wasn't up to it. Again they would call. Again he said no. After four times, maybe five they got the message and cut the cord. It was Lena who lost out most in this arrangement, of course. She was the social animal in the couple. But Morrie made the tough-love judgment call, throwing their friends overboard to keep their pride dry.

All this spilled out during our private shiva. We mourned together up in his fur trade room over a shared bottle of slivovitz. The sharing amounted to me doing the pouring and him doing the swallowing.

"Was there an insurance policy?" I asked him. It was my habit to stick to the practicalities on occasions like this. I never knew what to say over death, couldn't deliver the normal sympathy formulas with any conviction. Maybe it's because I maxed out on all those full-of-shit phrases when my dad checked out. For seven days straight after we put him in the ground they kept shovelling the platitudes in my direction until I thought I'd pass out from the stench they gave off. *Exemplary father, devoted husband, fine family man.* Christ! *Irreplaceable, a man of integrity.* Stop! Enough! But they misread the look on my face and kept laying it on thicker and thicker, those deluded relatives of mine, those duped friends of my family. Such a mensch he was, they'd whisper to me, a loving arm around my shoulder, assuming they had a receptive audience, *a pillar of the community.* Shut up already! He was scum. Shut up!

Sorry, sorry, I lost my train of thought. Where was I? Oh yeah, practicalities.

"Was there an insurance policy?"

"What do you think?" Morrie said.

"So you'll have to sell the house right away then."

"It's a bit premature to be talking for-sale signs on the lawn don't you think?"

"No, actually, I don't think. You'll be needing the income from the house right away, won't you?"

"My net worth is no worry of yours."

"Well, it wouldn't be, except my understanding was that you're net worthless."

"I get by."

"A money pit you always called it. I thought you'd be relieved to be free to dump the place. So you could do more in life than just get by. And it's not like there'll be any spare loonies and toonies coming in now that you're hanging up your cat-burglar skates."

He looked at me like I'd missed some obvious step in my reasoning.

"You *are* planning on hanging up your cat-burglar skates, right?" I expected an automatic yes. Instead, he waffled.

"I'll have to see," he said.

"What's to see? I don't understand. The payout you'd get from the house would cover all your debts and then some. You could relax. Have some cash in your pocket for a change."

His explanation for choosing to stay on the wrong side of the law had originality going for it if nothing else. "It's something to do," he said.

"You mean like suddenly you're going to turn it into your hobby?"

"What'll you have me do to fill in the time? Needlepoint?"

"Don't give me that. You could take advantage of all that extra time to beef up our plan. We both know it needs lots of work yet. You could buckle down to it with no interruptions. Tie up the thousands of loose ends."

"Quit handling me, Ben. I haven't lost my marbles yet."

"I just sort of feel in my bones that Lena would probably rather you gave it up. If she were to know about it I mean." Okay, so call me a flip-flopper. I'd sworn off meddling on this particular subject, but under the circumstances I felt I had to swear myself back on. Besides, the ground had shifted. I wasn't strictly speaking interfering in the life of a couple anymore, I was simply interfering one-on-one.

"I don't need you to instruct me in what Lena would say if she were here."

"You're right. You don't. So this here, it's coming straight from me. Have you gone crazy or what? It's way too dangerous and your luck's bound to run out."

"I'm willing to risk it."

"Why, when you don't have to? It makes no sense."

But then it did. All the pieces clicked together. "You want to get caught, don't you? You want to throw your life away. It's an easy out. That's it, isn't it?"

"All of a sudden you're a psychiatrist? I don't remember seeing your sheepskin on the wall at the museum."

Okay, so I didn't have a framed diploma. But I'd clocked enough couch time with shrinks over the years that I could diagnose with the best of them. "Why else would you be so stuck on an idea that's bound to end you up in jail? If you'd just sell the house you could relax. You'd have more than enough money."

"You're back on the house already?"

"Yeah, I'm back on the house and that's where you ought to be too if only you'd quit being so damn pigheaded about it. What do I have to do to ram some sense into you?"

"I'm old enough to make my own decisions."

"All evidence to the contrary."

"Thank you for your vote of confidence. I knew I could count on you."

Verdict in. I was a total screw-up. My role as under-mourner was definitely not to get the primary mourner all worked up. Where did I get off pushing his buttons? You'd think I'd know better, me of all people, when my father's shiva sent me round the bend. I remember wanting to chomp down on the jugular of all those sympathy callers who delivered me their higher wisdom. And now I was shmuck enough to be doing the same.

"I was out of line. I'm sorry." Morrie humphed his acceptance of my apology.

"It's just that I'm tired Ben. I'm so tired."

"I know." And I did know. Exactly. I was whupped too. Falling down on the job has a way of sucking all the wind out of you. It made me wonder how my dad ever got out of bed in the morning.

15

"So what royalty are we expecting?"

Rena was setting the table with the über good dishes, Mum's precious gold-rimmed ones. The ones she kept zipped up in special quilted china protectors. The ones she separated from one another with circles of felt to avoid chipping. The ones she nestled deep in the armoire instead of in the regular kitchen cupboards so anyone carelessly flailing a ladle or a serving spoon would be less likely to accidentally whack 'em one. Mum kept those plates better swaddled than she ever did us.

"It's Serge. Can you believe it? A first. An actual suitor at our dinner table. So what's he like, this charmer? Tell me. And don't leave anything out."

"How would I know? We've never had the pleasure, him and me."

"But you work in the same building."

"Yeah, me and a cast of thousands. Besides, he's new-ish. And the guys with the ties and me, we don't mix. Do you think the cleaners and the big shots from up on six ever talk to each other? In my lofty position I might as well be carrying a bucket and a string mop."

"Well Mum broke through the sound barrier somehow. Maybe he goes for the tightly-wound type and he saw through to Mum's inner, you know, sproing. Women like her, when you cut 'em loose they go bouncing off the walls. Could be his idea of fun."

"You're sick."

"If you've got a better idea of what drew them together I'd be glad to hear it."

Odd how the world unfolds. You do one little thing, and it gives a hip-bump to the next thing down the line, which then bumps into the next and then the next and then the next until before you know it you've bollixed up the future. I'm telling you, it makes you scared to sneeze. Who knows what that last domino might knock up against? Here I'd asked Mum to do me some simple research, and that rubbed her up against head office, and that put her in the path of Serge, with the result that now I had the guy coming into the house interviewing for the step-father position I wasn't even aware was being advertised. But maybe I was jumping the gun.

Poor guy. He didn't know what he was in for. How does that quote go? *Happy families are all alike. Every dysfunctional family is dysfunctional in its own way.* Those Russki authors got it dead on. Only it doesn't seem like dysfunction when it's just you around the table going about your family rituals. It takes the presence of a newcomer to shine a spotlight on how nutso your family actually is. For all I knew our visitor was the spawn of Kermit and Miss Piggy but he had the advantage because his folks were way the hell off in Blanc Sablon freezing their warped asses off and it was us on display. I hoped for Mum's sake that we'd all be on our best behaviour, keeping the opportunities for this Serge guy to witness any freak-show behaviour to the bare minimum.

Hold on. Look in the mirror, you're thinking. It's you who's the family fruitcake. It's you and all your fur trade garbage that snapped the family moorings. And you're hoping *they'll* keep a lid on? Talk about gall. Well, my detractors, I would beg to differ. By the time I threw my lot in with the voyageurs my family was already clinging to the ledge. My new avocation, shall we call it, well it just stomped on their fingers. Still, for the length of tonight's dinner I was prepared to keep my calling closeted in the interest of social peace.

Mum's heartthrob showed up at seven on the button, right on time. A good omen. In the Gabai house we're sticklers for punctuality. If you aren't fifteen minutes early you're late. We'd never give our family stamp of approval to anyone with too many tardy demerits on his report card.

Mum was busy introducing Serge to the cast of characters when I came in from the dining room. I recognized him right off. Not as a suit. What I'd told Rena was no lie. I'd never seen him bossifying around the store. Where I did know him from was the museum. He'd come in a couple of weeks before with his little girl. Élodie was her name. Cute kid. About seven maybe. She was on the shyish side, spent most of their visit under the protective custody of Serge's left arm. She had a head on her shoulders, though, that kid, and it was loaded with curiosity about the place. Clearly she had excellent taste. The way we worked it that day was that she'd whisper her questions into her papa's ear, he'd relay them to me, and I'd answer them back to her. After a while, when papa started ed botching her questions on purpose, she nerved herself up and proved that her voice really did have a few decibels to it. We passed a fun hour together, the three of us, and at the end she thanked me very politely with hardly any urging. In all that time the guy never introduced himself, never once mentioned any connection with our mutual employer. As far as I was concerned he was Monsieur Jean Q. Public.

"Good to meet you," I said as we shook hands in our front hall. "Same here," said Serge.

I was playing tit for tat. Childish? You betcha. But in a tight spot maturity was never my first port of call. Serge had held back on me at the museum, I was holding back now. And he was going along with the charade. I guess he figured he owed me. I couldn't tell you why exactly I was pretending that we'd never met, my mind operates in weird and mysterious ways, but I think it was because I wanted to start out on an equal footing with everyone else in the house who figured Serge was coming to Mum as a free agent. Why should I be the one to bring up the subject of Serge's progeny and risk drekking up dinner like a fly in the soup? Let the man himself reveal his encumbrances.

Now, vetting a prospect, this was new to us. Dad came to us fully formed. We kids never had any say, as is the way of things in the parental crapshoot. You get what you get. But this time around we had plenty of up-front time. Enough to run the full battery of tests. Too bad none of us knew what they were.

Things looked promising out of the gate. Mum's beau knew his p's and q's, didn't show up empty handed. But he wasn't a traditionalist. Flowers? Chocolates? Vino? Nope, none of the above. Instead, in front of all of us he handed Mum a small black velvet pouch with a drawstring, the kind meant to have jewellery inside if I knew my movies. All of us edged in closer. We weren't expecting such a dramatic turn of events before we'd even made it to the bruschetta. But when Mum reached into the bag she pulled out something rough and brownish, about as big around as a peach pit. It had the look of an overamped kidney stone. I'd seen one before on my Uncle Perry's dresser that he kept as a surgical souvenir. It sat there right next to the petrified foreskin pared off my cousin Jeff. But what the thing actually turned out to be was a piece of quartz that rock-hound Serge had dug up and hand-buffed. Mum didn't seem at all disappointed that the contents of the bag were geological. She gushed over his gift, turning it this way and that to admire the facets and then passed it around to the rest of us so we could likewise sing its praises. Maybe I didn't know how *my* mind worked, but Zach's was an open book. "A rock?" he was thinking. "He wants to make an impression and he brings her a rock?" The fingers of his right hand went shooting northwards so they could form a loser L up against his forehead.

Rena's Zach decoder worked way faster than mine. She swooped in beside him before his digital diss could make it past the impulse stage. She grabbed him by the right arm as if she needed an escort and together they led the processional into the living room where the appetizers were weighing down the coffee table. It was always a good tactic with Zach to park him near food so his hands and his mouth would be safely occupied. Mum borrowed Serge to go play muscleman with the wine cork in the kitchen before we dug in. Or maybe just to psych him up. I suppose en masse a newbie might consider us imposing even if two of us were octogenarians. While they were gone we did a preliminary scoring. Serge had three thumbs up, Rena, Nana, and Grandpa, and one thumbs down – Zach. I abstained. It did surprise me that the grandparents took such an early shine to him. I thought they'd be harder to bring around since it was their late son's chair Serge's derrière was angling to fill.

Serge had been well briefed by Mum. She'd fed him enough screenshots from our past so he had plenty of chat fodder. This lubed the path for him with everyone else around the table, but for me it was touchier. The guy had to know I wasn't a happy camper employee-wise and that I'd be holding him accountable. Indirectly, granted. He hadn't yet popped up on the scene when they made the decision to shut me down, but guilt by association and all that.

"So your mother tells me you run the store's museum?" he asked me after they'd exhausted Rena's starring turn in her college play and Zach's post-grad Bill Gates ambitions.

"That's right."

"What does that involve exactly?" I gave him the shrink-wrapped version since we were only play-acting anyway. Why waste my breath?

"And you, what do *you* do exactly?" Borderline snotty but Mum, chief of the tone police, was in no position to ream me out for it.

"Well, I troubleshoot you might say. That's what the job boils down to. They send me in to the stores that have an issue of some kind and I try to resolve it if I can."

"And what's the trouble you're shooting at our store?"

"The takeover. You know. The Americans' ways and ours, there's always some friction there. And then there are all the language issues. So I try to get us on the same page."

"You mean you help them out with the union busting, that kind of thing?"

"Ben, please," Mum said.

Jeez, Zach wasn't the only one who needed a handler. The thing of it is, I always knew when I crossed the line, I just couldn't do what it took to rein myself in. Ever since Dad did his number on me I developed this quirk where my brain sent out the proper signals to my mouth, but once they got there, my mouth would spit them out onto the sidewalk. Instead it would act on its own, without any direction from upstairs. I said a lot of stupid things was the upshot.

"A job like yours," Rena edged in, "it must mean you travel a lot." She might genuinely have been trying to gauge if the guy could be juggling a woman in every port, but more likely she was just aiming to cut me off at the pass. You had to feel for Rena. She'd always served as Mum's understudy, but lately running interference for me and Zach was taking up more and more of her time. Having another troubleshooter in the house, a professional yet, could lift some of the weight off her back. Even I could see this was a point in Serge's favour.

"It used to," Serge said, leapfrogging over my question in favour of Rena's. "I'd be on the road three weeks out of four sometimes. And I hated that part of it to be honest with you. I have a little girl at home and it was rough being away from her so much. But the good news is that new owners have offered me a different position once the transfer is complete, one that'll keep me in Montreal permanently. Believe you me I'll be glad to stay in one place."

"Élodie's a great kid," Mum piped up. "She's only six but she can already read anything you put in front of her." Hold on now. Mum had already done the step-parent tryouts on his end? We came second?

"You're divorced, then," Zach said, flat. He was running a quick spreadsheet. Crass maybe, but in his heart, and I was prepared to admit despite all our bad blood that he had traces of one, he was looking out for Mum. See, when Dad crapped out on us he hadn't left too much cash socked away in the mattress. Stay-at-home Mum had to go out and dig herself up a full-time job. The Bay gig she landed only paid so-so, but with that little influx of cash, her fifteen percent employee discount, and her genetic moxie, she pummelled us kids into adulthood. A rough assignment. In my case especially. Alimony payments could be a drain on the already stretched household economy. This wasn't exactly marrying up.

"Zach!"

"It's okay. I don't mind Carolina." He stroked Mum reassuringly on her arm. Nothing showy but intimate all the same. And what was with this pet name? He pronounced it Italianish, *Cahroleena*. I'd never figured Mum for the pet name type. Probably because Dad never saw fit to treat her to one. Stingy bastard. All those standbys like baby or honey or sweetie collected dust in his bureau drawer. He always just called her by her given name, Carol. He didn't shorten it. He didn't lengthen it. He didn't anagram it. With Dad, it came out sounding like a bark. But when Serge said *Carolina* it flowed like melted chocolate.

"Why shouldn't they know about me? It's only right and proper," he said to her. Then he turned to face the family. "I'm not divorced, no. I'm a widower. I lost my Maude when Élodie was three and a half. It's been just the two of us ever since."

That shut Zach up good. The rest of us too.

"This new job," Serge said, trying his damndest to save us from ourselves with a strategic redirect, "I can't tell you how thankful I am that it's come along. It means we can be together all the time now. The Bay's been very good to me, I've got to say. Very good. I've had offers here and there over the years, but I've never been tempted to work anywhere else. The Bay, well, it's my home."

So we didn't have to wait till we saw him at the beach to find out that the tattoo across Serge's heart read *God Bless the Bay*. The one inked across my deltoid had a slightly different message. *Piss on the Bay* it said. The gap between us wasn't plain old wide, it was titanic. Mum had once told me Serge was a serious employee. Okay, that I could live with. Wasn't she one too? Only she'd carefully sat on the fact that he was so disgustingly, everlastingly loyal to the Man, a veritable Bay suck. But now here it was, out in the open. I could see the dread in her eyes. She was waiting for me to let fly with the zinger that would send both dinner and her prospects swirling down the crapper. I mean how could I hold back after he admitted straight up his mad passion for the Bay? It all but qualified as inciting to riot. No jury on earth would convict me.

I let it pass. I just sat by while the conversation took a harmless turn minus yours truly and Mum's shoulders ratcheted down from her ears back to their at-ease position. It was that Carolina thing that did me in. Go ahead, call me sentimental, but it softened me up somehow. Or could it be I was belatedly growing up?

Mum had cooked her head off. Good thing. With her magnifico spread laid out in front of us, we had something nice and neutral to talk about while we recovered from our previous conversational cock-ups. And as recoveries go it didn't take long. By the time we were halfway through the soup, the laughing gas Mum had stirred into it started to take effect and things took a pleasantly loopy turn around the table. Serge offered us up a story about his incendiary first (and last) night as a short-order cook, the night that cost him half an eyebrow and his taste for fries. And since our guest so generously took the lead in embarrassing himself, the rest of us, in humble appreciation, put ourselves out there. Inhibitions? Out the window. Rena even opened up about the time she got all jumbled up in her cues, and walked onstage when the character she was playing was supposed to have dropped dead of consumption three scenes earlier. She had everybody cracking up. When the phone rang just as we were starting to dig in to the plum tart, we could hardly hear it for all the laughing. Rena was nearest, so she slipped out to the kitchen to answer it.

"It's for you, Benj," she said when she came back in.

"Tell whoever it is I'm busy, can't you?" For once I was happy wallowing in family and wasn't itching for an excuse to duck out. Used to be that I'd pray for the lifeline of a phone call to liberate me from the dinner table. But this night was different from all other nights. Tonight we were behaving like that other kind of family I'd heard rumours existed out there in the cosmos. The normal kind.

"I can't exactly," she said. Whiny.

"Why not? Who is it so important?"

Rena hesitated. She twitched her head toward the kitchen, signalling me to join her there for a private consult, but I was in no mood to budge. See how mellowness can mess with your mind? It kept me from reading the urgency in that twitch.

"C'mon Reen, spit it out."

She could have just fabricated up Renaud or Nick on the other end of the line, but she wasn't much of a liar, my sister, never had been. Dad hadn't rubbed off on her in that way. Her impulse when cornered was always to take a pivot towards the truth.

"It's sergeant somebody or other from Station Seventeen."

Mum rocketed up out of her chair like in the old days. She had to grip the edge of the table to steady herself. "The police! Why would the police be calling you? What's wrong? Oh Benjie." Her words were coming out all wheezy like they always did when the world was resisting her control. The grandparents, who most meals missed out on great swaths of what was being said around the table somehow made out the word *police* loud and clear. It must have been on the list of words that their hearing aid bouncers had been tipped to let through. "You're not in trouble, boychikel, are you?" Nana asked me, inspecting my face for clues out of the high-power slice of her progressives. She reached out towards me to reassure herself that I was still me. Grandpa, who wasn't much for physical contact, put a comforting arm around her even though it was hard to tell which one of them was more in need of support. Even Zach's jaw was hanging slack.

"Take it easy, Mum," I said. It's got to be a mistake of some kind. I'll go clear it all up." Serge's kishkes had to be doing the happy dance that he got to see behind the airbrushed version of our family before getting down on one knee to seal the deal. If he had even the least sense of self-preservation, he'd hightail it out of there before I got back from the kitchen.

"Monsieur Benjamin Gabai?" the voice said when I picked up the phone.

"Oui. Speaking."

"This is Sergeant Stéphanie Arbour from Police Station Seventeen. We have your uncle here. He asked us to call you. He needs some assistance."

"My uncle?" As far as I knew Uncle Perry was still down in West Palm working on his handicap.

"Monsieur Morris Shukert," she said.

"I'll be right over."

There were some basic questions I should have clarified with Sergeant Stéphanie while I still had her on the line. Like do I need to bring a gym bag stuffed with cash, or a lawyer maybe? Not that I had either. But I didn't ask. All I could think of was that I had to get over there. Fast.

Back in the dining room everyone else had stood up to cluster protectively around Mum. It was a pathetic huddle and I hated myself for being the one responsible. Serge had his arms around her. I caught him saying *"Calme-toi,* Caro. If it were anything really serious they'd have come by in a patrol car."

"A patrol car!" she burst out. Bam, the tears were brimming. If this guy was going to stick, he had a ways to go when it came to the ins and outs of Mum-handling. He was whipping her up instead of talking her off the roof. But he was a quick learner, Serge. He downshifted pronto to more white-bread soothing noises.

"Shh, it'll be okay, Carolina. It'll be okay. I'm here. Shh." He planted a gentle kiss on the top of her head.

They all froze when I came in. "Mum, can I take the car?"

"Benjie, what do they want with you? What is it?"

"Nothing to do with me. Absolutely nothing." Dummy me. I should have said that up front but this Morrie business had me majorly unglued. "It's a friend of mine. He's in trouble."

"Not Rossi I hope?"

"No, no one you know."

"Doesn't he have parents?"

"Look, Mum, I'm in kind of a rush. I'll give you all the details later. Okay?"

"Right. I'll get you my keys." Her face was so flushed with relief that I probably could have scored a car of my own if I'd pushed her for it then and there. But that would have been unseemly.

While Mum was upstairs rooting through her purse, Serge pulled me away from the others who were re-attacking their dessert with gusto now that peace had redescended on our table. "I know this isn't the best time," he said, "but I've been looking for a chance to tell you. I didn't want you getting your hopes up, you know, because of this ... situation between your mother and me. The thing is, I can't undo the decision that's been made about the museum. It's beyond my power. However much I'd like it to be different, the museum's going to close. There's nothing I can do to change it. I'm more sorry than I can say." If he expected me to be disappointed that he'd flubbed his first test of loyalty to the Gabai clan, he was way off base. Finally in this house I had an example of a stand-up kind of guy. If all my interfering had ended Mum up with Serge, then I guess I'd done good in the end.

16

It wasn't like on TV. They didn't pass Morrie back his shoelaces and wallet through a slot under the bulletproof window. There was no window. Just a counter. Weird. Even Place des Arts had a window where they sold you tickets to the ballet and you've got to wonder what their clerks had to be so afraid of. When I told her my business, the officer on greeter duty checked her online roster and called out into the public area, "Monsieur Shukert, your nephew is here." Morrie was slouched in a moulded plastic chair against the wall. His eyelids were fighting a losing battle to stay open. I was so focused on busting him out of the joint that I'd walked right past him without noticing.

"Let's get you out of here," I said. I reached down to cup him by the elbow to help jack him up out of his seat. The guy looked drained. He started talking but I cut him off. "You can fill me in out in the car." Even if it was way less scuzzy in there than I'd expected, decorated faux-perky in outdated Operation Red Nose posters, it was still a police station and I wanted us out. The desk cop waved bye-bye and we put the place behind us.

Well, not that far behind actually. We sat in the parking lot with the ignition off next to a lineup of blue and white cruisers on break from kettling demonstrators or whatever the hell they do. "Care to tell me what I'm doing here, Uncle Morrie?"

He shifted uncomfortably in his seat as if a spring from Mum's rattletrap Corolla was jabbing him in the back. "Let's just say they couldn't make the charges stick and we'll let it go at that. Then, just after they released me, I started having heart palpitations like I do, so they did me a good turn and called you."

"What? Why didn't they call an ambulance? Or take you to the hospital themselves with the flashers? You weren't their business anymore? Or were they too busy filing their nails?"

"Don't get yourself worked up. They did right by me. I just needed my pills but I forgot them back at home. I didn't want to pull up in front of the house in a police car and give the neighbours an eyeful. It would make Lena angry. So I asked them to phone you. Which they did. There, now you're all up to date." Hardly, but I'd pressure him later for all the gory details.

"What made you call the land line? I told you, always call my cell."

"I was a little confused I guess. I had your number mixed up. They had to look your house up in the phone book, or on the computer, however they do. Sorry if I messed things up on your end."

"It's okay," I said, even if it was no-kay. He'd mucked up the separation of church and state that I'd always tried to maintain between my fur-trade and non-fur-trade lives. "Forget it."

I started the car and drove us over to his place. He conked out the second the engine turned over. Was I being too cynical to suspect it was a strategic snooze? I wouldn't be able to give him the third degree if he was out cold, now would I? I know, I know. He didn't want to be grilled. Just wanted to turn the page. Said as much back at the station. But you can't always get what you want, like the song goes.

No problemo. I'd just wait him out. He'd have to answer to me eventually. And it wasn't as if my questions were all that mysterious or tricky. They were your joe-normal what-do-you-ask of-a-friend-who-just-pulled-a-botched-robbery-for-no-good-reason-and-landed-in-the-slammer-and-got-out-by-the-skin-of-his-teeth type questions. Didn't I deserve to hear the whole story? Me, his saviour? But the longer I drove with Morrie's snores drowning out the radio, that jumble of questions I'd been sorting and stacking jelled into just one. Prime and essential. One shining jewel of a question. A question that distilled all my curiosity to its syrupy essence. *What the fuck were you thinking?*

Only I never did get to ask it. At least not then. The timing was all wrong. We were men on a mission, so I could hardly object when Morrie shot out of the car at his house without letting another word slip. I tagged along behind. He headed up to his medicine cabinet to do his drugs and I wandered into the kitchen meanwhile. It was the only room on the first floor with any chairs in it outside of Lena's studio, and it was just too ghoulish to cool my heels in there. For something to do, I checked out the fridge. All that was in it were the beers we'd chug down after a canoe workout upstairs and a well-intentioned piece of fish that might have been just edible a couple of weeks before, masked under a goodly glop of tartar sauce. At least I thought it was fish. But was it a veal chop maybe? That hunk of protein was too far gone to know if it came to Morrie's fridge by land or by sea. I would have needed a HAZMAT suit to get close enough to make a positive ID.

The ex-con came back down in fresh clothes, slightly neatified. He must have passed a washcloth over his face and made a few half-hearted swipes with his comb but I have to say, in the interest of the truth, that he still looked rotten. His normal ruddy skin tone had gone all chalky and his jowls hung a good half-inch lower than I'd remembered. And did I detect a new stoop in his posture since this whole thing went down?

"They feed you in there?" I asked him.

"Yeah. Sandwiches with some kind of mystery meat. I took a pass."

"You mean to tell me you've been running on empty since they took you in?"

"Pretty much."

I sized him up closer, co-opting the patented Carol Gabai stare. It was a diagnostic tool I'd never had reason to try out before. I'd only ever been on the receiving end. But now I was seeing just how powerful it was. In the space of a few seconds the readout fed me the appropriate Rx for the situation at hand.

"You're coming with me," I said, expecting some push-back. But nada. Not so much as a blink. He just stood there like he'd checked out of his own premises. My mannequin buddy Alexandre showed more signs of life. "You're coming with me," I said again and waited for a reaction. Three beats, four. "Hell-o-o. Anybody home? Knock knock." I took hold of him by the elbow for the second time that evening. Normally I wasn't the touch-y type but this zombie act he had going had me worried. No joke. I figured a bit of human contact might snap him back to himself. And it did. Finally. Just as I was revving up my finger to call 911.

"Where're we going?" he asked me as if we'd never fallen into a conversational pothole.

"To my place."

"Your place?"

"Yeah. Got any objections, Unc?" He shook his head, too malnutrished to put up any resistance. Didn't matter anyway. I wasn't about to let him call the shots in his condition.

Serge's SUV was still in the driveway when we arrived home. At least I hadn't broken up the dinner party. "So look," I turned to my passenger, or my captive, depending on how you saw it, "as far as my family's concerned they don't even know you exist, so just follow my lead." He nodded his understanding but just how compos mentis he was at that moment I couldn't gauge. On top of his recent bout of out-of-it-ness, this was the guy who'd spooked me back at the station by talking about his late wife in the present tense. How he'd behave in the hair-trigger bosom of my family was anybody's guess but we couldn't turn back now. I opened the door to him. "Welcome to the fun house."

It felt like forever since I'd raced out of there after the phone call, but it hadn't been that long at all by the clock. Everybody was still sitting around the table sipping their decafs and chasing crumbs around their dessert plates. Here I'd completed a successful rescue mission to pry Morrie from the jaws of justice and to reunite him with his meds so his heart could quit its tipsy beat and I hadn't even missed a course.

I stumbled a bit over the introductions when I got to Serge. He was my mother's ... what exactly? *Friend*? Was that the right word? Nah. It felt too washed out to describe their relationship. Was *boyfriend* more precise? Maybe so. But that was a word with zits on its face. I'd seen the term *lady-friend* before in books I'd read, and it seemed to zone in on the right age bracket for Mum, but the opposite sex equivalent, *gentleman friend*, sounded too mint julep for down to earth, rock-digger Serge. So in the end I tossed them all and just introduced him generically, name alone, minus rank and serial number.

As for Morrie, *friend* was bang on and that's how I pitched him. Now I'd brought home friends before, nothing new there, but none of them ever had liver spots. Maybe that was why everyone rose from their seats when we came in, as if I'd walked into the room with Churchill or something. This demo of hands-across-the-generations was going to take them a little getting used to. Understandable. They were entitled. Totally. Before Morrie stumbled into my path, I'd have been first in line to think that a half-century age gap between pals had a kinky ring to it.

"Morrie had a pretty rough day," I told them, trying to break the geriatric ice. "He got robbed this morning by a couple of guys. They stole his wallet. Over by the Berri metro. They followed him away from an ATM. Manhandled him pretty good. He spent all day at the police station, going through mug shots, giving statements and stuff. I thought after all that a home-cooked meal would do him good. I know you always make enough to feed the immediate world when we have company, so I brought him over. That alright?"

"Of course it is." Mum oozed welcome. "Since when do you have to ask? Have your friend sit down. I'll warm him up a plate." They all pitched in to make Morrie feel at home. Zach instantly gave up his padded dining room chair to Morrie and got himself a folding chair from the front closet. Rena made up a fresh place setting with one of her fancy in-goblet napkin sculptures that was meant to look like a fleur de lis but always reminded me more of an erection. Serge spotted the cache of bottles in the breakfront left over from my aborted Bar Mitzvah and poured Morrie a stiff belt. Even the grandparents did their bit by exuding waves of sympathy over to their contemporary. After all, if there were goons out on the streets targeting the youth-impaired, they could be next. I have to say, for all that I have a tendency to kvetch about my family, that night they did me proud.

Mum brought out a plate so overloaded Air Canada would have slapped her with a baggage surcharge. "Am I the only one eating?" Morrie asked when she set it down in front of him and he looked around. "I hate to keep you at the table when the rest of you are finished."

"Now that you mention it," Serge said, "I could go for another help-ing." Mum jumped up. "Sit, sit, Carolina. I can get it. Anybody else?"

"I'm in," I said. "All this excitement worked me up an appetite."

"Okay, two number fours coming right up." Morrie's arrival scootched Serge up a notch on the food chain, brazening him up to edge in on the hosting duties, and once you have free rein in the kitchen, can the other rooms be far behind?

"Any leads on the guys who did it?" Serge wanted to know when he came back in.

"No," I said. "No luck. Chances are they won't ever find them. It's a needle in a haystack."

"They were probably looking to do a drug deal." This was from Nana, noted expert on crackhead behaviour.

"There're a lot of surveillance cameras out there," Serge said. "You look up in the air lately and they're everywhere. They'll track your thieves down once they review all the tapes from the neigh-bourhood. You heard it here first."

"But you have to factor in if they'll go to that much trouble," Zach said. "On TV they would, sure, but it's not like the Montreal police put themselves out much when it comes to the lower level stuff. Wallets, iPhones, bikes, good luck. Not to get you down Mr. Shukert, but their reputation for that kind of thing stinks."

"Did you have a chance to call and cancel your cards?" Mum wanted to know. It's her practical streak that filtered down to me. "Feel free to do it from here if you want."

"No need. Everything's taken care of."

"That's a good thing. You're all set then." Mum made the rounds of the table, topping up our drinks. "So I've been wondering," she said as she poured, "where did you two get acquainted?"

I should have been prepared for that question even though

she'd never asked it of me before. Why would she have? The answer was always understood. School. Where else? But clearly Morrie and I hadn't bonded in biology lab over our frog dissection. Everyone's ears perked up. Mum had done them all a favour putting it out there.

I went with the declawed version of events, skipping over the breaking-and-entering that brought Morrie and me together. In a way, I wished I didn't have to kiss that part of the story goodbye in the telling. You have to admit that as a beginning it had legs.

"Morrie comes in to the museum all the time," I said. "He's a huge fan of the collection. Knows everything about the voyageurs and the fur trade. A real authority, you might say."

"An authority. That's a nice change for Benjamin," Mum said to Morrie. "I'm afraid that around here, we're not especially knowledgeable about his favourite subject, and that's putting it mildly. Tell me, how did you come by your expertise? Are you self taught, like our Benjie?"

Morrie was returning to himself with every bite and had the wit to nudge us over to safer conversational ground. Mum's question regarding his expertise he parried neatly with a compliment.

"This meal is delicious Carol. I can't thank you enough. My late wife was a wonderful cook. This is the first time since I don't know when that I've tasted anything that held a candle to her cooking."

"I'm honoured you think so," Mum said. "May I ask, has she been gone long?"

"No, not really. It feels like just yesterday she was here for me to talk to. She was sick for quite a while before she passed away, confined to her bed. For the last few years I cooked for us both as best I could, which isn't saying much. Here," he said, looking more animated than he had all night thanks to the Lena-effect, "let me show you her picture."

Ay! No! Don't do it! No! No!

But he did it.

I must have forgotten to switch my subliminal warning system off vibrate. Morrie went right ahead and reached into his back pocket and pulled out his wallet. Yep. The very same wallet he'd theoretically been rolled for earlier in the day. Any idiot could see this wasn't a replacement wallet or a backup wallet. It was a comfy old friend of a wallet. His wallet and no one else's. Its arc conformed perfectly to the curvature of his right hemi-tush. It's a well-know fact that forensics can establish a billfold's paternity by matching up the two.

Luckily my family didn't have a suspicious bone in its body. Witness my mum's complete and utter cluelessness vis-à-vis my dad's moonlighting. I rest my case. Anyway, everybody was so focused on the photo of Lena, and it was a great picture I have to admit, that no one seemed to pay any attention to the enchanted wallet that disappeared and reappeared without rhyme or reason. Or if they did, they were discreet enough to keep it to themselves.

That bobble in the proceedings aside, the rest of dinner moved along without a hitch, all the chatter safely in-bounds. As soon as we set our forks down after dessert, I extricated Morrie from the table to drive him back home. No point pressing our luck.

"You said you live in Westmount right?" Serge asked him. "It's on my way. I can give you a lift. Ben doesn't have to run you back."

Uh-oh. A bad equation, the two of them alone in the car together with Morrie off his game. Loose lips and all that. But what could I do? So many lies had been streaming out of my mouth all evening that my cupboard was bare. I couldn't dredge up a single good reason not to let Serge play good samaritan. So it was settled.

Mum and I threw our coats over our shoulders and walked the two of them out to the car, leaving the rest of the family to get a head start on the post-game analysis over the dirty dishes. While I was helping Morrie balance all the foil care packages on his lap, Mum and Serge stepped outside the range of the garage light for a low-key goodbye smooch. I could still make them out fine, though. It wasn't all that dark. That kiss, I'd have to say, was one of considerable finesse. They'd obviously worked out on prior occasions whose job it was to tilt in which direction so there'd be none of that adolescent nose bumping, no awkward clacking of teeth. An easy 9.5 on technical merit. But it wasn't really the mechanics of their kiss that kept me gawking when I should have turned away and left them to their privacy. It was the tenderness of it, how they paused in the middle to look into each other's eyes and smile at their private joy before starting in again. See until that moment, the word *kiss* always tripped the same switch for me, the one that brought up on screen that damned Ritz elevator kiss, with its sloppy guzzling of lips, wet and wild, as if kissing were purely a salivary event. Thanks Dad, for yet another crapola legacy. But now I saw what a kiss was meant to be. I hoped that my brain would cut me a break for once and do the simple bit of rewiring required to bypass the old image in favour of the new.

"So what did you think?" Mum said once Serge pulled out of the drive.

"Supper was terrific, Mum. Your normal culinary triumph."

"Not supper, goofus. Serge. What did you think of him?"

"I liked him a lot Mum. Go for it."

"So you think he's a worthy successor to Daddy?"

Such an innocent sounding question. Except the answer to it was spiked with land mines, and no one ever gave me a map. One wrong step and I'd blow a leg off and probably bring Mum down with me. Her asking me straight out like that caught me with my guard down, and I'd spent every last ounce of my energy for so many years keeping it propped up that my back was permanently cramped with the effort. It would be such a relief just to tell her the truth, that a tree stump would be a worthy successor to Daddy. But my father had one hell of a long reach. After all these years, and from the grave yet, he could sense when my resolve was getting shaky. And that's when I'd feel it. A good twisting pinch in the arm. You think I was imagining it, do you? Then why was my arm black and blue for days afterward? A reminder pinch it was. A deal is a deal pinch. And so I'd can the urge to tell my mother the truth. It worked every time before and it worked this time too. Besides, it would be demeaning to Serge to lower the husband bar so far that even a cockroach could vault over it. Serge couldn't help it if he was following in the tracks of a scuzzball. Let the guy think he had big shoes to fill.

"More than worthy, Mum. More than worthy." I though that summed it all up with complete accuracy.

17

Papal dispensation had been granted to the Bay to stay open all night for the city's annual Nuit Blanche. Normally, Montreal's All-Nighter was for cultural stuff strictamente, but since the store housed a museum it was deemed artsy-fartsy enough to get full privileges. This was a seismic coup for my dear place of employment since no other stores would be allowed to stay open to cater to the dusk to dawn crowd. If festival-goers had an urge to do a little shopping and had a gap in their schedule between Poetry Slam at one a.m. and Glass Blowing at two, it was the Bay or nowhere. They had the market cornered.

Boy did they luck out in head office. Retail was so not the meaning of the night. But the Bay slipped between the Nuit Blanche cracks thanks to the very museum it was oh so happy to trash. At least it meant my place would finally be rubbing shoulders with the Big Macs of the city's museum world; museums with their own buildings, their own bankrolls, their own bathrooms. Too bad it had to wait to happen till just before they lit the funeral pyre.

Oh the Bay'd be raking in the bucks all right. The Nuit Blanche was a springtime mega-event. The streets would be gridlocked with people all night long, so many thousands that you'd think they'd taken the wrong turn for a Stanley Cup parade. And they'd be dressed up wild lots of them. Adding themselves to the show. After all those dreary months of greyscale winter, it was break out or bust. How really to describe it? Like Mardi Gras. But not.

We were expecting more visitors to pour in that one night than in the whole lifetime of the museum. Not that everyone attending the All-Nighter would choose to come see us of course. There were loads of choices of where to go, what to do. The printed program guide was a brick. A couple of hundred activities to pick from. A museum wasn't everybody's cup of tea. There were people out there who'd prefer to gumboot dance at city hall or build their own totem poles out of recycled tuna cans. Philistines. Their loss.

It was Mum who tipped me off that we'd be participating in the city's bedtime blowout for the first time ever. She heard it through the grapevine. So what else is new? By the time the top brass got around to notifying me officially via one of their afterthought memos, I'd already spent a week and a half scrubbing down the place. I'm not talking my ritual Monday morning wash either, soap and water with a shpritz of Windex chaser. No way. For this extravaganza I was treating everything to a facial and a pedicure too. Let no one presume that just because my museum ran on pedal power it was any less pampered than those ivy leaguers I was sharing the program with.

At least the bigwigs were trusting me to handle things on my end for once. They were too busy worrying if the Bay's clunky cash registers would be zippy enough to handle the mobs. Carte blanche they said I had for the event. Magnanimous buggers. Now they were giving me carte blanche? When my days were numbered? But I accepted the penny they tossed in my cup and kept quiet.

Those deadheads upstairs whose imaginations dribbled all the way from A to B, they figured it was unrisky to grant me my independence. What could I do in a museum beside set up a rope line? I'm sure they pictured me standing at the entrance like a lump, a fixed smile plastered on my face, doing your typical welcome/*bienvenue* bit. Yawn. I'd been to museums on Nuit Blanche before. It was way more than just an after-dark visit. Culture wasn't always an easy sell. You had to give the visitors some bang for their buck, even if it was free. Otherwise they might just as well have stayed home trawling for porn as usual.

I took my responsibility to heart. If they'd made this my baby, the museum was damn well gonna do itself proud. So what if the job was only mine for a measly two months more. That's right, two months. I was now in firm possession of the elusive closure date. Deep Throat had finally gotten around to worming it out of Serge and good little spy that she was she passed it on to me as promised concealed inside a cheese sandwich. Me of little faith. Just when I was starting to think that the assignment I'd given her had slipped her mind what with all the fizz of her new romance. I should have known better.

The date was firm, Mum reported. No wiggle room. The auctioneers from Toronto were booked in and they wanted to prepare the catalogue without any interference from *moi*. So it was only fifty-seven more days to x out on my calendar before the collection scattered to the four winds and the space occupied by the museum went to expanding the Bay's nail salon. Yeah, you heard me right. Nails. Those morons.... Well, don't get me started on them now. I have another story to tell.

I corralled Renaud, Nick, and Sam into playing supporting roles for the night of. Not that all that much strong-arming was really required once I laid out what I had in mind. It sounded like a hoot to them so they signed right up on the dotted line. I knew I'd be able to count on my kayak crew. Those guys didn't know the meaning of the word no.

My idea was this. In the back corner of the museum there was this diorama with three mannequins posed on a piece of scruffy astroturf. They're gathered around the birchbark canoe, going about their voyageur business. One is meant to be loading a pack into the canoe, another is smoking a pipe, and the third is hunched over a kettle cooking up brunch. A selection of fur trade *chazzerai* is set out in the foreground for verisimilitude, or whatever the hell that word is that means realism. You've got your rum kegs, your flintlocks, your fire bags, your oilskins, and a couple of stuffed beavers looking smiley and upbeat considering the fate that awaits them. Hanging behind this tableau is a set of four interlocking panels painted up to resemble a pine forest and all the little beasties that called it home.

Now I had a few issues with that diorama. Okay, more than a few. All right, let's just say many. Take the backdrop for one. The artist got the perspective all wonky. Or maybe he wasn't trying for perspective. Or maybe he wasn't even an artist. The birds and the animals did have a paint-by-number look to them if you put your nose right up close. And speaking of forest fauna, did those particular critters on the backdrop really pal around together? I could have sworn that some of them were tropical. It didn't do to cross-pollinate animals from the Canadian backwoods with animals from the Amazon in the same mural. There's a logical limit to biodiversity. But even worse than the we-are-the-world forest were the stuffed beavers dressed up in tuques and sashes. I mean come on. What was with this cutesy shit? Either you were aiming to be authentic or not. Which brought me to my last gripe, though definitely not my least, namely the three stooges sitting around the canoe. Voyageurs they were meant to be. You didn't have to tell me. But with the real and true canoe as the centrepiece of the scene, the plaster-of-paris voyageurs looked that much fakier by comparison. They were clearly twenty-first century implants, their clothing a polyester blend, and if you looked carefully at where their boots met their pants, you could make out that they were dressed in tube socks. What an embarrassment.

So I welcomed Nuit Blanche as my chance to upgrade that scene which I'd been forbidden from on high to fiddle with before. Now I was free to slap it into shape, make it less Disney-ish, more historically kosher. First off, I planned to take care of minor housekeeping details like putting the beavers back in mufti. Easy enough done. But the sumo revamp I had in mind, my proudest brainwave, was to ditch the mannequins altogether and parachute in real people to replace them. Sort of like those living statues you see on street corners downtown, except mine wouldn't have their faces bronzed. Actually they wouldn't even be statues either. My thinking was that they'd move around in front of the piney backdrop as if they were genuine voyageurs in camp. A living crèche kind of thing, but minus Jesus, Mary, and Joseph.

I could count on at least one fan of this plan. Alexandre. He and the voyageur mannequins didn't get on, you might say. For sure they never mixed outside of office hours. He found them too dumb. If they had baseball caps on instead of tuques they'd be wearing them backwards. And even though it was all part and parcel of their gig, he looked down on them for their sweat-soaked clothes, their matted hair, and their lowbrow habits. For their part, they saw Alexandre as snooty and limp-wristed. So there was no love lost there. Junking the voyageurs who stank up the joint would make Alexandre a happier camper for the duration of my tenure, brief as it was going to be.

As to my role in all this? Well, aside from being producer, director, set designer, prop master, gaffer, and best boy, I'd be playing the archi-voyageur. The bossman. I'd be the one doing most of the talking. My three live recruits would just be backing me up. I figured the kids attending would go for it big time. The four of us voyageurs would stage a little activity every hour on the hour all through the night, although kiddly attendance tended to fall off after midnight so I'd been told. Yeah, kids were my real audience, I calculated. Or rather families. My experience in the museum taught me that mums and dads loved it when their little darlings soaked up history au naturel, rather than from the pages of a book. So that was the description I had them put in the Nuit Blanche program. I called it *Little League Voyageurs*. Catchy, wouldn't you say?

Not everyone in my nuclear family was as high on the plan as Alexandre when I let them in on what I'd dreamt up for Nuit Blanche. We were sitting around chewing on duck bones when the subject came up. It was the anniversary of Dad's funeral. On that day Mum always rounded us all up so we could drive out to the cemetery and put a pebble on Dad's marker. Then we'd go out for Chinese. To VIP where Dad used to take us because we kids liked spinning the lazy Susan and it was dirt cheap to feed a family of seven. It was Mum's homage to the old régime. Personally, I didn't see the point of going to the graveside. You could think or not think about Dad anywhere. He hardly deserved a special trip out to the boonies. I only went along on the outing for the Kung Pao chicken.

Predictably, Mum thought my plan was brilliant and Zach insane. He didn't so much object to my idea for the night as to the fact that I was putting myself out to do anything at all. "I give up," he said. "I'll never understand you. Why in the world are you going to all this trouble for the Bay? They're letting you go. All you ever do is complain about how they treat you. And what do you in your infinite wisdom decide to do? You get down on your knees to them and say, 'yes massuh, anything you say massuh, of course I'd love to help you squeeze more pennies out of the buying public before you toss me in the dumpster, massuh.' Jesus. Grow a pair, why don't you? Sorry, Mum."

"It's not for them, this, it's for me," I said. "That's the crucial difference."

"Yeah right. Well, what we've got here, I'd say, is your classic self-destructive, love-hate relationship. You really ought to go see someone about getting that straightened out." Here Mum lifted her eloquent eyebrows. They clearly stated that I'd seen too many someones in my life and this line of talk was unfunny to her in the extreme. Zach picked up on her message and shut up. But Rena took over right where he left off. Turns out she was pissed off. "Why didn't you ask me to play one of the voyageurs? All my experience on stage and you skip right over me? Correct me if I'm wrong but do you have any other sisters who happen to be studying acting? You know I could nail a role like that." She was more steamed than I'd seen her in a good long while. "It's because voyageurs didn't wear bras, right? I wasn't true to life enough to suit you. That's it, isn't it?" Shit, they were coming at me from all sides.

A little footnote here on the question of historical purity. Rena was way off the mark with her Victoria's Secret crack. I'd come across quite a few cases in the literature of cross-dressing voyageurs, in the woman-to-man direction I mean, who went out as members of fur-trading crews for years on end incognito. Or would that be incognita? Anyway, some of them were actually known to have taken native wives. Started families even. Somehow. But this discussion I so didn't want to prolong.

"Sorry, Reen. Really. I should have thought. I'm full up with voyageurs now, but you'll be in my next production. Swear to God."

She thawed partway with my apology, however worthless it was. "I just wanted to help out," she said, leftover moody, and in fact I did need help, but none that she could give me. It was Nana I had my eye on.

See, my Nana was a bit of a pack rat. She had balls of wool that she'd picked up on sale squirreled away all over the house. And since me, Zach, or Rena didn't show any signs of procreating, she had no immediate need to knit the baby blankets they were intended for. That kind of thing you didn't do on spec. That we knew. She'd taught us those old-country rules and regs. Pre-knitting could rile up the evil eye. Get it thinking of harelip, club foot, what have you. She couldn't put a future great-grandbaby at risk, so the wool just sat there, waiting for her plugged-up grandkids to get with the program.

What do you call it when you have a need that matches up perfectly with someone else's supply? Kismet? Capitalism? Whichever. This was a perfect example. Nana had the wool and I needed tuques. Lots. I wanted every kid who came to our voyageur open house to put on a tuque to get them in the mood. They'd have to give them back before they left the museum of course, so there'd be enough there for the next group. Yes, I was aware that the sharing of hats was frowned upon in the world of kindergartens and daycares who operated under the shadow of the big L. I'd seen the commercials on TV for those special combs. But if the kids left the museum itching and scratching, at least I'd be sending them out into the world with a real sense of what it was like to be a voyageur. And wasn't that the point of it all?

I found Nana a free pattern on the web. It was for a Santa cap actually, but the tip drooped authentically, and minus the pompom and white trim it looked pretty well right. She absorbed the instructions through her pores, seemed like, and the tuques started coming off her needles so fast she could have outfitted the whole North West Company given half a chance. She fixed me up with a stash that more than covered what I had in mind, filling my empty rum barrel to the brim. I was ready. In theory that is.

You know those recurring dreams people have? Or nightmares I guess they'd more accurately be. The ones where they're running down the street being chased? Or they're endlessly falling, falling, falling? Or they walk into class one day, look down, and see that they're completely naked? Those ones? Well I'd been having one lately. Different from those though. Personalized. It had me waiting at the museum door on Nuit Blanche, all expectant and welcoming, and no one showing up. All night long. Not a single solitary person. Discounting, of course, the Bay's big guns standing by, taking in my nonsuccess with what-did-you-expect expressions on their faces. Well I was about to see if it was nightmare or prophesy. The time had come to boogie or get off the pot.

18

You'd have thought we were giving the merchandise away, judging by the crowds. The store was packed to the gills. Way fuller than I'd ever seen it. More crammed even than on Boxing Day when shoppers streamed in by the truckload to exchange Christmas gifts that were too long, too short, too tight, too plaid, didn't heat up, didn't turn on, didn't shred, didn't froth, didn't liquefy, didn't fast-forward, didn't crimp, didn't exfoliate, didn't whatever. Mum dreaded that day like no other. Lines were long and tempers short. But the mood of the store was different for Nuit Blanche, that is if a store can have a mood. Everyone seemed bouncy on both sides of the counter.

It didn't hurt that the Bay had put on its party shoes for the event, really tricked itself out. The window dressers and the stylists rose to the challenge considering they didn't have any set theme to fall back on, not like Donner and Blitzen at Christmas or Cupid on Valentine's Day, although if they'd really wanted to go thematic for the night they could have just decorated with dollar signs. None of the designers jumped for that idea. Go figure. I guess they didn't want to get themselves sacked. So instead they stuck with the literal, all stars and moons and constellations, *some enchanted evening* with fairy lights and disco balls. And it worked, I thought. Didn't look sow's earish at all. The place sparkled.

I was in my finest voyageur apparel for the event. Authentic from tip to toe. Okay, I stand corrected. Authentic *style* from tip to toe. I'd even gone so far as to tuck my glasses away for the duration. I didn't want any present day accessories spoiling my look. Besides, I figured it would blunt some of my stage fright if my audience was a bit hazy out there in front of me. My team was outfitted in my image. I'd issued a fatwa on anachronisms for the night and the guys cooperated by cobbling together outfits that passed my take-no-prisoners modernism inspection. We were four awesome looking voyageurs. IMHO.

At five minutes before the festivities were slated to begin, just coming up on nine, I forced myself to head towards the door of the museum to fling it open to the hypothetical masses. I'd been holed up inside all day with Sam, Renaud, and Nick putting the finishing touches on our moves. "You look like you're off to your own execution, Bennie boy," Sam said while I hesitated with my hand on the door. "Forget that stupid dream of yours. They'll be there, the rug-rats, all fired up to be entertained by that world renowned theatre troupe, the Wannabe Voyageurs. Go. Open up already. Let's get this show on the road."

I couldn't put it off any longer even though my stomach was petitioning for an eleventh-hour reprieve. I understood from its gassy toots that all it wanted was for the two of us to crawl into the canoe, hide ourselves away with a hot water bottle under a Hudson's Bay blanket and wake up when it was all over. Sam had no patience for our squeamishness. He was stoked. "Move it," he said taking charge. "It's time." He reached past me to push the door open and gave me a good shove out into the world of Nuit Blanche. And there lined up before me was a straggly row of kids stretching out as far as the eye could see, which granted was only as far as the Luggage Department across the floor, but still. I could let out my breath. If they kept showing up at that rate, we'd be packing them in all night long.

Per plan, I handed the kids tuques as they trickled in all giggles, their parents playing paparazzi with their iPhones. What really blew me away as they filed past was that most of them had taken the trouble to dress up special for the event, like it was a Harry Potter opening night or something, but instead of Voldemorts and Dumbledores I had voyageurs, Amerindians, and beavers. There was even one kid outfitted as a missionary, his ex-bathrobe soutane swishing against the floor like he genuinely had a vocation. I don't mind telling you the scene got me all choked up. These kids were keeners, the re-enactors of the future, keepers of the voyageur flame. I hoped to hell we wouldn't let them down.

The guys started singing "La Belle Lisette" right on cue as the kids settled themselves on the floor in a horseshoe facing me, with their mums and dads hugging the edges. The tune was a fur trader classic. My fellow voyageurs were lined up side by side behind me, in profile to the kids, each one plying a single paddle in rhythm to the music like they were my personal doo-wop girls. It was Nick who'd pushed for the musical intro. He was lead drummer in a spectacularly unsuccessful and tone-deaf band called Heisenberg Express, but he insisted that even the lousiest music, performed live, earned you bonus stamps on your loyalty card. I knuckled under even though I was afraid the kids would find their a cappella warbling too cornball. But there they were the little nippers, sitting goggle-eyed and expectant and we'd hardly even gotten under way.

When the song trailed off, my three glee club members sat down tailor style and made themselves quietly busy around the voyageur camp so I could take over. I looked out over my audience in their hand-knitted tuques. I felt calm suddenly, sure of myself, like I was Grand Marshal at an elf convention. I was ready.

"*Missi picoutau amiscou,*" I said, deliberately low, so the kids would have to lean in to catch it. I said it again, a little louder. "*Missi picoutau amiscou.*" I had them chant it after me like it was our secret password into the past. They didn't have a clue what they were saying but it didn't matter. I could have been asking them to repeat *kish mier in tuchis,* Grandpa's favourite posterior obscenity, and they would have belted it out loud and clear. I had them in the palm of my hand.

"Hundreds of years ago," I began, "not so very far from where you're sitting, when there was nothing at all around here but forests and rivers, the Montagnais trappers used those very words. In their language it meant *the beaver makes everything. The beaver makes every thing.* Now I want you to tuck that idea away in your brain where you can get at it. And tonight, what we're going to do you and me, we're going to go back in time together, to let you see first-hand what they meant. How the beaver really was at the root of it all, how the beaver really did make everything happen." That was Renaud's cue to come up and tap me on the shoulder. He'd performed one of the few wardrobe changes slated for the night so that now he was dressed up like a well-to-do British bloke of the eighteenth century, cape, cane, and a top hat on his head. He preened in front of the kids, smarming it up something fierce, until I snatched the hat off his head and held it up to them.

"It was fashion that did it," I said, putting on Mum's storytelling voice, all low slung and warm like a mug of cocoa. "This simple hat, made out of beaver felt, is what set off the European frenzy for furs from our side of the Atlantic that shook up everything. And we voyageurs, if I may say so, we were the most important link in the supply chain that led from the beavers to the hat shops of merry old England." My two fellows at the canoe nodded vigorously at the truthfulness of my statement. "Without us," I continued, "those dandies in England would have had to wear this." Renaud reached under his cape and pulled out a cowboy hat which he put it on his head. "Or this." He replaced it with a pith helmet. "Or this." A beanie copter. "So you can see how crucial our job was. To fashion, to commerce, and to the world.

"Which brings us back around to our friends the beavers, because we all know," and here I spread my arms out like a choir conductor and my wee charges came back in perfect unison, *"missi picoutau amiscou."* Ah, the headiness of power! I hadn't been planning on it, but since I had a pair of mascot-sized rodents in the audience, twins from the look of it, I invited them up to the front for my demo instead of using the stuffed beaver I'd planned on. In my current pumped state I could handle a little improv. Piece of cake.

"You might not think it, but it wasn't the long outer hairs, the guard hairs we call them, that were so valuable in producing hats." I stroked the front of the plush beaver costume one of my twin volunteers was wearing. "Oh no. It was actually the under-felt that the hatters used, the ground hair as it's known. The ground hair is softer and easier for the hat-makers to mould into shape." I rubbed the plush upwards against the grain on beaver number two to give them the idea of where the ground hair came from. While I was rubbing the tummies of my two beavers, it flitted through my mind that I might have made a strategic mistake. Would the parents accuse me afterwards of diddling with their little cherubs? Well, I'd know better for the ten p.m. show. I'd go less pedophilic, totally hands free.

"Now just at the point that demand for hats like these was exploding in England, when anyone who was anyone absolutely had to have one, the European beavers were dying out from overhunting and disease." My two beavers, a pair of hams who had their twin telepathy going, clutched their throats in slow but showy death throes and sank to the floor where they enjoyed a few last-ditch convulsions, real floor-thumpers, before croaking. It was sweet of them to accommodate me. It so suited me to have them dead. I thanked them for their buck-toothed participation and dismissed them back to their places while the audience clapped their appreciation and rubbed them up within an inch of their lives. I forged ahead solo.

"So what happened then was that our fat, healthy New France beavers stepped up to the plate. They were trapped by the various tribes and stripped down into pelts like these." I passed a few around. This was a risky move but I decided to go for it. Some kids didn't have the stomach to handle pelts that still had heads and tails attached. These were the same kids who cried bloody murder when their parents put a whole fish on their plates. But this night not a one of them squawked so I moved right along. "The pelts were traded to the Europeans in exchange for manufactured goods like beads, knives, hatchets, guns, and ammunition. The Indigenous peoples thought the Europeans were missing something upstairs, trading eight nice sharp knives or twenty metal fish hooks for one beaver skin. That was the going rate. The Europeans, well, they had similar doubts about the sanity of the native peoples. But both sides had their particular needs, and the fur trade, for many years, benefited them both.

"Now we voyageurs, where did we fit into all of this? Well, it was our job to transport the pelts by canoe from the interior to the trading posts and to ferry trade goods back in the opposite

direction. If you think it was easy work, a quick zip down the wa-
terslide, then you better think again. There were dangers lurking
at every turn. Raging rapids that could rip the bottom right out of
our canoe sending us to a watery grave. There were grizzlies the
size of houses, and wolves who were anxious to take a chomp out
of us to see if we tasted like chicken. We had to put up with fever,
disease, and swarms of black flies so thick you could hardly see
your hand in front of your face. Being a voyageur wasn't for sissies
my friends. It took a certain kind of man."

I signalled to Nick. He ducked behind the foresty backdrop and
came back out wearing a white smock with a stethoscope round his
neck and rolling a tall doctor's scale which he parked beside me.
"There were height limits," I informed my audience. "Too tall and
you were out of the running." Nick directed Sam onto the scale,
pulled the height-measurer stick down onto his head, studied it,
and put a giant check mark on his clipboard. "And weight limits
too. No blubber butts accepted." Nick balanced the weight marker
on the scale, bobbed his head yes, and marked another check on
his paper. "See the ideal voyageur couldn't be so big that he took
too much room away from the trade goods. The more freight we
could cram into the canoe the better."

Nick motioned Sam off the scale as if to continue the exam-
ination but they froze in position while I kept up with the com-
mentary. "Okay, so on top of coming in at the right size and shape,
there was another, slightly more unusual test you had to pass before you could join the voyageur fraternity. And that was, you had
to be able to sing. Yes, you heard me right. A halfway decent singing voice was way up there on the list of necessaries for a would-be
voyageur. I know it might sound silly to you. I mean it wasn't the
opera these guys were wanting to sign on with. But we voyageurs,
we sang for a reason. Did you know that we paddled our canoes for

sixteen long hours a day? Think of it. More than two school days put together. And we had to keep up the pace if we expected to reach our destination before winter closed us down for business, one stroke per second, no slacking off."

I clapped my hands to give them a feel for the tempo. They all joined in, and repeated my refrain to the beats.

"From dawn (clap) to dusk (clap)."

"From dawn to dusk."

"From dawn to dusk."

Oh, we were into it. "Now imagine yourself not just clapping at that rate, but paddling, paddling, paddling." My arms made the switch to match my gestures to my words. The kids on the diapered end of the age spectrum figured that if Herr Leader was up there paddling away then they should be too, as if we were all playmates in some flaky mashup of Simon Says and Pattycake. They jumped up and imitated my row-row-row-your-boat movements, but on overdrive, which had the unfortunate spillover of blocking the view of the kids in the back and whapping their neighbours on each side who got cranky as a result.

Things were starting to get a bit shaky control-wise. Among the underage spectators in the room there was clapping, there was paddling, there was pushing and there was shoving, all of it overlaid with a veneer of shouting and whimpering. The little red tush-cushions that I'd set out so carefully were threatening to become projectiles. The kids were reverting to a state of nature and we weren't even half-way through the program. From my vantage point up front it looked to me like I had a budding insurrection on my hands and I didn't have a flaming clue how to go about quashing it. But luck was on my side that night. The group turned out to be self-policing. Before things could go completely *Lord of the Flies* on me, the older siblings swooped in to my rescue and yanked the little ones down and out of the way. Then they silenced them with glances that foreshadowed all manner of tortures back at home if they didn't settle down stat. My enforcers saved the day. The show could go on.

"So like I was saying, you're out there in the canoe. All the live-long day. In the rain, in the wind. You're cold and you're damp and you itch and you ache and you've got bugs between your teeth. The only relief you get is a ten-minute break every hour to smoke your pipe and do your um ... personal uh ... well, you know what I'm trying to get at. And then back to it. How are you supposed to keep up the rhythm under conditions like that? Well, we voyageurs, we figured out the answer to that one pretty quick, which was to row in time to music. Our hands weren't free to play an instrument. We didn't have an iPod. So what did we do?"

"You sang," a bunch of them cried out.

"Right you are. We sang. If you couldn't sing, you didn't make the cut." I snapped my fingers at Nick and Sam to pop them back to life. Nick pulled a pitch pipe out of his pocket, blew into it for a G, and stood ready with his clipboard. Sam launched into a wild and woolly rendition of "My Baby Does the Hanky Panky," his hands flying over his air guitar. He had the kids rolling in the aisles.

Sam reached out to accept the tuque and sash Nick had dangling from his hand, the tokens that marked his acceptance into the tribe, but he dropped them pronto when he heard me yell out, "Hey you! Wait. Not so fast!" The kids all gave a jump at my stop-thief tone. "Sorry," I said as their little bottoms dropped back down to the floor, "but here we are running through all the qualifications to be a voyageur, and I nearly forgot to mention the most important one. More important than how high and wide you were, more important than carrying a tune, more important than being able to put up with the kinds of hardships that would break a lesser man. To be an A-1, crack voyageur, more than everything else put together, you had to have the strength of a superhero." At this Sam swung into a series of Hercules poses behind me that tipped the scales in his favour and allowed him to graduate. "But maybe all this was obvious to you. You strike me as a very intelligent audience.

"Of course you had to be more than strong to row a fully-loaded canoe over thousands of miles of rivers and lakes and live to tell about it. And to toss around packs that weighed in at ninety pounds each like they were so many pillows. But portaging? That's where your muscles really kicked in. Who here knows what it means to portage a canoe?" A sea of hands shot up. These fur trade groupies knew the score. I called on the dwarf missionary who was practically jumping out of his cowl to supply the answer.

"It's when you have to take the canoe out of the water and carry it till you get past the rapids."

"Exactly, *mon père*. Portaging, ah, what a business that was. We dreaded it like nothing else. Whenever we spotted foam churning up on the surface of the water up ahead, our stomachs sank, because that lather meant rapids, no two ways about it. And rapids and canoes don't mix. So what we'd do, we'd have to hustle up on shore and empty the canoe right down to the bottom. Remove every single solitary thing. And a canoe like ours could carry four tons of cargo, easy. You heard me right. That's eight thousand pounds we're talking. So what did we do with it all? Well, we had to load it on our backs. What other choice was there? Most of us, we carried two or three packs at a time, way more than our own weight. And don't forget, on top of that, some of us had to carry the canoe itself. Water soaked, it weighed a good seven hundred pounds or more. Now there was a job. We carried it turned upside down on our shoulders, four of us usually for a canoe this size. Take it from me, portaging was pure torture. Overland, burdened down, for miles and miles and miles, however long it took till the river calmed down and we could relaunch, reload and paddle on."

I moved over closer to the canoe. It dwarfed our poky makeshift stage as if it were a felled redwood. The kids could see the boat was the real deal, weighty, not a dinky prop. It radiated heft, as if it had a personal magnetic field that was bear-hugging it to the floor. Renaud, Sam, Nick, and I took our pre-arranged places on either side. We shook out our arms to loosen them up, did a few neck rolls right and left, and performed some bravura knuckle-cracking. Then, at my signal, we grabbed hold of the canoe and hoisted it up over our heads into portaging position. Even the parents gasped. It was as if we'd clean-and-jerked a grand piano. We marched in place with it over our heads to give them the general idea. As a party piece it was damned impressive if I say so myself. That canoe was one heavy sonofabitch but we'd practiced for hours to get the lift just right. The experience taught me why the voyageurs had pushed to have their health plan cover hernias. The guys and me, we expected a certain amount of clapping after we set that sucker back down, but the waves of applause practically blew us off the stage, followed by a standing ovation no less.

We flew through the rest of the script surfing on a high that Olympians must feel when they've turned in a performance that'll snag them a gold. And before we even registered that the time had gone by, bang, it was over. One of the kids asked me to autograph her arm on her way out of the museum. I'm telling you I felt like a rock star.

We did a threepeat of the production, but for the midnight show we were planning to shake things up. The crowd massing outside the museum entrance was even bigger than for the earlier shows. Whoever it was who'd told me that the kidlets stop coming as the night wears on had it all wrong. No way we'd be able to cram them all in. The overflow would just have to hang around till one a.m. if they were determined to see us in action. Considering how late it was, past their bedtime and then some, I figured this batch of kids would be dozy, but I was dead wrong. They were hyper awake, fuelled on all the sugary *bouffe* their parents had been stuffing them with all night long from the food trucks along Ste. Catherine Street. Well, they were in for a special treat.

The four of us kept on script till I got to my mini Q&A with the audience. "Does anyone here know what it means to portage a canoe?" I asked for the fourth time that night. I pointed at a kid who reminded me of Serge's daughter Élodie. Could even have been her, with those liquid eyes so like papa's. This little girl had screwed up costume-wise, she was wearing a coonskin cap à la Davy Crockett, but her heart was in the right place. "It means to carry the canoe on land to get around something dangerous in the water, like rapids or rocks. You put it up in the air like this," she said. And she lifted her stick arms to demonstrate.

"Right you are," I said. She beamed as if I'd given her a gift. I went on to deliver my same little lecture, portaging-is-torture blah blah blah, and then moved over to the canoe for the guys and me to do a rerun our feat of strength. On three we heaved the canoe up over our heads to the gasps that were old hat to us now, but this time around, instead of marching in place, we slalomed our way through the kids and portaged the canoe right out of the museum and into the store. It was a tight squeeze, but with both of the double doors open, we just made it through without even scraping the finish.

I could sense a bit of a commotion behind me in the museum as we made our exit. The parents were thrown. Was this the end of the performance? Should they take off for the next event on their Nuit Blanche schedule? I couldn't blame them their confusion.

Ambiguous endings always burned me too. But in the midst of the parental dithering one pipsqueak with ADD jumped up to follow us, and that's all it took to convince the rest of the pack to join in our slipstream. That settled that. The parents couldn't just let their precious bambinos hotfoot it off unsupervised so they tacked themselves onto the end of our conga line and off we went.

Even for a night when it was in to be out, we made one helluva spectacle. The Nuit Blanche crowds in the store clapped us on as we trotted through the aisles at a rickshaw clip. We could hear them all hooting and whoo-whooing as we passed like they were cheering us on at a marathon. Who knows, maybe after this indoor portaging would catch on. There were more demented sports out there for sure. We circled through all the departments on the museum floor, even Fine China and Stemware. Me and my compadres, we were staking out new territory. Voyageurs weren't trained to manoeuvre through breakables, but we managed it without a single wine glass crashing to the floor. Our cornering was impeccable. Neat, tight turns. And our footwork was Bolshoi nimble.

Once we'd hit all the departments on five, we pointed our canoe towards the *down* escalator. Our cockiness knew no bounds. Navigating on terra firma was one thing, but with the earth shifting under our feet? We had no choice the way I saw it. We owed it to Nuit Blanche, to the museum, and to all the voyageurs who art in heaven to give it our best shot. Getting on the escalator went okay. Just. I gauged the speed of the top-most sliding step perfectly and got my foot planted on it solid. But then the combination of the movement, the angle, and the pressure from the canoe overhead made me feel like I was in a 747 coming in for an emergency landing. I got all light-headed and wondered when the little yellow oxygen masks were going to pop out. Good thing the descent only took a few seconds. For that long I could suck it up. Our dismount?

Steady if not elegant. Small victories.

The voyageur roadshow hit all the departments on every floor. We portaged ourselves through Intimates and Sleepwear, Plus Sizes and Petites, and Boxers and Briefs. You'd think we'd slow down as we went on, toting a dead weight like we were, but instead we whizzed along faster and faster, in full show-off mode. The kiddies who were playing tail to our comet could hardly keep up with us with the result that after a while they started to crash and burn; a tantrum here, some puking there. Their parents had to pluck the casualties out of the line as they dropped. By the time we got down to one to do a flypast of Mum's counter for her to see what her son had come to, there were just a few diehard imps still trailing us, and once we finished our rounds of the first floor at the door marked *Personnel Only*, we didn't have a single tailgater left. Not a one.

I flashed my employee ID at the card reader and the door popped open all hospitable to welcome me and my guys in. The staff locker room just inside was deserted for once. Made sense. Who'd want to be hanging out back there BS-ing when all the excitement was out in the store? Same deal just beyond at the cleaners' assigned space. The equipment was all there, yeah, but no sign of life. The carts with their buckets and mops and swiffers were backed in for a change so they'd be ready to shoot right out in the morning to deal with the strata of schmutz the Nuit Blanche revellers had dumped in their wake. We breezed right on through unseen. From there we sprinted past the ghost town of the heating plant, and then skirted building maintenance where the absent operators had bedded down their forklifts and skyjacks for the night. At the recycling hub we hooked a sharp left and that's where we picked up the corridor that led to the loading dock. Rossi was there to meet us, perched on the edge of a plasti-wrapped sofa that was waiting to be shipped out, its toe tag marked Dorval.

He jumped up when we got there.

"You ready?" he asked me.

"Ready as I'll ever be."

"Ya sure?"

"Now you're asking me? Yeah I'm sure. C'mon. Let's get on with it. We don't have all night."

"Because you can still change your mind, you know." Rossi, my backup conscience, wasn't making any headway in rescuing me from myself. He had a nerve even trying. He knew the rules. Hell, he'd taught them to me. Once you shake on it, there's no dismantling a deal. If he was suffering from accomplice's remorse, tough shit.

"Okay," he said, shaking his head. "You're the boss."

Rossi stepped over to the control panel next to the loading dock door and punched in the code on the key pad. We all looked up so we could catch the great door rumbling to life, lifting overhead on its runners. Not an easy thing to do with the canoe constricting our sightlines. But it didn't matter in the end. There was nothing to see. The thing didn't budge. Not so much as a jiggle. And the light on the panel never switched off of no-go red.

"Try it again," I said. "You must have punched it in wrong."

So he did. Same result. Meaning no result. The door hugged the ground so tight you couldn't have slid a dime under it. The Bay must have paid out plenty to get the top-of-the-line weather stripping.

"Quit doing it from memory," I told him. "You probably reversed a couple of the numbers or something." At least I hoped he had, though as far as I knew Rossi wasn't one to dyslexify. He hesitated at my suggestion. Which worried me. "You do have it written down somewhere, don't you?" I asked him. But no sooner had I said it than a vision came to me of no-loose-ends Rossi in the fifth floor can, flushing the scrap of paper so it wouldn't be around to incriminate us.

Rossi stood stock still in front of the keypad, like it had put a hex on him. "I memorized it right," he insisted. "I punched in the right sequence." Was he scamming me? Had he mixed up the numbers on purpose to kneecap my scheme? My poker face clearly needed work. It was letting some signals leach out. Rossi picked right up on my suspicions as if Siri had whispered them into his ear. He reached into his jeans' pocket and pulled out a crumply piece of the Bay's official letterhead to show me. "Here," he said, smoothing it out against his leg. "This is the code I lifted from head office when we lost power during the flood. Put your glasses back on and read it out to me. Or better still, punch it in yourself."

"No need," I said. "You do it. Go ahead." Jesus, as a friend I could be a real shmuck, but there you go. For the third time in as many minutes he punched in the numbers, slow and steady, taking the time to check each one against the paper. Same story. The garage door didn't know from those numbers. It continued its snooze while the rest of us ratcheted up into panic mode. Or I should say I ratcheted up. My kayak guys were just along for the ride. They sympathized, sure, but the panicking privileges were mine and mine alone. Okay, mine and Rossi's.

Instead of keeping a cool head like I should have, I jumped down his throat. "You didn't know enough to test it out?"

"I *did* test it," Rossi said. "I know my business."

"My ass. If you knew your business the door would be open."

"I tested it over and over since you put me on it. Three days ago it went right up."

"Three days ago? That's the last time you tried it? That was what? Wednesday? And now we're Saturday?"

"Yeah, Wednesday. And it worked like a dream, I'm telling you. Up, up and away."

"It didn't occur to you to test it any more recently? Like today maybe? The crucial day. The day we actually needed it to go up? The day that mattered more than any stupid Wednesday? Would that have been too much to ask?"

"You don't get how it is," he said. "I couldn't just come in and test it every day. It would attract too much attention, me being down here where I have no business to be. I had to stay under the store's radar."

"Well let me be the first to congratulate you, O master of your craft. You stayed so far under the radar that you fucked up every-thing. What was I thinking? I never should have trusted you with anything higher level than slicing a tomato. Of that, you're capable. Two jobs I gave you to do. Two stinkin' jobs to be responsible for. The code and the security cameras. We already know that you bombed out on the code. You're not going to turn around and tell me that they're filming us right now, are you, in all our glory?"

"The cameras are dead. Trust me."

"Trust me, he says. A real comedian. Well what do you suggest we do now, pardner? Try to wedge this damned canoe out through the revolving doors maybe?" The canoe was gouging permanent coolie divots into my shoulder, and my knees were torquing in such a way that prophesied a lifetime of appointments at Concordia Physio Sport. We didn't dare put the boat down. We had no juice left. If we set it on the floor now, we'd need a derrick to lift it back up again. The sweat was streaming off me. It was probably the first time in my career as a voyageur that I genuinely smelled like one. My body was in no mood to treat Rossi with kid gloves. Besides, I wasn't one of those magnanimous-type bosses who's prepared to absorb all the blame himself because he stinks at delegating. I needed a scapegoat. I couldn't bear the weight of so much failure on my own head. I had to delegate it too.

"All that time, all that work, all that planning, shot to hell.

Thanks to you and your dollar store criminal instincts we're screwed with a capital S. That's it. Game over."

Rossi never wanted this assignment. He'd hung up his criminal spurs for good by the time I met him. To my eternal shame I convinced him to dust them off for this one final job. I painted it as a humanitarian act. A righting of historical wrongs. Knowing him, he probably only agreed to come on board so he could keep an eye on me and here I was using him as a punching bag. Need a three letter word for *turd*? It's B-E-N.

But that didn't stop me from laying into him. My rant was running on a loop and I made no effort to pull the plug. Hysteria does weird things to a guy. I was back to chewing Rossi out about the code when we heard a rustling right behind us. What with all the flap over the stuck door nobody'd remembered to play lookout. As gangstas we were shleppers, pure and simple.

"Allow me," Serge said, coming out of the woodwork. He circled wide around us portagers. The canoe's hind end was fishtailing on Nick and Sam's depleted shoulders and he didn't want it to conk him one on his way to the control panel, for that's where he was headed. Serge, turns out, was a man of parts. Who'd have thunk he was the Elton John of the keypad? His magic fingers tripped lightly over its numbers and the door responded presto by rolling upwards in a graceful arc as it was meant to do. The puff of fresh air it let in from the outside revived me, but not half as much as the sight of the U-Haul truck idling on the ramp with Morrie tapping his fingers impatiently on the steering wheel.

Me and the guys jumped back into action, our case of the wobbles miraculously cured. We eased the canoe down into the truck onto the nest of straw Morrie had prepared for it. Not for him the bubble wrap or packing peanuts most DIY movers swear by when they need shock absorbers. Morrie didn't want the canoe to suffer any more culture shock than absolutely necessary he'd explained to me earlier. So straw. Once we had our birchbark baby snuggled in all cozy and safe, we lifted out the kit canoe to ferry back upstairs to the museum. The whole swap only took a couple of minutes and when it was done I gave Morrie two take-off thumps on the roof and he was out of there. I poked the *close* button on the control panel and now that the door had been newspaper-trained by Serge, it rumbled obediently down at my command to settle at my feet. By the time we had the ersatz canoe firmly settled on our shoulders Serge had taken off so I couldn't thank him, but I'm guessing my benefactor knew how I felt about his drive-by act of kindness.

19

Permit me to introduce Morrie 2.0. Or maybe it would be minus 2.0, considering.

The Morrie I reconnoitred with early the next morning at our favourite secluded cove wasn't my Morrie. This Morrie, the one standing in the glare of my headlights when I drove up, was resplendent in the full voyageur. A major shock to my system. In all our endless envisioning of this day, he'd never once let on that he was planning to go native. Not that he owed it to me to tell me what he'd be wearing. What was I, his mother?

Ooh, he was one dapper sun-of-a-gun I had to admit, decked out in a primo outfit like he was heading off to some fur trader cocktail party. He had on an eye-popping pair of mukluks, not lowly moccasins like mine which are the voyageur equivalent of Keds. His boots went all the way up to his knees. They were tied around traditional style by criss-cross thongs, and lined in some rich, dense fur that tufted out at the top. Beaver? Lynx? I'd drooled over mukluks like those on the web. The cheapo ones, relatively I mean, were lined in serviceable, everyday rabbit, but the high flyer versions had inners of coyote, or silver fox even. A pair of those babies could set you back all right, a college education would run you less, but they'd keep your toes warm and dry on a long voyage, that's for sure. No point asking Morrie how he came to be in possession of such extravagant footwear. That was usually an unprofitable line of inquiry to pursue with him.

Morrie's face was in perfect sync with his getup. Ever since Lena died he'd boycotted his razor so his beard had come in unsculpted and free-range, woodsman style. So bushy you could hang ornaments off it. If only my cheeks would be half so cooperative. Or my chest for that matter. But now wasn't the moment to repine about my inferior shagginess. We had other fish to fry.

"Any trouble with the truck?"

"No. No problems. I drove at leaf-peeper speed the whole way. I didn't want to risk being pulled over or anything."

"Good thinking. Nice duds by the way."

"Thanks. I thought an occasion like this deserved some special recognition."

We sat on the riverbank for a while and waited for the sun to come up. Mother Nature must have been feeling pretty peppy that morning because she whipped us up a made-to-order sunrise, way heavy on the pinks and purples. Its beauty was beyond any words at our immediate disposal so we just followed its progress in silence. Which suited me fine because I needed to unwind, and bad. I'd raced straight over from my nightlong shift at the Bay. I was boomeranging between exhaustion and exhilaration. Morrie? He'd be wiped out I figured. After all, he'd spent the better part of the night inspecting the canoe from stem to stern and performing field surgery. He couldn't have grabbed any shut-eye either. But somehow he looked like he'd just stepped out of a spa. How'd the guy do it?

"So the repairs, how did they go?" I asked him.

"Easy-peasy. This boat is one fine specimen like I told you all along. I just had to daub her a little here and there with some spruce gum, do a minor bit of patching and job done." Spruce gum? But again I didn't ask where it came from. Today we were in a no-pry zone.

I peeked inside the truck where the museum's canoe sat waiting patiently to receive its new marching orders. "It was something to finally see the two canoes side by side last night," I said. "Two peas in a pod."

"We made it happen."

"Nah, not me. I hardly did anything on that score. It's you who deserves all the credit for the cloning, you with all your magic aging formulas. I wouldn't have known where to start."

"Come on, Ben. Take some credit where it's due. You know I couldn't have done it without you. You were the one who banged and battered all the newness out of the kit job. You were my main man."

"Your only man, you mean."

"Same difference," he said. "We did it together. A team we were."

With all this backslapping going on, leave it to me to be a killjoy. But this particular line of talk always swung me around to my ground-zero worry in all this. "Do you think they'll notice the switch back at the store?" We'd gone over this territory again and again, but I needed to hear him run through it one last time.

"Listen. The Bay won't have any reason to believe that it's a phony on display. What do they know from anything? It's the auctioneers who'll notice something fishy when they show up. That's a given. But I'm betting they'll conclude that the store got shafted somewhere way back in the mists of time, and they've had a fake one on display all along. End of story." I was always convinced when he put it to me that way. Till I wasn't. But even if they did clue in that the original had been lifted somehow, how would they know where to send the repo man? I'd just have to keep my fingers and toes crossed that the trail wouldn't lead back to my door.

"Son," he said, "let it go."

Letting go. Not my forte. When it came to worries and hurts I was cursed with a Velcro personality. They landed and they stuck. But if ever there was a time to move on, it was now.

Morrie set his hand on my knee. "The moment of truth is upon us Ben," he said in a new, formal tone that carried me along in its confidence. "Shall we?"

We shall, I decided. We set the ramp up against the truck and gentled the canoe out and onto the scrub. With just the two of us on moving detail it wasn't easy, but we managed without a fender-bender. The canoe sat ungainly on the ground, looking every bit her age. Maybe we should have fashioned her a sun bonnet of some kind. Back in the days when she was a working canoe UV rays hadn't been invented yet.

It was quiet on the riverbank so early except for one insomniac trail runner who slowed down as he passed to give our canoe a good ogle. You could just tell he was sniffing at it, judgmental SOB. If it were up to him he'd probably feed it nose first into a wood chipper for a lifetime's supply of toothpicks. Okay, so maybe it did look well-used compared to those slick fibreglass jobs he was accustomed to seeing on his runs, the ones painted up all twinkly in lip gloss colours. But those were the chick cars of the canoe family, beneath contempt. They didn't deserve to be mentioned in the same breath as ours. To Morrie and me our canoe was beautiful. In the same way we'd both seen Lena as beautiful. A guy like that, all microfibre, he'd never get it.

"Do you think we should say a few words first?" I asked.

"You do the honours."

Speechifying. Not my thing. When I'd said *we* what I'd actually meant was *you*. I thought sure Morrie would want to be the one to officiate, giving the little homily that preceded cracking the bubbly over the bow. Metaphorically speaking that is. As feisty as our boat might have been, it couldn't withstand getting clocked on the head with a bottle of Dom Pérignon. But I called it wrong. Morrie didn't grasp that ring for himself. The assignment to hold forth canoe-side fell to me, so I strip-mined our history for commemorative material. It didn't take long for me to hit on what I was hunting for. Not long at all actually. I bent my head and delivered my speech. Nano but heartfelt.

"Acabris, Acabras, Acabram."

"Well put," Morrie said after a respectful pause.

The ceremonials behind us, we slid the canoe into the water and held our breath. It bobbled a little at the start like it was on its first trip without training wheels, but then it got its groove back and floated straight and proud, its bed bone dry. Morrie grabbed me into a hug. It was all I could do to keep from crying. Crying wasn't referenced in the voyageur handbook. But Morrie, he didn't bother holding back the tears, just let 'em gush. We tore into the water and scrambled in, where we were always meant to be.

The boat was way too big for just the two of us, but it didn't matter. She handled so smooth it didn't feel at all like we were out paddling the *Queen Mary*. Morrie helped me rejig my kayaking stroke and once I had it down we made for the open water, singing our hearts to bursting. The fish must have been putting their hands over their ears, but we were in the mood to belt, and nothing could stop us.

The perfect weather egged us on. The day's windsock was flaccid and there was a nice taste of warmth in the spring air, just enough to keep our limbs loosey-goosey. So maybe we didn't manage the one-stroke-per-second standard, but damn near. Not half bad for a pair of rookies. Full speed ahead we paddled, so far out that we could imagine we'd made it up to Lake Superior. Water water all around. We paddled and we sang and we lived. When we were thirsty we cupped up H_2O from the river (okay, so maybe not brilliant) and when our bladders hit full, we pissed over the side in festive arcs. I had so much adrenalin shooting through me that I wished I had some rapids to run to prove my mettle.

I could have gone on forever if not for my lungs. They finally lodged a complaint. All my training in a runty kayak was nothing to prepare me for this. Morrie must have heard my breath coming in coughing rasps. "Now would be a good time to break for breakfast don't you think?" he said. He looked to be in fine shape for all our exertion, hadn't even broken a sweat, which for a few seconds made me feel like the sissy boy of the voyageur world. But I understood that wasn't his intention in suggesting that we turn back. At least not his main one. Morrie was simply abiding by the time-honoured schedule every self-respecting voyageur kept magneted to his fridge. Crews traditionally left camp in the wee hours of the morning on an empty stomach. They'd get a few solid hours of paddling under their belt and only then put ashore for breakfast. That's the way it was always done, and that's what we would do too. So we turned around to paddle at a leisurely pace back to the cove where we'd laid by our grub, the current helping us on our way.

I'd whipped us up a batch of breakfast rubaboo the day before in the cafeteria kitchen at the Bay. Rubaboo, you've got to love a name like that. It's kind of like voyageur polenta. See what they would do, they'd stir the ingredients into a big kettle of water the night before and then let it all burble super-slow over a banked campfire. Come morning, whoever was on breakfast detail would wrap it all up in a blanket to keep in the warmth and then load it onto the canoe where the rubaboo would get thicker and thicker as it sat. When a wooden spoon stuck in the middle stood straight up, that was the sign to clang the breakfast gong.

Truth be told, it was Rossi who did most of the rubaboo cookery. I was pretty much *nul* in the kitchen. We worked out a division of labour that had me supplying the groceries and Rossi overseeing the porridgy mixture's progress even though its ingredients were an offence to his palate. And that was *after* I'd semi-modernized the recipe out of necessity. See, the dried peas and corn I could come by no problem at the natural foods store. Even pemmican was out there for the buying. But bear grease? Where the hell was I supposed to find that? Morrie, acquisitor par excellence of all things fur trade, would probably have known how to rustle us up some, but me? Uh-uh. The recipe did list pork fat as an alternative, but I was culturally unable to make myself buy it, so in the end we used Crisco tinted into realism with a glop of tahini (Rossi's bright idea). Just watching it simmer I could feel my arteries gumming up.

"Is it ready you think?" Morrie asked me as I was lifting the pot out of the back of the truck. "I could eat a horse." I took off the lid so we could check it out. Morrie rubbed his hands together as if he was genuinely eager to dig into what could only be referred to as glop, despite Rossi's heroic efforts to crank it up a few gastronomic notches. I performed the official wooden-spoon test. The handle listed at about an eighty-degree angle. "Almost there. Another forty-five minutes I'm guessing. An hour maybe," I said. Since that gave us some time to while away, I staked myself out a sunny patch of ground and laid down for the catnap my spent muscles were craving. Morrie, on the other hand, was buzzy.

"Let me take her out once solo since we have some dead time," he said. "Otherwise I'll tighten up."

"You think you can manage that much boat all on your own?" I asked him. A born sailor he might have been, but our canoe would still be a handful for a single paddler.

"Yeah, I'll take it easy."

"Okay, let me help you push off. A fine repast will be awaiting you upon your return, sir."

"I expect no less," he said.

He paddled away with ease, the ur-voyageur. His image belonged on a postage stamp. Or on a Molson's label at the very least. I settled myself back in on the grass after he disappeared from sight, pulled my tuque down for eye cover, and conked right out. It was a dreamless sleep for the first time in I can't think how long, bottomless and deep. My sleep-demons must have finally squeezed every last drop of nourishment they could out of me after so many years and gone hunting for a new roost. I never thought the day would come. Life was good.

I might have slept the sleep of the dead till Morrie came back if not for the aroma that crept up on me and hovered over my head like my personal cloud. I couldn't disperse it, not even using that reflexive black-fly swat common to all voyageurs. It clung there in the air above me, coaxing me back to consciousness. Once it had me good and awake it beckoned my nose snake-charmer style over to the pot of rubaboo and the rest of my body tagged along for the ride.

I plunged the spoon in to confirm that the dish was à point, and it stood up at attention. Done. I licked some off my finger expecting not a whole heck of a lot. It was just fuel right? But whoa! That taste. Rossi, my prince. He'd nagged and nagged at me to let him throw some herbs into the pot, legit ones that probably grew wild along the river back in the day. Likewise some berries. The full locavore. The result was out of this world, rich and tangy with a nice little sweet and sour riff going in the background. *Layered*, foodies would call that flavour, or *complex* even. This, my readers, was a whole that beat the pants off the sum of its parts.

What a revelation. I'd always understood that voyageur food holed up in the culinary doghouse with prison food. You had all those uninvited critters doing the backstroke in your bowl. Serendipity protein. Voyageurs stuffed down their gullets whatever was put in front of them. When you're wrung out and empty, your tastebuds'll give anything a pass. All the books said so. But now I had scientific proof that it wasn't so. All that time they were feasting on ambrosia. Maybe some day with my discovery I could add to the literature. Behold my revisionist future.

I was dying to dig in. The last thing I'd eaten was a Kit Kat just before Nuit Blanche and a lot had gone down in my life between that chocolate bar and now. If I had to wait much longer for that rubaboo my stomach would start feeding on itself. But eating on my own would be a serious breach of voyageur etiquette. Or any etiquette I suppose. So I laid back down on the ground and clamped my eyes shut to try to trick my hunger into thinking it was fatigue, but it wasn't so dumb as to fall for that. So I sat. Scanning the horizon for the blip that meant I could start doling out breakfast.

Or would it be lunch? Could have been. It felt to me like Morrie'd been gone a good few hours at least. Way longer anyway than the hour we'd agreed on when he took off. Now I didn't blame him for breaking curfew. I'd probably have done the same if the situation had been reversed, out there slicing through the water in a real and true piece of history, unhitched from civilization, conditions perfecto. I wouldn't have had my eyes on the clock either, not that there was one. If anyone had earned an extension, it was him.

Still, I had to pass the time somehow till Morrie pulled a U-ey and headed back. Since I couldn't eat and I couldn't sleep, I paced up and down along the shoreline. And paced. So many back and forths that I eventually tamped down a whole new path in the brush where there wasn't one before. Which got me to thinking again about how much time had gone by. Now telling time by the sun was an art I was a little shaky on, but I guesstimated it had to be high noon. A little past even. Ages since Morrie took off on his own. I wasn't exactly what you'd call worried. I had a pretty fair idea of what was keeping him out there. The guy'd paddled so long and so hard he was too pooped to pop. Pulled in the paddles and drifted. Dozed off maybe. He'd be back once he treated himself to some R&R in the canoe.

I held out for what felt to me like another hour or so. By then clouds were starting to clutter up the sky so the sun couldn't back up my hunch. I checked out the rubaboo under its blanket. My baby. Corpse cold. The wooden spoon stuck straight up in it all right. Like a flagpole planted in cement. The stuff was way past eating. Unless you had a chisel handy. I used my voyageur wits to deduce a thing or two. Rubaboo was designed to be forgiving, no? I mean it's not like voyageurs broke for meals at set times. The stuff had to be able to sit and sit and sit till they got around to wolfing it down. If my rubaboo was by now so hardened up that I could climb up a tree and use it to bean a bear passing below, then a shitload of time had gone under the bridge since Morrie left. Okay, so now I was worried. Seriously worried. No, scratch that. Panicky is what I was.

The car. I needed the car. My cell was in there. I had to get the search going. Have Sûreté come out in their cutters and helicopters. Radar, scuba. The works. Enough playing around in the past. I wanted technology and lots of it. How many different kinds of idiot was I, waiting so long?

I shot over to where I'd parked the car to get my phone out of the glove compartment. Jammed. Dammit. I'd have to drive for help. Waste more precious minutes Morrie might not have. You could only cling to floating wreckage for so long. While I was struggling to get Mum's junker to turn over, a knock on the side window practically gave me heart failure.

It was Morrie. Dry. Safe and sound. I didn't get how I could have missed him approaching when I'd had my eyes glued to the river all along. I got out of the car. I couldn't make up my mind whether to hug him or sue him for emotional distress.

"Ben," he said, "Join us. We have room for one more."

"Us? Who's us?"

He gave a whistle and one by one they materialized from between the trees to gather around him. Ten men by my count. We'd never once set eyes on each other but I knew who they were right away. I'd nearly made their acquaintance once before not so very far from here. I stared them up and down, trying to convince myself that some mondo hoax was going on, but they were the real deal, these guys. I wasn't being had, no way. Lots of things were fakeable if they wanted to put something over on me, but there was no mistaking those eighteenth-century teeth. Shit! He'd found them. Or they'd found him. Whichever. They'd hooked up fully and completely this time. What were the odds?

"We came back for you, Ben. I couldn't leave you behind. You ready?"

Excellent question. Was I ready? Back in the days when it all qualified as a pipe dream, I used to think that hanging out with my voyageur brothers up in that celestial green room, or wherever the hell they passed the time between earthly appearances, would be the very definition of ecstasy. But now that I had proof positivo that that other world existed, a previously undocumented slice of the universe wedged in between the then and the now, I was spooked. Most definitely. What I needed before I made the leap was a sneak preview of what it would be like, a trailer that ran through the nuts and bolts of flipping centuries.

Morrie wasn't so gutless. Clearly he'd signed right up without even requiring a shpiel from the recruiter. He was ready and willing. Why shouldn't he have been? What was the downside for him? Not to be too ageist about it, but he was on the downward slope. This would give him one final kick at the voyageur can, an unmatchable adventure. We'd been playing T-ball him and me, but now he had a chance to suit up with the Yankees.

But what about me? Voyageurs had a notoriously short shelf life. A broken arm, a wrenched back and boom, I'd be off the job, still in the flower of my youth, if you'll pardon my literary pretensions. What then with no home to go back to? I'd be the has-been voyageur, the tag-along with no people to call his own, my canoe dreams dashed and stuck in pre-flush-toilet times. Did I want to take that chance? Why did I have to be so practical, weighing it all out? Why couldn't I just jump for it like Morrie. Boldly go where no man had gone before, or sort of. But that wasn't the way I was made. A fantasy was one thing, a one-way ticket another. No, I couldn't accept it. What exactly was anchoring me I couldn't say. I just had this urge to see how my future would play out on this side of the International Date Line.

"You go on ahead, Morrie. By yourself."

He looked at me as if I'd suddenly become a stranger to him. "What's come over you? This is our dream here. If you don't come now, the chance'll never come knocking at your door again. You'll regret it. For the rest of your life you'll regret it."

"Maybe so. But my mind is made up. I'm staying put."

"Ben. Think. It's all we've ever wanted. Handed to us on a silver platter. Who else in the whole wide world can say that? We've been chosen. Us alone."

"I know, I know. And I'm grateful. Really I am. Honoured. But I can't do it. I can't go. You'll have to be my representative. Hold up our good name back there. Show 'em what we're made of."

"It's normal to have cold feet Ben. You think I don't? But once we get ourselves into it, we'll forget we ever had a life here." That was the draw for him. But it wasn't mine.

"I guess I'm just more firmly planted here than I realized."

"C'mon Ben. It's like everything. The first step is the hardest."

"I'm staying behind, Morrie. I have to."

"There's nothing I can say to convince you?"

"No. I've thought it all out."

"You're sure now?"

"I am." And I was. My mind, so prone to decision reflux, was at peace. Somehow I sensed that in years to come, I wasn't going to be haunted by my habitual *if only's* over my choice to stay behind.

"I guess this is goodbye then my friend," Morrie said.

"Looks that way."

"Be well."

"You too. Don't go pushing that heart of yours too hard."

"I'll be sensible."

"You? Sensible?" I said. "Those two words don't jibe."

"Don't worry wise guy. I'll take care of myself."

"See that you do, or I'll have to come out there and do it for you."

"You'll be more than welcome."

The memories were washing over me. It was hard to believe that Morrie, their starring character, wouldn't have a role in any new ones I'd be accumulating. "It was a wild ride for the two of us while it lasted, wasn't it?" I said.

"The wildest."

"I'll always be grateful it was me you chose to burgle. Don't ever forget that."

"I won't," he said. "And I'll always be grateful that you called them to come."

"What are you talking about?"

"Today. They swung by for us special when they heard your speech back at the canoe before. I'll never be able to thank you enough for that. You were inspired."

What? I was the one who'd summoned them? It wasn't chance that brought them to us? This bombshell that Morrie dropped in my lap as by-the-way as if it were a weather report sent me reeling. Morrie's new paddling mates appearing in the flesh before me was nothing compared to this. Here they'd been out there listening. To me. The satellite dish they'd whittled on slow nights around the campfire had pulled in my signal. If that could happen then where did prayers go? The question just jumped into my head. I wasn't very religious, that's for sure. I don't think I ever prayed in my life. Praying was retro. It was what grizzled old men did in *shul* under their *tallises*. Or immigrants. I guess I never really believed anyone was out there on the receiving end. But now I'd have to give the whole subject a major rethink.

"Does this mean I can sort of give you a shout if I want to talk to you sometime," I said, "check up on how you're getting along?"

"It's a nice idea, but I'm not sure if we normally operate on an on-call basis. This might have been a one-off."

"Too bad. I would have liked us keeping in touch."

"Me too."

"Well, make my apologies then." I felt a bit guilty that they'd troubled themselves to make a detour and only wound up with one new paddler instead of the two they'd been counting on.

"I will."

Morrie and I reached out to each other. I thought my hands would just pass through his body, that he'd no longer have any substance considering he was half-here half-there, or whatever the proportions might be in such a situation. But he felt the same as always. One hundred percent present. His new companions looked anxious to be on their way so we could only clutch one another for a few seconds. When we broke apart, he turned to head back to their canoe, wherever in the wild blue yonder they'd moored it, and I headed back to Mum's car to drive off to wherever I was intended to go in this life.

ACKNOWLEDGEMENTS

You can't paddle a voyageur canoe alone. I was lucky to have support in the venture, and to all my fellow paddlers I give thanks here.

An early draft of My True and Complete Adventures as a Wannabe Voyageur was workshopped in a Quebec Writers' Federation seminar led by Claire Holden Rothman. Subsequent versions were scrutinized by my writing group, Frank Babics, Joanne Gormley, Kim Darlington, and Imola Zsitva. Kendall Wallis, as always, gave me invaluable suggestions, as did Ivan-Michael Juretic. I also owe a debt of gratitude to Lonnie Weatherby and Halyna Carpenter for services rendered, and to the crew at NeWest Press, notably Merrill Distad, Claire Kelly, and Matt Bowes.

Thanks to my son David who mercilessly blue-pencilled Benjie's dialogue so I could convincingly sound like a smart-mouthed 23-year-old. If any clunkers remain in the text, it's because I foolishly chose not to listen to him from time to time.

Finally, thank you to my husband Ron, who encouraged me in this as in all things. However many fur-trade museums and canoe exhibits I dragged him to, he was always up for more. It's handy being married to a historian.

ABOUT THE AUTHOR

Phyllis Rudin's writing has been published in numerous periodicals including The Massachusetts Review, Agni, Prism International and Prairie Fire. Her short story "Candlepower," which appeared in This Magazine, won its Great Canadian Literary Hunt in 2010. Her first novel, Evie, the Baby and the Wife, a fictionalized account of the Vancouver to Ottawa Abortion Caravan, was published by Inanna Publications in 2014. Phyllis Rudin has lived in the US and France, and now makes her home in Montreal where she is engaged in a project to walk every street in the city.